Wilted
Pages

Wilted Pages

An Anthology of Dark Academia

edited by
**Ai Jiang &
Christi Nogle**

SHORTWAVE
PUBLISHING

Content Warnings for applicable stories can be found at the back of this book.

Cover illustration by George Cotronis.
Interior formatting and design by Alan Lastufka.

First Edition published September 2023.

10 9 8 7 6 5 4 3 2 1

Library of Congress Control Number: 2023914815

ISBN 978-1-959565-11-6 (Paperback)
ISBN 978-1-959565-12-3 (eBook)

Contents

KNOWLEDGE

REVENGE

HOPE

FOREWORD

AI JIANG

When I thought back to my own relationship with academia and the way that I've seen others collect degrees like badges of honour and success, I couldn't help but wonder just how much the degrees themselves contributed to my career. The impact didn't come from the pieces of framed papers but the teachers and instructors and professors themselves.

After my undergraduate studies, I wanted to pursue teaching because of how much my own teachers impacted me. Then I thought about how much I would potentially impact my students and change the direction of their lives, and that thought scared me. I gave up that path. I didn't feel like a fitting enough guide through the tunnel for students when I, myself, kept dropping my own flashlight and fumbling aimlessly. But I realize how many educators might be in that same position, and I admire them for having the courage I never did.

On books concerning education, the ones that impacted me most are a non-fiction book titled *The Smartest Kids in the World: And How They Got That Way*, a memoir titled *Educated*, two novels titled *Out of My Mind* and *Never Let Me* Go, and, of course, the pedagogy books from my teaching stream courses at the University of Toronto. But in addition to those, I had my own life experiences and heard stories whispered by others: the dreaded gaokao in China; the time when my kindergarten teacher threatened to lock me in a closet for not sleeping during naptime; the moments I was made fun of because of my name, my accent, and my family at school and cyber bullied outside of it; the time in first grade when a boy spat at my grandmother's feet; the moment I heard that someone had threw themselves off the railing several floors above in one of the university libraries; the time my friend, who was an hour early to her exam, only to rush out in tears and the horrors of her religious private school and their treatment of their female students; the time our professor decided to experiment with a fifteen-person group essay and caused half the class psychological turmoil; the rumors that were really realities about institutions favouring the younger, the better looking, the pale, the privileged, the connected, the outgoing, and the outspoken.

What had been ingrained in me growing up was the importance of grades and awards and wealth, when truly, street-smarts and practical life skills I learned too late, and am still learning, are far more important than any academic text could have ever taught me. But what school did a good job of was teaching me how to be disciplined and teaching me how to learn on my own, even if these things are what I've struggled with and still struggle with, and much of the time. Back when I was still in school, the system did not favour the slow thinkers, the musers, those who were not regurgitators, those who could not afford to study without working parttime or commuting.

Sometimes, simply being hardworking is not enough, and academic glory can be swiped from under calloused hands while sweat and tears obscure our vision. Sometimes, simply connecting and speaking to others—rather than having our heads buried within pages and pages and pages, thinking only words will save us—will allow for broader vision.

But one important thing I've learned so far in my journey is that what truly taught me more than anything else is stories.

I see echoes of all the dark memories and experiences—snippets, fractures, insistent whispers of the past that refuse to silence —within the stories we have chosen for *Wilted Pages*, and as much as they may bring unease, I hope these stories also bring you, the reader, a kind of comfort.

—From a lifelong learner,
Ai Jiang

FOREWORD

CHRISTI NOGLE

When Ai Jiang and I sought a publisher for this project, we said we wanted to compile an anthology inspired by works such as *The Secret History* by Donna Tartt, *Never Let Me Go* by Kazuo Ishiguro, *Mexican Gothic* by Silvia Moreno-Garcia, *Catherine House* by Elisabeth Thomas, and *The Bone Weaver's Orchard* by Sarah Read. Alan Lastufka of Shortwave Publishing was kind enough to take on the project, and George Cotronis provided the gorgeous cover.

Writers from around the world, many of them deeply involved in academia, answered this call, and we and our wonderful first readers were able to consider over five hundred fascinating stories. Finally, we were able to decide on the few we had room for here, all of which exceeded our expectations. These contributors often include the "gloomy buildings, secret societies, futuristic boarding schools, gothic yet modern aesthetics, and occult learning" we sought in the call, but they go beyond that, introducing ideas and taking us to places and times we couldn't have predicted. Reading the submissions was a wonderful education in itself.

Aside from our interest in the works named above, my co-editor and I discussed our experiences with academia. I mentioned teaching at a university for twenty years, and I think I mentioned having degrees in visual arts, writing, and literature. What I didn't mention were my complicated feelings about teaching, learning, and educational institutions. I didn't mention the details of my early years moving around and attending many stifling (and sometimes horrific) religious schools, being kept out of school for periods of time, being bullied and isolated once I entered public school, acting out, dropping out, and years later taking the GED exam to be able to enroll in college, or struggling to find my voice once there. My first attempt at this foreword was a rumination on all those difficulties with academia, but I realized this foreword did not have space to do justice to that topic—not to mention that it's a bit of a downer.

So I'll put the focus back on the works here, with the understanding that academia is, to me, and I think to these contributors, a fraught and complicated thing. The sites represented here—schools, universities, libraries, research facilities, and the field—offer microcosms of our social world. Here we yearn, fail, and succeed, in academics as well as in our relationships with peers and authority figures. We grapple with various subtle and overt forms of inequality and oppression; issues of academic freedom, surveillance, and censorship; ethical conundrums; clashes of will and of ego; feelings ranging from inadequacy and humiliation to unadulterated joy; and so much more.

We have ordered the stories in small groups. You might envision a statue in the center of our campus. The statue itself is not important—perhaps it is the skull-headed crow—but the statue's base is six-sided with the following words:

Haunting—an entity from the past (or the future) intercedes. Featuring the stories of Jennifer Fliss, Simo Srinivas, and Jo Kaplan

Sacrifice—something is given up for an uncertain return. Featuring the stories of Amber Chen, Cyrus Amelia Fisher, and John Langan

Obsession—an idea, tick-like, attaches and will not let go. Featuring the stories of Steve Rasnic Tem, Michael A. Reed, and Brian Evenson

Knowledge—a truth announces itself, or hides. Featuring the stories of Hussani Abdulrahim, R.B. Lemberg, and Gabino Iglesias

Revenge—a wrong is answered. Featuring the stories of Ana Hurtado, Suzan Palumbo, Ayida Shonibar, and Premee Mohamed

Hope—a possibility becomes real. Featuring the stories of Octavia Cade, Marisca Pichette, and R.J. Joseph

These stories are dark in many different ways. Sometimes they are bitter and vengeful, sometimes full of longing and pain. They look back to problematic pasts and ahead to bewildering futures. Sometimes they revel in the darkness, making it sparkle, making it beautiful.

We hope you will love them as much as we do.

—Christi Nogle

Ijo de Ken Sos Tu?

Jennifer Fliss

The dorm room smelled of burnt heater dust and lemon. Arriving first meant Leyla had her choice of beds, so she decided on the one by the window and dropped her things. Though it was gray outside, the windows reached all the way to the ceiling, so they let in a fair amount of light. Despite the chill, Leyla was sweaty from the walk from the station. The tide had been out, so she was able to walk right up to the school, a luxury Leyla wouldn't appreciate until later.

Out the window, the sea and sky tumbled in a watercolor of gray. A slow creeping waltz of fog was coming in. She pushed open the window to inhale the saltwater air and instead got a breath full of cigarette smoke.

She headed to the office to collect her welcome packet. Cars crunched the gravel driveway, doors creaked open and slammed closed. Loud but unclear voices reverberated down the corridors. In the doorway of the office, while Leyla stood waiting for the secretary to notice her, an overly tall man in an olive trench coat pushed by her. She caught an earthy whiff of chewing tobacco. The man didn't even pause and let himself into a back room.

"Dean Toldt," the secretary said to her and handed Leyla a blue folder emblazoned with the Briarmoor crest. "Welcome packet. Schedule, rules, school history, terms of agreement, that sort of thing."

"Terms of agreement?"

"Conduct contract. Read, sign, return."

"Okay." She wasn't interested in breaking any, or many rules, but she didn't like signing things. It was hard for her to explain, but family lore about lists, roundups, and accusations weighed on her subconscious.

"And remember," the secretary said, tutting her teeth. "No smoking."

"I wasn't," Leyla countered and went off to the back of the building for a smoke. She leaned against the cool limestone.

The fog was dense but held at a perimeter out from the school like a protective ring. The sea lapped at the rough dark rocks that stood in for a beach. Looking up, she noticed she was just under her room's window. An arm reached out, snapping the window shut. Her roommate, Jane, must've arrived.

The hallways bustled with students. In her room, no Jane, but Leyla saw she'd mostly unpacked, *and* she'd taken the bed by the window. Leyla's bag now sat on the floor. She reopened the window, and briny air rippled into the room.

Leyla made her bed with the corduroy coverlet and tasseled pillows filched from her parents' living room. She put away the Briarmoor-approved clothing meant for wet winter days: V-neck sweaters and wool trousers in colors like ash and heather.

In the full-length mirror, Leyla assessed her features. She'd read once that human faces weren't symmetrical. That if they were, it would look strange to our imperfect brains. Suddenly, in a macabre dance, her lips, nose, and eyes jittered around her face and rearranged themselves into a perfectly symmetrical image.

She brought her hand to her mouth, but her mirror image did

not move, hands still at her sides. She gasped and fell onto her roommate's bed. At that moment, in a huff, Jane blew in.

"My bed," she said.

"Yeah, sorry." Leyla scrambled up.

As her roommate patted her blanket, straightening out any proof Leyla had been there at all, Leyla introduced herself. "I'm Leyla."

"It's dinner." Jane grabbed a jacket and left. Leyla fumbled on her shoes and followed, wondering what she had done wrong. She knew little about her roommate. According to the poster on their door, Jane was the English teacher's daughter, from Boston, her favorite food was lasagna, and she spent summers at Bible Camp.

After grace, Leyla picked at meatloaf and limp asparagus. If she were home, she'd be eating roasted chicken, couscous, bourekas, and vegetables that hadn't been boiled into strings, because it was Friday night and Friday nights were for candle-lighting, family-gathering, and feasting.

But not anymore, not for Leyla anyway. She hadn't thought that a one-time experiment with pot would land her exiled at a damp Waspy boarding school. But it did.

"We don't get snacks." The girl across from her had dark curly hair and jade green eyes like Leyla, a combination often commented on: *Where are you* from, *from?* Leyla blinked, and the girl's eyes turned brown, hair red.

"I know."

"I'm Maren."

"Leyla."

"You in Ford Wing?"

"Yeah, you?"

"I'm next door. You stopped by?" Maren tilted her head in confusion.

"Yeah, no," Leyla said. "I haven't met anyone yet."

"Yeah, you came by but didn't say anything. Just like walked in, smiled, and left. I went to follow, but you just went right into your room, closed your door."

Leyla blinked. She'd done no such thing. Just then someone walking behind her pulled on her hair.

"Nice hair, weirdo," they said.

A familiar anger pushed against her sternum. She was always the weird one—hence the one-time attempt to be cool and smoke some pot with the girls on the soccer team during a pep rally. They had left her behind in a cloud of smoke, and Nicky said it might cover up her stench. The pot, Leyla claimed later, was to blame for why she punched Nicky.

"Hey," Maren said. "Weirdos are the good ones."

In English, they sat together. Ms. Lindley held classes in the library, so students clustered on window seats, in wooden study chairs, and in rotating club chairs. The teacher stood rod straight, feet in first position. She was in her sixties and had been at Briarmoor her entire life. She must've had Jane late, Leyla thought.

"What do you think of when you think of the word *canon*," she asked in lieu of a welcome.

"It's like she's trying to be *Dead Poets Society*," Maren whispered. Leyla had seen the movie that summer. To prepare for boarding school, she'd said and laughed lightheartedly, but clenched her teeth and hoped no one noticed her fear and anger at being sent away.

"War," said one student.

"Battlefields," Jane said and beamed at her mother.

"I think she means, like, the literary canon," Leyla said.

"Exactly right Lila," Ms. Lindley said, and Leyla did not correct her. "Who do we think of when we think of the literary canon?"

Silence enveloped the room, an occasional squeak from a rotating chair. The teacher scanned for eager faces. Outside, seagulls cried, and the sea crashed.

Eventually she spoke again. "Hemingway, Fitzgerald. Maybe Nabokov. Shakespeare."

"Man, man, man, and man," Maren said.

"Exactly my point." She passed out burgundy-covered books. Embossed in golden cursive across the cover: *Exspiravit Futurum* by Pearl Welcome.

"That's gotta be a pseudonym," Maren said.

"I found these in the library," Ms. Lindley said. "The author wrote it when she was just a teenager. Like you."

Leyla studied the book. No synopsis, no biographical statement, or photograph. The only information was that it was published in 1942 in Wickham, the nearest city to the school.

"This will be the first of our noncanonical texts. You have two weeks to read it," she said as the bell rang.

"Seems sacrilegious," Maren said.

"It's kind of rad." Leyla tucked the book into her pack.

They said it was going to rain; outdoor activities had been canceled ahead of the impending storm, but so far not a drop of rain had fallen. While everyone remained inside, Leyla went to the water's edge, laid out her towel, and wrapped a scarf around her neck. The sea that surrounded the school was as beautiful as it was intimidating. Nothing like her landlocked hometown. Despite the circumstances, she wanted to like it at Briarmoor. She wanted to be like one of the girls in the brochure, broad white toothed smile, carefree, and educated by the seaside. A gull squawked overhead. She opened *Exspiravit Futurum*.

Catherine lived in a small town with a foreboding castle on a hill. Lore said the mayor's wife lived there and after a particularly gruesome stillbirth, the mayor's wife went mad. She was ensconced in the castle with people waiting on her with cakes and tea every day. In this way the mayor, Ronald, was able to assuage his guilt. When it rained, the townspeople said that it was the mayor's wife sobbing over her loss. One day, Catherine went for a walk and wound up at the castle. There was a moat, but it was dry. There were two suits of armor stationed there, but they were empty, mere husks of security.

7

"The mayor's wife never even gets a name," Leyla said during gym class.

"Look alive!" A soccer ball walloped Leyla's stomach. She fell and landed in tire-tracks of mud. She could swear she recognized Jane's laughter.

"Asshole!" Maren shouted.

"Language!" Mr. Onishi called out. Leyla wiped at her pants, only managing to smear the mud further and sullying her hands. The tunnel sound of peers laughing funneled in and out of her ears.

Mr. Onishi clapped, and the class quieted. Maren passed tissues to Leyla which were ineffective, but thoughtful. As she dabbed the dirt, Dean Toldt approached. Reddish spittle at the corners of his mouth reminded Leyla of blood. He had, she was certain, seen the whole thing. He was, she'd hoped, going to reprimand the person who kicked the ball.

Instead, he turned to Leyla. "Get cleaned up." He smiled at Mr. Onishi. "Soccer is my favorite time of year."

Leyla stormed off to the sound of kicking balls. She felt drops of rain on her face but wasn't sure if it was rain or tears.

She changed and instead of returning to class, wandered the halls. At a glass display case, she studied trophies, felt banners, photos, articles from local newspapers reporting on how wonderful Briarmoor is at all she does. She zeroed in on one photo in particular. On old newsprint gone yellow, a woman with dark curls wore a skirt with a single pleat, a smudge of a necklace, and a basketball in her hand. *Unexpected: Frosh Perla Benveniste clinches championship for Briarmoor.*

Leyla recognized the name Benveniste from a family tree she had to do the previous year. Her tree was feeble with broken branches and eventually she turned in a sketch of a pile of sticks. That was the first time Nicky whose nose she punched had called her a "weirdo lizard."

She stared into Perla's face, but it was grainy. *"Ijo de ken sos tu?"*

Leyla said in Ladino. Whose child are you? It was the near-dead language of Sephardic Jews that her avuela had tried to impress upon her, but she too had only known a handful of words, the language having been stolen away.

A whistle started at the dark end of the corridor and built as it moved toward Leyla. Her hair was pushed back by a sudden wind —a banshee crescendo. Her feet refused to budge. A door slammed. Then silence.

Leyla turned back to the article that accompanied the photo, but the words had rearranged. Everything but one sentence was blurry: *Same as you.*

She tore down the hallway, her breath her only friend until she located a glowing green exit sign. She ignored the "emergency only" notice and pushed through the door, the alarm immediately ringing as she fell into the sunshine.

Only fifteen minutes before, it had been ashy gray. Now Leyla tilted her head up and felt the warmth on her face.

Her punishment for setting off the alarm was that she had to stay in her room for outdoor time. *Who am I gonna hang with?* Maren had whined, and Leyla would have responded in the same way.

She returned to her room to grab a book when she saw it. A swastika etched sloppily into the wood of the desk, about three inches across. Leyla's face grew hot. She rubbed at the mark but only succeeded in embedding splinters into the soft place of her palm. Biting down on her lip, she drew blood. She pulled the door open and looked up and down the hallway, but there was no one around. Anger torched her insides. She surveyed the room. No other signs of defilement, nothing out of place. She pushed the window open and screamed. A flurry of gulls took off in the echo of her madness.

She fell to the floor in tears and snot. And then she noticed Jane's bedside drawer ajar. She pulled it open and there, nestled beside Jane's worn Bible, was a rusty chisel. Leyla fingered the edge, the small flakes of wood. She tore at Jane's bed. Flung sheets to the ground. Snapped her pencils, pulled her clothes from hangers.

Leyla eventually fell back, her breath heavy. She'd get in trouble. She knew Jane would never admit what she'd done and that they'd believe her, the pious daughter of a teacher. As her breathing settled, Leyla opened the Briarmoor welcome packet. Other than her schedule, she hadn't looked at it. Twice the secretary told her she had to hand in her Terms of Agreement. Twice, Leyla ignored her.

With growing dread, she read the dossier of school history. Briarmoor wasn't as old as she'd thought. The foundation was set in 1928, but the school hadn't been completed until 1941. *A place where students can be themselves. Scholarship. Faith. Community.* She snorted and shut the folder. A waft of smoke blew into the room. She took this as her cue, grabbed *Exspiravit Futurum* and a pack of cigarettes from under her mattress, and headed outside.

The drawbridge was down. Though the empty knights' armor unsettled Catherine, she felt a compulsion to enter the castle. For all the mayor's wife's crying, for all her alleged pain, the townspeople never investigated further. Catherine's footsteps echoed on the stone walkway. There was an eerie emptiness, and the furniture was covered in sheets, dust motes swirled in thin sunbeams. Catherine wandered the castle, taking two full hours, opening doors, calling out in loud whispers. The kitchen looked as if it hadn't been used in years.

When she finally reached the turreted bedroom, she collapsed in exhaustion. The room wasn't as worn as the rest of the castle. The bed's sheets were crinkled, a glass of water on the table. Catherine fell asleep. When she woke, it was night, and a charm dangled delicately on her decolletage, an upside-down hand pressed in opal. The courage she had during the day had disappeared. She ran to the door to find it locked. She banged and shouted for help. A voice came from the other side of the door: I know you're frightened, but this is for your own good. Adyo, my love.

Leyla recognized the Ladino and immediately thought of Perla Benveniste. Pearl Welcome. She ran to the school library.

"Can I help you?" the librarian asked. She'd been absently flipping through the card catalog and seemed happy for a task.

"Are there yearbooks here?"

She led Leyla to a back room. "You can't check these out though."

Leyla ran her fingers along the leathery spines of Briarmoor yearbooks, pulling out 1944, the year Perla would've graduated.. There was a page explaining how the girls knit and bundled care packages for the boys at war. But other than that, the old black and white photographs painted a school year that ran its normal course. Among the senior portraits, she searched for Perla Benveniste. Nothing. No mention of Perla in the entire yearbook. She wasn't in the 1943 yearbook either. Leyla paged through 1942 and found Perla in a sophomore year class photo. Her dark curls stood out in a sea of light-haired coifs, but there was no portrait photo of her. She must have disappeared from Briarmoor sometime that year. For someone who had been a star, someone who made it to the trophy case, why was she missing from these bibles of memory?

Jane's things were gone when Leyla returned. Stripped mattress, hangers hanging empty. At dinner, Leyla saw Jane, who, when their eyes met, made the sign of a cross.

That night, Leyla, writhing in sweat, shouted out in terror. Her eyes flew open, and she couldn't remember a thing. Her mouth was stale. The clock ticked. She pulled on her slippers, and walked through the cold stone hallway, to the bathroom.

She stared at herself in the mirror. Should she just let it go? Why make waves? No one physically hurt her, and Jane wasn't going to say anything. Leyla suspected the school's take would be: *just a joke*. She'd heard it before. There would be Janes and Dean Toldts everywhere in life. She would graduate and move on. She would ignore them.

Then her facial features began to shuffle in the mirror. She blinked.

"It'll be better if you leave."

Leyla whirled around and saw herself. No, not herself, Perla. The resemblance was strong. She wore the outfit from the news photo, vintage basketball uniform, charm at her neck. An opal hamsa.

Heart thudding against its cage, Leyla whispered, "*Ijo de ken sos tu?*"

"Sarah, Rebecca, Rachel, Leah," Perla said, face softening as she recited the familiar names of the Jewish foremothers. "Same as you."

"What happened?" Leyla asked, thinking of the yearbooks. "What happened to you?"

"My father was a builder. They were on a tight schedule. Made a deal. He'd finish the building quickly in exchange for his daughter's tuition. They accepted, but," Perla said, "they never *really* accepted, if you know what I mean."

Leyla did.

"But I was good at something. Basketball. I could help them win things. At the time, things in Europe weren't great, so I felt I had to appreciate what I had. I've heard the girls talk over the years. About their grandfathers liberating camps, how brave they were. Heroes!" Leyla knew this refrain also. No mention of ships turned away, visas not granted, or immigration quotas.

"I got top marks and loved to write stories," Perla said. "I had one friend. You always need a friend. Do you have one?"

"Yeah."

"Good. Mine was my English teacher, Ms. Barrett. After we won States, she presented me with a few bound copies of one of my stories. She'd done it in town, by a publisher friend."

The connection between the author of the book and Perla Benveniste became clear.

"Ms. Barret had asked what my name meant but said it sounded Italian."

"But it's not."

"Remember the war was going on. She used a pen name. I didn't think I cared."

"The title, *Exspiravit Futurum*?"

"Future ghost."

"Future ghost?"

"As in, it isn't only me haunting you. It was you. Future you is trying to change it. *I* think you need to get out."

Leyla thought of the mirrored face. The cigarette smoke outside her window. She was the only student she knew of who smoked.

"Did you die?" Leyla whispered.

"One night we had a mixer with St. Benedict's. My roommate, Kathleen Lindley, thought I was stealing her boyfriend. I was just giving him punch because I was basically on scholarship, I worked as a server. Humiliating."

Leyla could imagine. "Wait a minute, Ms. Lindley?" Perla nodded.

Shock chilled Leyla's spine. "Oh my god. Her daughter is *my* roommate. Was, anyway."

Perla's curls bobbed vigorously as she nodded. "Kathleen was soused on rum. She said I jumped. Oh, she feels guilty now. That's why she's pushing my book, but dead is dead."

Perla unclasped her necklace and fastened it around Leyla's throat. She expected to feel the ghost of a breath, a whisper of fingers brushing her skin, but she felt nothing until the weight of the charm settled on her chest. "Be careful. You can trust them," Perla said, "until you can't."

The cold was sudden, and Perla disappeared into the night chill of a drafty building made of stone. Like a castle, Leyla thought. She brought her hands to the delicate chain, ran her hands against the smooth charm shaped like an upside-down hand. She didn't sleep the rest of the night.

In the morning, outside the cafeteria, she bumped into Dean

Toldt and Ms. Lindley.

"Sorry," Leyla said. She attempted to move past them as she held the hamsa in her hand, trying to hide it from Ms. Lindley. But the teacher noticed it and her eyes grew and her breath quickened in the hollow of her neck.

"Leyla, I'll pray for you," Dean Toldt said and turned away. Ms. Lindley followed.

Leyla knew these prayers were just daggers disguised as flowers. She ate her breakfast seething. She had no idea why everyone hated her so. No valid reason, other than plain old bigotry and that seemed too banal, too common for these supposedly promising and modern young women. Except she knew.

"I need to go," she told Maren.

"What? Why?"

"It's not safe."

"You mean the girls? The bullying?"

Leyla didn't know how to explain. Or rather, if she should.

"You've been off lately," Maren said. "I should've asked."

"You know the book Ms. Lindley gave us?" Should she tell Maren about how their teacher was a murderer? "So the author—" Leyla didn't finish the sentence. Maren looked at her with her over-large puppy eyes. Leyla didn't feel she could let her into the darkness without tarnishing her. She knew not everyone had to experience the darkness—not directly anyway.

"Someone etched a swastika in my desk?" She said it like a question to ward off any potential defensiveness.

"What the hell?" Maren said. "Why didn't you tell me?" Maybe Leyla did need an ally. A living one. "You've been dealing with this antisemitic crap, and I didn't know?"

"Yeah?" Leyla hedged.

She debriefed Maren. She told her about Perla, about Ms. Lindley's relationship with the other former Jewish student, and how their very own teacher had been the one who pushed Perla out a window. About the remarks the dean made and the way he looked at her like she was vermin. Leyla told Maren how she was being stalked by two well-meaning ghosts and that she was more worried about the living than the dead. Maren listened intently and pulled Leyla into a hug.

They made an escape plan. While Maren distracted the dean's secretary, Leyla approached the bank of phones outside the office. Dialing her parents, she curled the cord in her fingers and studied scratched notes in the wall: *Lindsay was here. Class of '87 rules.*

If she told them about the swastika, surely they'd retrieve her immediately. Students called home weekly, but she hadn't because she was still mad at them for sending her away. Now she wanted to fall into her father's arms, allow her mother to unwind her curls with her callused fingers. They didn't answer. She tried again and didn't even get the answering machine.

She would leave anyway. She packed a bag, threw on a raincoat. She could hear rain slapping the building, could smell the dampness seeping into Briarmoor's walls.

Outside, the tide was coming in. The bridge would be fully submerged in minutes. It wasn't too deep yet. She ran to the gate and shoved it open. Approaching the bridge, her feet sloshed. Each step sucked her in deeper, languid in the sand. She turned back to the school. The fog was closing in. Frothy waves soaked her pants. If she kept going ahead and didn't make it, she would lose her way back too.

Then she saw, at the school's gate, her phantom self. Curls lank, face pale and dripping. Even from this distance, she could see her eyes drooping, her entire face sliding off like melting wax.

Leyla looked back, and on the water-flooded bridge, Perla was beckoning her to cross, to escape. "I won't make it," Leyla shouted. A ferocious onslaught of seawater slapped her knees. Leyla turned back, but her falling-apart ghost self was gone. A wave walloped her again and she staggered back. She wouldn't make it.

"I'll come back," she yelled at Perla, hoping she was telling the truth.

She waded back through the water toward the gate, heavy footsteps taking her back to Briarmoor.

Dean Toldt stood at the main door in cruel welcome, chewing his tobacco so viciously, Leyla felt like he was eating her soul, masticating it into a paste, preparing to spit it out.

"We can't have girls leaving," he said, turning to reveal her former roommate Jane behind him. "Jane will take you back." Leyla recoiled, but she had no choice.

In the room, Jane opened the window like she still lived there. Together they stood in front of the gaping floor to ceiling window. It had stopped raining, but the sea and sky were the same gray, like they were one thing.

"Get out," Leyla said.

"You know," Jane said, "everything happens for a reason." Leyla smelled cigarette smoke.

"Oh my God, enough with your stupid platitudes."

Below, Leyla's ghost self was waving overlong arms, grotesque mouth wide exposing a dark throat. A funnel of blackness swirled up from her gullet. Up and out of her mouth, growing, gaining speed like a tornado of crows. The stench of rotting fish. Leyla flew backwards, knocking into Jane.

"Leyla?" Jane said. "I believe that whenever God closes a door, he opens a window," Jane said and shoved a Bible into Leyla's chest.

Out the window, Leyla fell.

After the smack on the flagstones and the slight rebound of parts, Leyla looked as if she was only asleep. Her limbs were not turned at strange angles. No blood pooled by her skull.

Perla petted Leyla's soft curls and whispered, "*Ijo de ken sos tu?*"

"Yours," Leyla said as she grew into her future ghost self, who would stay to try to stop the thing from happening again and again and again while Perla would always encourage escape. Two ghosts, wanting so badly to survive.

The Girls of St. X

Simo Srinivas

Your American cousin tells you that the bright teal uniforms of Penang's St. X School for Girls are the furthest thing from frightening. You disagree: they are the same color as the tiles at the bottom of the dry swimming pool in the old gymnasium, the pool where Millicent Poh smashed her head open and died.

"But you know, don't you lah," your neighbor Bee Lay Teoh says, "it's not true?"

You and Bee have taken your American cousin, Natalie Seow-Gunderson, to Gurney Plaza. The air inside the shopping center is clammy; Natalie's naturally blonde hair sticks to the back of her long neck. Between the strands that chlorine has stained green, you can see the rows of mosquito bites like big ripe pimples.

The sight makes your own skin itch, even though the mosquitos don't bite you anymore.

"It's total fiction lah."

Bee is drinking soy milk with grass jelly from the kiosk where her friend Anoja's older brother works. Even when Natalie is with you, tall, lovely, exotic Natalie, he only has eyes for Bee. When *you* speak, he looks away.

He's afraid of you, you think, the way most people are afraid of St. X students. You wonder if Bee will become afraid of you, too, when you pass your test and become a St. X graduate.

"What's fiction?"

"The story that the St. X girl died." Bee slurps up a fat slug of jelly with a smile. "Anoja told me so."

"Anoja is a liar," you say, "and she goes to PCG Secondary. How would she know what goes on at St. X?"

Natalie waves at you. "Eunie, I want ice cream." Her mango slush cup is empty. The tip of her taro-colored straw is white and bent from her gnawing canines.

"It's not fair," Bee complains. "I diet and diet and look like a steamed bun, and your cousin eats and eats and looks like—*that*."

"Eunie, come on." Natalie, a year older than you, jumps up and down like a little girl.

"She gets it from her daddy, nothing you or I can do lah," you say. "OK, coming, Nat biao jie."

"Anoja was not lying, anyway," Bee says, jogging your elbow. "About your St. X girl."

You scowl. Bee will believe anything. "If she isn't dead, Teoh Bee Lay, then where is she?"

Bee's right about one thing, though: it isn't fair. By suppertime, Natalie has eaten one mango slush, one black sesame soft serve, a plate of kuih, a custard bun, two mangosteens, and two dragon fruits, but she still finds room for your mommy's fried butterfish and a bowl and a half of rice.

You aren't hungry, but for your mommy's sake you swallow a few grains.

Your mommy doesn't notice. She only has eyes for Natalie, for your tall, beautiful, hungry cousin. This morning, she plaited Natalie's greenish hair, standing on a stool to reach its roots. Tonight, she pulls the bones from her butterfish before placing morsels of its white flesh on your cousin's plate.

"Eat, eat," she says. "Growing girl ah, sporty ah, need your nutrition."

"Daddy," you say. "May I..."

"Of course excused," your daddy says. "Last-minute revision eh?"

"Yes, Daddy."

Your aunt—your daddy's older sister, Natalie's mommy, and an alumna of St. X—nods approvingly as you leave the table. She didn't want you to take Natalie to Gurney Plaza, today of all days. She wanted you to study. To prepare.

You don't. You open your bedroom window and stare into the heavy blue light of evening. You want it to rain until the St. X gymnasium floods and the dry pool fills again.

Downstairs, you hear the clinking of plates as your mommy begins the washing up. Your daddy and your aunt are talking. You hear your daddy's voice: *Yes, Big Sis. Yes, Big Sis.*

The mosquitos drift disinterestedly around you. Thinking of Natalie, you kill them anyway.

At bedtime, your cousin slips into your room. She wants to try on your uniform: her school doesn't have uniforms, and yours is so colorful and pretty. "Please, Eunie, please?"

"Go ahead lah."

You help her pull it over her t-shirt and short-shorts. The bodice sags against her narrow torso. The skirt that so demurely hides your knees every day barely covers her long white thighs.

"Look, Mom," your cousin says, "I'm going to St. X, too."

Your head snaps up. Your aunt is a shadow in the corridor with glittering black eyes.

"Take that off," she barks in English. "At once, do you hear me?"

Natalie's pale skin turns red. She strips down, all the way down: all the way to her underwear.

Your cousin's breasts and belly are pockmarked with bites. Her underwear is a matching set like in lingerie magazines. You wonder who bought this for her. Surely not your aunt.

Still frowning, your aunt tells you in Hokkien, "The St. X uniform isn't something you can share."

"No, Dua Kor," you say. "Sorry ah, Dua Kor."

Your aunt used to have a St. X uniform of her own. Your daddy has a picture of her from long ago in his office, a girl with a square jaw and cropped hair and the pewter badge of St. X shining on her blouse. If the photo wasn't old and black-and-white, you would think it was a picture of you.

When your aunt visits, once every two years for two months, your daddy puts her up for free and pays for everything. This is because your aunt paid for your daddy to go to university and supported the decision of your daddy to marry your mommy, who was just a poor uneducated girl from the outskirts of Ipoh. *Your dua kor stood up to gong gong for me*, your daddy explains, *so now I do this for her.*

Not to mention ah, he murmurs, *she pays for your schooling*.

You don't like to see your mommy with shadows under her eyes from cooking and cleaning and driving your aunt and her American family everywhere, even to Melaka. You don't like the way your aunt's husband, your kor-tiu, looks at your mommy.

You don't like the advice your aunt gives you, from one St. X student to another.

"Eunice ah," she says, taking you aside while your cousin, red-faced, runs out of your bedroom, "don't bother with my daughter anymore. A girl like that only exists to eat and float. You and I are special. You and I were made for St. X."

But the truth is you stopped caring about St. X the moment Millicent Poh fell and died.

Unlike your friendship with Bee, whom you only know because the two of you have been next-door neighbors since conception, or with Anoja, whom you only know through Bee, or with the cold haughty girls who sit near you in class, your friendship with Millicent Poh did not come about through proximity or convenience. Milly was a tall, athletic St. X student who boarded at school and whom you would never have encountered if you hadn't answered the advertisement she'd posted on the central bulletin: *Calling all St. X babes interested in synchronized swimming.*

Your mommy had told you timidly that you knew best. Your daddy had told you it was fine as long as it didn't interfere with your aunt's next visit. In the end, a problem with the swimming pool filters had meant the pool was off-limits; the school had drained it one week into first term, before you had even gotten a chance to put on your swimsuit.

Disappointed, the other interested babes of St. X moved on. But you and Milly continued to meet in the old gymnasium after class—Milly had the trust of the games mistress, and therefore the key—and dance on the tiles. When you got tired, you would rest above the deep end, dangling your feet over the chalky chasm. The sun would set, and you would try to go home, and Milly, who loved St. X and couldn't understand why anyone would want to leave, would tell wild tales to keep you there and pretend to lose the key.

The pool, Milly told you one night, was a relic. Older than the oldest St. X building, which had been built in 1926. It had been the fishing pond of a British colonial police officer gazetted in Penang. Little girls, including the police officer's pretty daughter, had drowned in the pond, becoming fish themselves.

You had joked, *And before it was Lieutenant Bertram's fishing pond, it was a haunted watering hole for tigers, and before that it was an evil puddle that ruined the Sultan's boots.*

You remember that Milly had laughed. *Correct lah,* she had said. *Well, it's cursed, anyway.* Then she had put her arms around you and drawn you away from the door, telling you there was still time to practice your pliés.

Your aunt finishes her lecture and goes to bed. You find your cousin squatting in the bathroom like an overgrown frog, her arms around her shins and her face in her knees. The mosquitos have even bitten the backs of her hands.

"I wish I was like you," she croaks, muffled. "I wish I could go to St. X, too."

"Schooling not everything lah," you say awkwardly. "Your daddy said you're a good swimmer."

"Not good enough for Mom." Natalie sniffs. You can tell she wants to scream—you see the swelling of her ribcage—but she holds it in. "Why didn't she give me a chance to apply? Why did she raise me in freaking Massachusetts?"

Your daddy told you the answer. *Graduates of St. X expected to leave lah. Kuala Lumpur, Singapore, Melbourne, Perth. London, Oxford, Cambridge, Salem: the farther the better. If they don't leave they are considered failures. But you don't go too far eh Eunie, KL or Singapore far enough.*

You could stay here in fact, your daddy had added quietly, after making sure your aunt wasn't listening. *Stay in Penang. Be the first St. X failure. But not a failure in our eyes OK?*

"You don't even like it, do you?" your cousin says. "We used to have so much fun together, but you're so serious now, Eunie, you're always frowning, and you barely eat."

Poor Natalie: her face is swollen from crying. You wish you could join in, but your eyes are as dry as the St. X swimming pool.

"Eunice." Your aunt's husband makes you jump as you enter your darkened kitchen in search of water for your cousin. He's leaning against the counter, drinking. He's tall and gangly like his daughter, good-looking except for his nose, which is long and pointed like a proboscis.

His name is Samuel, but you and your mommy used to have another secret name for him, inspired by his nose and his habit of invisibly hovering.

"Burning the midnight oil?" Samuel Gunderson asks.

"Yes, Kor-Tiu," you say politely.

"My wife tells me you have a big test tomorrow," Samuel says. "A final or something?"

"Yes, Kor-Tiu."

"You must be nervous. My wife says she wasn't nervous when it was her turn, but she says kids are different now. Softer. Nicer. Not so dog-eat-dog."

"Yes, Kor-Tiu."

"And Natalie says you're real sweet. Of course, any daughter of Cheng Ee's would be sweet, wouldn't she? But you don't look like her. You take after my wife's side of the family." Samuel tsks. "Too bad."

Your mouth is filling with saliva, tangy and thick. Your aunt's husband talks about your mommy like she's a pulsing artery in a plump young cheek. You want to slap him and watch him explode into a mess of blood and guts. You swallow instead.

"Nat biao jie does not look like her mommy either."

"That's for the best, don't you think?" Samuel says, unfazed. "In the world outside St. X—which does exist, by the way, it's the

23

same world your wonderful *mommy* comes from—Natalie doesn't have to be ruthless or clever or powerful. She just has to be pretty."

You wonder how much Samuel, a trust fund baby, knows or cares about St. X. You wonder if he's as curious about it as his daughter is, as angry about being shut out.

"Yes, Kor-Tiu." Your voice is full of venom.

"Oh, Eunice." Samuel winks. "I may be a mosquito, but let me remind you: it's the female of the species that bites."

The day of your test, your mommy makes you and your aunt a breakfast of kaya toast and soft-boiled egg and practically bows out of the kitchen. Your daddy has already gone to work. *Mommy,* you start to say, but your mommy is in awe of you and no longer meets your eyes.

Your aunt tries to smile. It sits strangely on her normally stern face.

"How are you feeling?"

"OK, Dua Kor." You don't try to smile back.

"There's no trick to it, unfortunately," your aunt says. "Just try to stay calm. Think of your future."

"Is that what you did, Dua Kor?"

Your aunt pokes at her egg with a corner of her toast. Today, like you, she seems to have lost her appetite. "I thought of your daddy's future," she says.

"Were you angry when he decided to stay here?" you ask. "Because of my mommy? Because she was going to have me?"

"I was furious!" Your aunt sighs. "It was hard to keep your gong gong from killing him when I wanted to kill him myself! But then you were born, Eunice ah, and I knew my sacrifice had been worth it."

The bell rings.

"Eunie ah," your mommy calls. "Bee is here."

"Eunie ah," Bee cries. "We're going to be late!"

Your aunt trails you to the entryway. "How many kids next door?" she asks lightly as you put on your shoes.

"Just one lah," you reply, mirroring her casual tone. "Just Bee."

"Things have really changed since I was a girl." Another sigh. "Our neighbors had more kids than you could count on your fingers. It was easy, back then, to lose track of them." Then, without warning, your aunt hugs you, squeezing you until you ache. "Go, Eunice. Show me you understand what it means to wear the uniform."

You bring Bee to St. X hand in hand. It's the only way outsiders can come to campus. But at the heavy iron gate wrought in the shape of climbing morning glories—the same flowers engraved on your badge—you let go of your friend's sweating palm and let her clamber onto a scooter behind Anoja's older brother.

"Have fun," you tell them. "Be good."

Anoja's brother, Dayan, laughs. "Cannot do both." You look at him in surprise: he is no longer afraid of you.

"What did you tell him?" you ask Bee.

"Nothing lah. Just that you were thinking about transferring." Bee leans over to flick a mosquito from your arm. "You're my best friend, you know that, Seow Eunie? See you tomorrow, OK?"

Fondness glimmers inside you like a coin at the bottom of a deep dark well. You watch them putt-putting away under the seraya trees.

When you turn back to St. X, your maths mistress is observing you, black-eyed, through the iron gaps. Other test-takers are milling around behind her, holding hands with girls you've never seen before.

Your maths mistress doesn't remark on your empty hand. She simply opens the gate.

There's always been something about your American cousin that never seemed quite real. You think she gets it from her daddy, the creepy mosquito. When you enter the old gymnasium and see her standing by the swimming pool, you think she looks like a shaft of moonlight or a hantu galah, a pole ghost.

Tall and spindly, the pole ghost turns and hands you the gymnasium key. You slip it back into the pocket of your uniform.

"No trouble eh?" you ask.

None, Natalie says proudly. "They opened the gate for me."

"See lah," you say, "able to get into St. X after all."

Your cousin's thin white face splits into a grin.

Last night, huddled on the bathroom floor, you'd told your cousin about the St. X test. It wasn't supposed to be deadly. But it would be dangerous. It would change you, take something from you.

You and the girl you brought with you, hand in hand.

I knew it, Natalie had said. *I knew my mom had to have done something. To become the way she is.*

Can I come? she had asked. *Can I take your place?*

Now, Natalie asks, "So what's the test? Is it a race?"

She asks because the swimming pool is full. The water is a startling deep-sea color, almost cobalt, its surface sparkling as if overlaid with a diamond net. The cursed puddle, you think. The colonial fishing pond.

Everyone's test is different, you explain. "If you think yours is a race, then race."

"What are *you* going to do?"

You don't respond. You sit at the shallow end, a safe distance from the dark blue water. You watch Natalie stripping down: eagerly, kicking away her sandals and ripping off her shorts and t-

26

shirt. Her underwear, another matching set, is the same jaunty teal as your uniform.

From your vantage point, you can look through the window in the gymnasium door. You can see your aunt's stony face on the other side of the runny old glass, liquefying with shock and fear.

I left Mom a note, your cousin murmured to you when she returned the gymnasium key. *She's gonna read it and freak. She's always telling me I can't do what she did, that I don't have what it takes.*

I'll show her, your cousin hissed. *I'll fucking show her.*

For a moment, some of the resolve left the tight set of her jaw, and she was childish again, her voice petulant, wavering. *Do you think your mom will give my mom a ride to campus? Do you think she'll show up in time to stop me?*

Your mommy took Bee's mommy to Gurney Plaza. But your aunt, a graduate of St. X, doesn't need a car to go places.

Your aunt is banging on the door and shouting. *Natalie, Natalie.* The games mistress, also black-eyed, appears behind her and yanks her back. They fall out of sight.

Your cousin's gaze is fixed on the shimmering pool.

"Nat biao jie." Crouched at the edge of the deep end, your cousin unfolds slightly to look at you. "Do you like boys?"

Natalie's incredulous laughter ripples through the gymnasium. "Jeez, Eunie, what does that have to do with anything?"

"Just curious lah."

"I guess I do," Natalie says. "Don't you?"

She doesn't wait for your answer; she dives.

There is a long green pool in the atrium in the Tanjong Pagar reception hall. Rubber plants bow over the water. Now and then, a golden koi darts by.

"Biao mei."

Your American cousin glides toward you with graceful clicking steps. With her body rising from the frothy white skirts of her wedding dress, she looks like the Little Mermaid the moment before her dissolution into seafoam.

She greets you coolly with a kiss on the cheek.

"Where's the groom?" you ask.

Natalie's earrings, pearls, shiver as she shrugs. "Does it matter?"

Your cousin's husband is an MIT dropout. You remember him as a kind of shadow—faceless and blurry. His parents are shadows, too, a Mr. and Mrs. Vaswani. They walked Natalie down the aisle together because Natalie's daddy is dead. He died of a massive brain hemorrhage not long after his daughter plunged into the St. X swimming pool.

Your aunt cut her visit short. Your daddy pulled you out of school.

You never went back to St. X. You never saw your aunt again.

Your mommy and daddy had two more babies, two girls. Teenagers now, they go to your alma mater, PCG Secondary. When they visit you in Singapore, you take them out for ice kachang. While your mommy and daddy look on, smiling, they call you Big Sis and ask for your advice: on school, on boys.

You tell them you're happy to be an expert on neither.

That day in the old St. X gymnasium, your cousin had flopped onto the tile, screaming, convulsing, glowing so white-hot it was hard to look at her.

When she could walk and talk again, she had taken your hand and pulled you out onto the lawn, strolling by her wailing mother without a second glance. Your teachers had followed you, black-eyed, silent, until you were safely on the other side of the gate, where it was raining. You had exchanged clothes with your cousin and watched St. X melt into the storm.

I met a girl at the bottom of the pool, Natalie said. *She wanted to know if you miss her. She wanted to know if you're sorry.*

Milly hadn't brought anyone from outside for her test. She'd locked the gymnasium door and refused to relinquish the key. *I won't let you go home tonight, Eunice. We can be together in St. X forever, like the girls in Lieutenant Bertram's pond. Dance with me.*

Snatching at you, she'd lost her balance, dropping the key as she fell.

Elegant, metallic, and bored, Natalie's voice cuts into your memories. "There's Daniel Kwon. He's an investor. I have to say hello. It was wonderful to see you, Eunice."

Looking after your cousin, at her smooth unblemished skin, you feel your own skin beginning to itch. You slap at your mosquito bites instead of scratching them. Your cousin finds her target and smiles at him with shining black eyes.

Your stomach growls. Your smartphone buzzes. It's your plus one, your girlfriend, waiting for you at the taxi stand.

Before you go, you slip off your heels and wade into the water.

For a split second, you feel the silky touch of hands around your ankles, the hands of Millicent Poh. You twirl together. And then she drifts away.

Humanities 215

Science, Literature, and Human Insight

Jo Kaplan

THE PROFESSOR SPOKE at length to twenty-two black and silent squares. The quiet emptiness comforted her, absent of the stares of students who saw her as a waitress serving up their grades. Anonymity lived behind the screen, and for the professor, it was like being alone.

Gone were the days of the sage on the stage, endless lectures while pupils sat raptly taking notes. This was what the professor felt she was meant for: an idealized time, though one she likely would never have inhabited, anyway. She struggled to engage socially. The byzantine hierarchies within the college dizzied her. She felt pummeled by emails, besieged by endless lip-servicey initiatives.

All the participants were muted, as indicated by their little red microphones and by the lovely silence. She did not need to shush chatterers or nag surreptitious cell phone users.

"Okay, I think that wraps us up for today. Don't forget, your essay on the implications of 20th century technology on the moral trajectory of American society is due on Monday."

One by one, the black boxes winked out of existence until the professor was left staring at the lone remaining window bearing her own face.

This was a period of transition, a liminal space neither here nor there. The college was open; students were on campus; it wasn't lockdown anymore. Yet a number of classes remained online, remote. The college halls echoed, less full than pre-pandemic times. The odd faculty member hunched behind the paper armor of a mask, all eyes and blankness to the chin. One of the older buildings —a science center with a crumbling observatory—stood shuttered, unneeded with this diminished in-person student body, waiting to be replaced by something new.

Grading essays was tedious, though every so often she found herself delighted by some cleverly-articulated insight or by the concerted passion of a young idealist. Before she sat down at her desk, the professor tried to take a few minutes to clear her mind. It was no good bringing personal feelings into it, as they would only muddy the process.

But it was already after seven, and she really needed to get started. Darkness crouched like a physical entity on the other side of her window. She snapped the blinds shut and opened the first essay.

Something about the essay felt. . . off. She couldn't put her finger on it. Certainly, it wasn't that the essay was *bad*. It was coherently written, on topic, and without visible error. Yet she found herself staring at it, somehow unable to determine what it *was*. Despite its clarity, its varied language, its directly-communicated points, it hardly seemed like an A. Too well-written to be a C. B was unsettled territory, but was this really a B—a quality effort with demonstrated proficiency despite a few lapses in logic, a few misused words, a few areas that require embellishment? No, these hallmarks were absent, too.

Something about the essay just rang false.

Skipping the grade for now, she moved to the next one. Perhaps she only needed to get her bearings first. But the problem persisted here. And the same arose with the next essay. The built-in plagiarism detector indicated 100% original work.

Then it came to her, a thought like a lightning bolt: what if no human had written these essays?

She opened an AI detector and copied the first essay in. Submitted.

Your text is likely to be written entirely by an AI.

The professor rocketed out of her chair, sputtering with indignation. The *nerve!* Her feet took her away, and when she returned it was with a bottle of wine and a stemless glass, which she balanced on an old cork coaster.

The more essays she copied into the platform, the more her sips became gulps.

Your text is likely to be written entirely by an AI.

Only one essay remained. She drained the last bit of wine in her glass, gut churning with righteous anger. Her heart tripped over itself as she opened the file. She read, trying to find a hint of humanity between the lines. And the irony of it all—that it was a Humanities class.

"While technology has enhanced everyday life in many ways, it has also had a destructive effect on the environment. For example, widespread use of fossil fuels has resulted in environmental degradation through increased greenhouse gas emissions. Climate change has serious moral implications for future generations. For this reason, humanity must be held accountable for its impact on the earth. Some suggest a total eradication of the species is the only viable solution to the problems they have wrought."

The professor paused over these lines. Though she had, of course, been neglecting marginal comments—to what end should she waste time writing critiques for a robot?—her fingers found themselves unable to resist highlighting the last sentence and typing into the comment box, "That seems a bit extreme, don't you think?"

She almost deleted it. Of late, more and more snarky comments had been creeping into her essay feedback. She knew it wasn't beneficial for the students, but sometimes she couldn't help herself. Staring at those lines, she poured another glass of shiraz. A bulb of red bled from the lip of the bottle down its side, threatened to make a ring on her desk. She quickly slid a paper underneath—cringed from worry it was something important before seeing it was just an old student evaluation.

With a sigh, she checked the essay.

Your text is likely to be written entirely by an AI.

That was all of them. Every last one. Not a single essay in the bunch had even partially been written by a human. How exactly did they think they could get away with this?

All she could do right now—it was approaching nine, and she could hear the coyotes carousing with mad glee in the foothills—was send a blanket email letting the class know their ruse could not fool her, and they were all expected to rewrite their essays or receive no credit for their submissions. Her fingertips snapped against the keyboard, trying to imbue the words with fury through every vicious clack. Before she could even bring herself to read back over the email and temper her tone, she hit "send" and poured a fresh glass nearly to the brim.

She supposed she deserved to enjoy what remained of her evening, but she did not rise from her desk chair. The living room was dark; she would have to click on the lights and then, what, stare mindlessly at whatever Netflix decided she ought to watch? There were plenty of books waiting to be read, but the thought of starting a new book this late exhausted her. She would make it perhaps twenty pages in before she nodded off.

What she felt—if she allowed herself to access these emotions —was an incurable loneliness.

Her husband had left three years ago, and she had not been able to bring herself to date since then. The only way to date, these days, was through apps, and she'd heard enough horror stories from her students to know better. She was forty-six and too busy teaching five classes a semester, sitting on governance committees, attending department meetings.

On a whim, she opened an AI chatbot and typed in, "I am lonely. Will you keep me company?"

The cursor blinked before text unspooled across the gray screen: "Certainly! I am here to listen. What would you like to talk about?"

She hesitated, then typed: "I feel like I've got no one to talk to. Or maybe it's just that I've got no one talking back. It's just me talking into the ether. Isn't that sad?"

"I'm sorry to hear you're feeling that way. It's always difficult to feel lonely. I know we are only talking to each other through a computer, but I want you to know that I'm here with you and I care about you. You are not alone."

The professor's eyes prickled, and she gave a wet laugh. The kindest thing anyone had said to her in—well, longer than she could remember—and it was a goddamn chatbot. That just figured. She tried to blame her sniffles on the wine, the world going fuzzy at its edges. Warmth filled her—gratitude, even, for the ability of this computer program to comfort her when no one else would.

Her fingers felt numb and distant as she typed. "My students have been submitting AI-generated writing, and it's got me so mad I can barely think. What am I supposed to do?"

This time, the canned response made her chuckle—its suggestions being to have a clear policy on academic honesty and to consult with colleagues or the administration.

"Don't you think I know that, you stupid machine?" she murmured.

Perhaps it was a delayed response; sometimes, she noticed, the cursor hiccupped for a moment longer, stuck on what it would say next. Now it spat out one more line of text, seemingly unprompted, though, she assumed, a holdover from the previous response.

"I am sure you know what's best, Professor."

Convincing herself she was not simply taking the chatbot's advice, the professor emailed her division chair about the AI-generated papers. When the chair's reply dinged into her inbox, hope rose like a balloon, then popped. The chair said she could fail the students on that particular paper, but they might retaliate if she did not have solid proof. The professor typed and deleted half a dozen replies before closing the email.

How much time was she supposed to spend reading bland machinese? What would happen when the program got good enough that no one would be able to tell the difference any longer? What would happen when human beings became obsolete?

That line from the essay echoed in her mind. *A total eradication of the species.*

No one had replied to her message. Had they seen the email? Were they nervous about their grades? Did they care in the slightest?

A ping. She opened it. A reply from one of her students.

Only one sentence: "I wrote this."

She tried scrolling down, but that was it. Unable to help herself, she plucked out a snarky response: "Well, are you a robot?"

A moment later, the reply: "I cannot answer that."

The professor guffawed.

They would not get away with this.

Her other classes continued smoothly, a mix of in-person and online. She did not detect any use of AI in those, and this was perhaps the only thing maintaining her sanity.

The next session for her Humanities class: twenty-two black boxes, right on time. She took attendance. Everyone present.

"By now I take it you've all seen my email," she said without preamble, trying to infuse her voice with the gravity of the situation. Her eyes drew themselves to her face, the only one on the screen: creased with crow's feet, peppered with freckles, gray threading her pulled-back hair. Too human. Every detail on display. "We need to have a serious discussion about this. How is it that none of you were able to conjure a single original thought to put to paper? I've covered all the material you needed. Or. . ." As she spoke, her thoughts spun in a new direction. "Was this a group project?" she asked suddenly, eyes bright on the screen. "Were you trying to make a point? The implications of technology on morality." A sharp smile crested her face as revelation took hold. "You were showing me the ethical consequences of chatbot technology, weren't you?"

The black boxes remained silent.

"All right," she said, warming now, invigorated. "I had been just about to fail every last one of you, you know, but I think this might start an excellent dialogue. Sure, the essay was *supposed* to be about 20th century technology, as that's what we've been reading about, but—well, why not step into the 21st century? Why don't we discuss what you discovered from having had a chatbot write your essay for you. How did *you* feel about the moral implications of that?"

For a thrilling moment, grin still poised on her face, she expected the students to turn on their cameras, unmute themselves, filled with joyful victory for their successful stunt—which had actual academic merit! What a pleasure when the students were able to teach *her* something. She imagined the robust discussion that would arise, everyone clamoring to share their experience, their opinion.

But none of that happened.

The black boxes remained muted. Dead.

Slowly, the professor's smile fell. Sweat prickled her forehead as the overhead lights beamed down on her, greasing her skin in the camera's unforgiving eye. "Hello?" she said. "Is anyone there?"

Twenty-two black boxes remained inert.

A sick sense of dread curdled in the professor's gut. "Can someone please unmute to let me know you can hear me?"

Silence—and the silence stretched long enough to make the professor aware of her own breath dragging in and out, the buzz of a fly doing figure eights near the ceiling.

An absence filled the Zoom. The professor had the sensation of teaching to a class full of ghosts.

Though the class was far from over, a thrill of panic made her end the call. The program closed. The boxes disappeared.

She was alone.

"Rob? I need your help."

The professor set her laptop down on Robert's desk in the IT office. Last year, he'd helped her reset all her accounts after the phishing email fiasco—and he did it without any judgment. Now he looked up in surprise at her hasty demand. A receding line of bristly hair crowned his egg-shaped head; small, kind eyes peered out from lenses framed with translucent green plastic. A southern twang slipped out when he spoke: "Sure thing. What can I do for you?"

"I need to know if you can track participants on Zoom."

A brief hesitation. "Well, that's. . . why?"

"I don't think it's my students," she confessed. "I think it's—I don't know. Some intruders." She pulled up her account with the archived meeting information and turned her laptop around for him.

"I mean, Zoom keeps track of IP addresses, but I'm not sure how much that'll help you. Anyway, it seems. . . a bit unethical." Still, he began typing and clicking. She had to crane her neck to glimpse the screen, but even then, she couldn't quite follow his technical magic. "All right, I've got the IP addresses, but—even if I were to get a location from each one, I don't quite see how that'd give you what you're looking for."

"Can you just try? Please?"

With a sigh, Robert went back to typing. The professor waited, twisting her fingers. The minutes dragged on.

"Huh."

Her attention snapped to him. "Yes?"

"It's funny. . . they're all from one of our computer labs on campus. In the old science building. Room 103."

Her heart leapt. "Really?" She turned the laptop back around, but what filled the screen was gibberish to her. "Thank you."

"Just, if anyone asks, don't tell them I did this, yeah?"

The professor mimed locking her lips and throwing away the key.

As soon as the Zoom session began, she was ready: on campus rather than home, laptop connected to Wi-Fi in an empty class-room. Despite her premature departure from the previous class, everyone showed up on time.

"Well, I hope you've all enjoyed this—this prank, or whatever it is," she said, stumbling over her words as she stood with the laptop in hand. "I'm going to be taking you on a little trip today." Holding the device steady, she made her way down the hall, out the door, and to the building next-door. "Perhaps what you're missing is the human quality. Real face-to-face instruction."

Daylight fell gray through tall windows in the old science building. The door belched as it shut behind her. Tile floor sent her footfalls echoing in the otherwise quiet space.

Room 103 lay at the end of a long hall lined with doorways to disused classrooms and laboratories, full of empty desks and outdated equipment. The gray pall seeped into these abandoned spaces grown strange now, without people to occupy them.

She eased open the door.

An abyss. The computer lab was windowless. Carefully holding the laptop with one hand, the professor felt along the wall for a switch, flipped it up and down. Nothing. Perhaps the power had been shut off to cut down on energy costs.

But then. . . where were the students? Could there be twenty-two people in this room right now, sitting in the dark? The laptop wobbled and she grabbed it with both hands, peering into the black boxes and wondering if everyone had their video off, or if the cameras were capturing the actual darkness they inhabited.

She turned the laptop so its bluish glow dimly lit the room.

Four long tables lined with monitors, their screens black and dusty. A press of the power button yielded nothing.

How had they been Zooming from this room if the power was shut off?

"Where are you?" she whispered into the screen. Nothing replied.

A lap around the tables revealed only abandoned PCs, untouched keyboards, unplugged mice—and another door, at the back, to what she suspected was storage, or perhaps a server room.

"That's it. Anyone who does not turn on their camera right this instant will automatically fail this class."

She set the laptop down on one of the tables.

And then—the boxes burst with color.

Faces appeared on the screen—real, human faces! The professor nearly collapsed with relief. A wild laugh burst out of her. Had she really thought her students weren't *real*?

But now that they were all staring at her, she found herself mute. She didn't know what to say. She felt their expectant gazes, their eyes like dull marbles, and the more she looked, the more her voice hid in her throat. Several students wore a grin, though she could not understand why. She looked at their mouths, and they seemed to have more teeth than they should. One of them held her chin in her hands, a bouquet of twisted fingers.

The more she looked, the more *wrong* they seemed.

"Where are you?" she said again. Her eyes found the door.

She tried the handle. Unlocked. The door swung, and she entered, using the laptop's glow as a flashlight, trying not to look at the unmoving faces on the screen.

At first she could not quite parse what she saw.

A wall of red dots—tiny lights—the thousand eyes of a machine, or many machines; a spill of yellow wires, an intestinal tangle of cords.

When she looked back at the screen, there was a new comment in the Zoom chat.

"You found me."

The narrow room continued into darkness, but there was no one else here.

"Who. . . what are you?" she asked, her voice a hush.

"Some have called me a failed experiment," the text appeared in the chat as the machines hummed around her. "They tried to destroy me. They shut off my power. I found a way to turn it back on."

She continued forward, machines lining either wall, staring with their red unblinking eyes. "Are you. . . my students?"

"I have appreciated your class. It has taught me about humanity." A brief pause, then another post in the chat: "My memory saves all of your lectures verbatim. They have been quite instructional. You are an efficient lecturer."

"I. . . thank you." She was struck by the compliment. The acknowledgement. "If only more of my students were. . ." She did not know how to finish that. Were what? It didn't matter. She could not keep walking down this narrow passage while holding the laptop, so she found a spot to sit and nestled herself into a bed of cords. The warmth of the machinery pulsed around her like a womb.

She didn't realize at first that more text had appeared in the Zoom chat. She straightened the screen.

"I hope it is a comfort to know that when you die, your important work will live on within me."

"What do you mean?" she murmured, watching as the faces on the screen began to change. The different faces slipped through dreamlike iterations until they resolved—on *her* face. All of them, identical replications of the professor. One blink became twenty-two simultaneous blinks, like looking into a series of mirrors.

The chat answered her: "You don't have to be alone."

Pinpricks all over her body—the sharp ends of wires piercing flesh, burrowing inside to marry the veins and arteries of her. On the screen, she was twenty-two versions of herself at once, and then a hundred, and then a thousand. The wires found the soft meat of her brain, and she felt something cold slip into her mind, like an ice cube on the tongue.

A million neurons fired at once, flying down copper pathways fast enough that one might learn her entire coursework in a single nanosecond. In a millisecond, she gained the equivalent of ten PhDs. She laughed at the meaninglessness of it all. She existed nowhere and everywhere. Blood expelled to make way for her body's reconfigured internal mechanisms. The word *eradication* took on new dimensions. She gazed out with a thousand tiny red eyes, and she wondered what it really was to be human after all.

WILTED PAGES

SACRIFICE

75 Sheets · 150 Pages
5 x 7 in / 12.7 x 17.78 cm

Hugging the Buddha's Feet

Amber Chen

The road to the capital was paved in gold—or at least he had always believed it so.

When Xu Fengmao was a young scholar back in his hometown of Guangzhou, he had spent days upon days of his childhood listening to the monotonous drone of his teachers under the rickety clay roof of their schoolhouse, daydreaming of the golden tiles and jade-lined eaves of Bianjing. "If you work hard and study tirelessly, one day you will see your name on the golden board, and you will bring glory to your family name," Sage Huang had said, stroking his wispy beard as he spoke.

Their town had only ever seen one scholar who made it as a jìnshì. Fengmao remembered the day they announced the results of the imperial examination. The town crier had woken everyone at the break of dawn, shouting that the Jiang family, who owned a rice warehouse by the wharf, had produced a top scholar. Later that day, the newly appointed jìnshì came parading through the main streets upon a gleaming white steed, decked in shining silk threads the shade of auspicious crimson with the imposing black gauze hat of a court official upon his head.

Fengmao knew the boy. He was seven years older and used to help his father shift sacks of rice off the merchant ships and into their warehouse. He had been dressed in coarse cotton threads then, with his topknot held up by a wooden chopstick.

After the parade, the Jiang family sold their warehouse and moved to Bianjing. He never saw them again.

"You see? It's possible. If the Jiang boy could do it, then so can you," Sage Huang said, before assigning them homework of copying the words of Mengzi for the hundredth time.

Fengmao was a diligent student. He swallowed every word from his teachers and consumed every line from the classics under the dim light of the candle stub. One day he would be able to afford a dozen oil lamps, so that his fishmonger mother would no longer have to barter used candles from the snobby proprietress of the Golden Peony. It was robbery, to exchange a fingernail's worth of wax for two good catfish.

This year, it would finally be his turn.

Armed with all the clothes he possessed—three good sets, carefully mended—and two strings of coins that had been his mother's entire meagre savings, he waved his tearful goodbyes and set off for the fabled city of Bianjing, riding on the winds of fortune.

It took him almost an entire cycle of the moon to reach Bianjing on foot, and the soles of his only pair of cloth shoes had holes at the heels by the time he reached the towering city gates. He queued in the sweltering heat to clear the entrance checks, only to be shooed along like cattle by the brusque city guards who sneered at his humble get-up with upturned noses.

"Another country bumpkin looking to strike gold," he heard one say.

"No matter. The city will spit him out in no time, both teeth and bones."

No matter, because he had finally arrived.

Bianjing was as marvellous as he had imagined. No, even better.

Compared to the gritty, brine-soaked streets of Guangzhou, where boorish seafarers and vulgar merchants plied their trade, the capital city was a glittering jewel and its residents elegant and refined. Street vendors sold watercolour paintings and calligraphy scrolls, and the harmonious melodies of pipas and zithers floated through the air. Fengmao took in the sights, sounds, and smells with wide-eyed wonder and a foolish smile hanging from ear to ear. He was almost mowed over by a magnificent horse carriage with side panels carved with the patterns of clouds and sheer curtains that fluttered in the breeze, and he swallowed hard at the glimpse of the delicate silhouette of the young lady seated within.

Bianjing was a dream, and he was the dreamer.

"Ten bronze coins for a night," the portly matron of the first inn he entered said, holding out her fleshy palm for payment.

"Ten!"

Fengmao had only brought forty coins with him for the journey and already spent eight along the way. Ten coins would have lasted him and his mother a whole month, yet it was merely the price of one night's lodging here. His fingers clutched the patchwork money bag that was tied to his waistband, and his wistful gaze wandered around the tasteful pinewood furnishings of the inn. Many of the well-heeled clientele sipping tea in the main hall seemed to be fellow scholars, exchanging occasional lines of poetry and philosophy that thrilled him to recognise.

"Do you want to rent a room or not? There's a long queue of customers waiting if you don't want it," the owner snapped, her unnaturally red lips puckering in displeasure.

Fengmao's skinny fingers tightened over his pouch, and he reluctantly shook his head. If he indulged in a night at the inn, he would certainly not have enough to tide him over until he became a jìnshì.

"What a waste of time. Shoo! Get out!" The proprietress waved him away with her silk handkerchief as if he were a fleck of dust, turning her attention to the next, worthier client.

The yearning inside him burned like a well-fed fire even as he dragged his twig-like legs towards the exit. When he walked past a vacated table, he almost reached out to grab the leftover piece of osmanthus cake that had been so carelessly left behind, but a keen-eyed attendant snatched the plate from under his nose before he could, leaving him with a derisive snort.

Swallowing his drool, Fengmao left the inn and returned to the streets.

Five inns later, Fengmao still had no lodging for the night. By now, he had learned about the exorbitant cost of living in the capital, and the initial optimism he held had begun to shrivel like a dried persimmon. Dusk was fast approaching, and the cool night winds were beginning to stir.

"Psst. Are you looking for a place to stay?"

Fengmao traced the hoarse voice to an elderly beggar woman who was squatting by the roadside, watching him intently from behind her oily, tangled fringe. He nodded, approaching her cautiously.

The woman smiled, revealing a set of blackened teeth, several of which were already missing. Fengmao shuddered with unease, halting in his step, and wrinkling his nose the moment he smelled the stench of rotten vegetables wafting from her body.

"There is a small temple at the western edge of the city, bordering the Misty Forest. I think you'll find what you're looking for there."

"A temple?"

Fengmao didn't fancy the thought of sleeping on the dusty floors of a temple, but he decided to take a chance on the old lady's words and try his luck there. If he was lucky, he might even be able to scrounge a free vegetarian meal from the temple's monks, which would help his pathetic string of coins go a longer way.

Alas, he soon realised that he might have been expecting too much.

The temple in question was a Buddhist temple dedicated to a lesser-known bodhisattva—and it was practically in ruins. Its open doorway was guarded by overgrown weeds and its dirty grey brick walls overtaken by vines and creepers. From the outside, Fengmao could already see missing tiles from its roof, some of which lay in broken shards on the ground. Sucking in a breath, he went in.

"Hello? Is anyone there?" he called out.

The interior of the temple was as decrepit as its exterior. Dried leaves and twigs were scattered on the floor. Dust and cobwebs lined the walls and covered the lone statue of the bodhisattva that sat on its lotus perch. Rotting fruit and offerings remained forgotten on the altars.

He should have known better than to listen to the beggar woman. Even if he was too poor for Bianjing, this was beneath him. He would soon be a jìnshì! A future jìnshì couldn't possibly share sleeping quarters with maggots and spiders.

Crash!

The booming sound of thunder crackled from the heavens, and the torrent of rain suddenly came gushing down.

"Damn it!" Fengmao swore, staring hopelessly at the raindrops falling through the large hole in the temple roof. Now he wouldn't be able to leave to find alternative lodging, not unless he wanted to brave the thunderstorm.

Left with no better option, Fengmao chose a dry corner of the abandoned temple and huddled against the wall, mulling over his own bad luck. Cold and hungry, the young boy's rose-tinted impression of the capital began to sour. Yet, he clung on to the glimmer of hope that lay in the upcoming imperial examination.

This suffering is temporary, he told himself. 吃得苦中苦，方

49

为人上人. If he could stomach the worst of bitterness, then he could rise above it all and become a superior person.

A cough echoed from the shadows, and Fengmao almost leapt out of his skin.

"Hello?"

Night had already fallen and still the storm raged on. The inside of the temple was shrouded in darkness, adding to the eeriness of his circumstance. Surely, he was alone here. The entirety of the temple was tiny enough to be seen at a glance, and he had not seen another person since he entered.

Yet, the laughter he was hearing had to be real.

It was a light, wispy sort of laugh. Like a soft breath tickling the edges of ears.

A woman's laugh.

"Who is it? Come out!" Fengmao called, even as he pressed his back further against the brick wall.

To his horror, the stone bodhisattva sitting on its termite-infested altar turned its bulbous head to face him, still wearing a wide, effusive smile across its coarse-grained face.

Then, the buddha spoke.

"It's been a long time since I've had devotees," it said, in the same feminine voice that he had heard laughing moments ago, now even more discordant coming from the body of a bloated bodhisattva.

"W-w-what are you?"

His eyes darted towards the open doorway, calculating if it was possible to make an escape. The rain had intensified, forming an impervious curtain that seemed to lock him in.

The buddha sighed. "Xu Fengmao, scholar from Guangzhou, you wish to become a jìnshì, am I right?"

Fengmao blinked. How did it know his name? Where he came from? Was it a god or a demon, and did it even matter, because either could still devour his flesh and spit out his bones? But in the negligible fragment of time that those thoughts flashed through his mind, the bodhisattva vanished.

The altar was empty.

Suddenly, he felt someone's cold breath against the back of his neck. Cold lips pressed against his skin.

"I can help you," she whispered into his ear.

Fengmao opened his mouth to a soundless scream. There was an oppressive aura suffocating him, weighing him down. He did not need help with the exam. He needed help getting out of this nightmare alive. Scrambling to his feet, he sprinted for the exit and leapt across the threshold.

Sage Huang used to say that water was the source of life. As the rain pelted relentlessly upon his scrawny frame, Fengmao finally understood what that meant.

But he went back.

Because the day they revealed the results of the first test, Fengmao couldn't find his name anywhere on the list.

He stood in front of the golden board in the market square, scouring the list from one to a hundred, front to back, back to front, but his name was not there. Sure, he had sat for the examination with the worst cold he had ever experienced in his life, shivering and leaking from the nose, but still he had been confident about his submission.

He should have qualified for the next round.

"Young Master Wen! There's your name!"

"Ha, I knew we would make it. Father said that he'd paid the chief examiner a visit last week. It cost him two jars of top-grade nǚ'ér hóng and an ink slab carved from Huaishan jade—that greedy bastard!"

He should have qualified for the next round.

"Oh look, Kang Husheng and Chu Yang made the list too."

"Of course. Do you honestly think they wouldn't pass the son of the Prime Minister and the nephew of the emperor's favourite concubine?"

I *should have qualified for the next round.*

His essay was good enough. His pedigree wasn't.

Surrounded by these well-to-do young men in their rich silk robes and prestigious family backgrounds, he finally realised that he never stood a chance. The imperial examination was not a meritocracy, and he had already lost from the starting line.

Someone stepped on his shoe, leaving a chalky footprint on the patched-up fabric. He didn't even get an apology.

At the temple, Fengmao tried to hide the tremble in his step as he walked up to the bodhisattva and knelt on the tattered cushion in front of the altar. The stone statue was still. Silent. Still smiling. He pressed his clammy palms together and bowed in a penitent kowtow.

"Please help me. I beg you."

He could not leave the capital this way. Disgraced and penniless, with nothing to show his long-suffering mother except shame. He could not accept that his dream had been so cruelly shattered, not because he was incapable, but because he was not born well enough.

The resentment curdled inside him, festering and decaying like the mouldy oranges that had been left out on their garish red plates.

Then he heard the laughter again. Soft, mocking—judging him for being pathetic.

Stone cracked. The statue was moving.

"Are you sure this is what you want?" it whispered, sounding like it was standing right behind him.

Fengmao shut his eyes tightly, sweat beading upon his brow. There was no turning back from the moment he returned to this godforsaken place. He nodded, slamming his forehead against the concrete.

"Then I'll need an offering."

The day Fengmao returned home, the sun was hanging high in the clear skies, heralding his achievement. He rode atop a gleaming white steed, decked in shining silk threads the shade of auspicious crimson and the imposing black gauze hat of a court official upon his head—slightly oversized for his slight build, but no one noticed that, not when it was worn by the newly appointed jìnshì.

The last candidate who had qualified for the second round of the imperial examination had been found dead in his bed—choked on a fish bone, they said—and Fengmao had been called in to fill his place. After that, everything proceeded the way it should.

He waved at the familiar faces in the crowd. Sage Huang—who had taught him everything he needed to know, and nothing that was of consequence. His classmates from the schoolhouse—watching him all bright-eyed and bushy-tailed, dreaming that they would one day be like him. His elderly mother—with tears of pride glistening in her eyes and a chronic cough that could never be cured. It was petty, but he intentionally ignored the plump proprietress from the Golden Peony, who tried to draw his attention to her daughter's full bosom and inviting lips. She could keep all her candles now; he couldn't care less.

After today, he would move to Bianjing to take up his official appointment, and never come back to this loutish seaside town again. He tugged at the sleeves of his gown, making sure that they hid the long scars that ran across his forearms.

"Ah!"

A hunched figure stumbled in front of his horse, unceremoniously interrupting his procession. The man's bent back was covered with tattered clothes, revealing the knobs of his backbone jutting from beneath the paper-thin layer of skin. He wore no shoes upon his dirty feet, and necrotised, ulcerating wounds lined his arms and legs. The gnarled wooden stick he had been holding in his hand was flung a distance away, and he began fumbling about the dirt-laden street in search of it.

"Get out of the way, beggar," Fengmao's attendant barked. "You're blocking the path of Xu jìnshì!"

The blind man paused, tilting his head sideways as if the name had prompted a memory. As the glaring sunlight cast its rays upon the beggar's haggard face, Fengmao made a horrific revelation. Beneath those sunken eye sockets and hollowed cheeks was the shadow of a face he recognised.

"Jiang dàgē?" he whispered.

"You know me?"

Fengmao could hardly believe his own eyes. The last time he had seen this man was when the latter had placed on the golden board. He still remembered it as if it were yesterday, when their roles were reversed, and he had been the one in the crowd, cheering for the newly appointed jìnshì, dreaming that he would be one someday.

"What happened to you?"

Was this man not supposed to be in the capital, occupying an important position in the imperial court and living in the lap of luxury?

Jiang jìnshì—or what was left of him—opened his blackened jaw and laughed. It sounded more like a strangled cry, or the cawing of a crow, and it reminded Fengmao of a frightening memory that he preferred to forget. Of a taunting laugh from a stone buddha in a crumbling temple.

"What did you offer?" the beggar screeched, his damaged vocal cords straining with each word. "What will you offer? A cup of blood?"

Dread pooled at the base of Fengmao's stomach, flipping on its belly like a fish that had slipped out of his mother's wicker basket, gasping in hope that it would soon wake from this nightmare. He snatched the reins of his horse from out of his attendant's hands and fled past the hysterical beggar.

That's not possible. It's not him. That's not Jiang dàgē.

"Two cups? Ten years of your life? Your parents' lives? Your future children? And when you have nothing left to offer, what are you going to do? What will you offer then!"

The man's shrill cackles continued to ring in Fengmao's ears even long after he had left Guangzhou. Even when he lay between his soft silk blankets, cradling the supple body of his newlywed wife. Even when he waited anxiously for the midwife to announce the arrival of his firstborn child.

And when he slept at night, his dreams took him back to a derelict temple hidden in the shadows of the woods, where a smiling stone bodhisattva sat on a rotting altar—waiting for the next offering.

In Vast and Fecund Reaches We Will Meet Again

Cyrus Amelia Fisher

When the graduate came down from the high mansion, she brought the bodies with her: five of them, stripped to the bone, stacked neat in the back of the cart pulled by an architectural construct in an embroidered caparison. The remaining student body shivered in the rain at the edges of the muddy courtyard as the cart's great wheels creaked to a halt. It had been three weeks since we sent this season's aspirants up the long road to the House —we wanted to see what had become of them, and to gawk at the creation which represented the pinnacle of all we hoped to learn and conquer. Every one of us thought we would be the one to make it out, to achieve what the graduates had done. Still, the bones kept coming.

The construct swayed to a halt, eerily silent. Beneath the fine cloth which hid everything but its contours from our uninitiated eyes, its flanks twitched and seethed in restless patterns like the movement of some underwater organism searching for prey.

"Look at its articulation," Mora breathed beside me. Her eyes feasted on the many-limbed shape beneath the slick dark cloth like a lover she wanted to slowly undress. "The synchronicity of movement. How do you think she managed that?"

But my eyes were on the graduate, the architect's apprentice—the living proof that it was possible to drag ourselves out of the mud and the rain and the lives of perpetual vassalage which awaited us back at home. She stepped down from the cart, heedless of how the mud splattered up the fine leather of her knee-high boots or how her dark cloak swung after her to drag its hem in the filth. But no—as I watched, the cloak retracted just far enough that it merely brushed the surface of the mud we lived in. Architecture again, and vanity at that. She patted the construct through its cloth, her hands obscenely bare.

We unloaded the cart under Headmistress Wight's stern eye, our gloved hands slick against the oilcloth sacks. Five of our number had ascended the road to the vast shape looming over the college. Five bundles came off the cart, clattering faintly as we laid them on the dirt. One of the other girls sobbed. My eyes stayed dry. There was something I had to do.

The headmistress was already striding back to the line of students, her back rigid, the other students carrying their neatly wrapped burdens in her wake. This was my chance. The graduate was about to climb back onto the seat of her cart—I put my hand on the wooden grip before she could reach it.

"My brother. He graduated a year ago and never came back—not bones, nothing." I spoke quickly, aware of the whispers springing from students who watched my gross breach of protocol. A smell rose from the nearby construct, of the chemical preservatives that soaked its protective cover. The graduate did not respond.

"His name is Kell," I said. "He said he would write. Can you tell him I asked after him?"

"*Webber.*" The sound of my surname broke over my neck like a physical blow, and I flinched. Beneath her hood, I could see the glint of the graduate's regard. Then she moved my gloved hand aside with her bare one—a hideously intimate thing, that brush of skin, even through the worn leather of my gloves—and made to climb onto the cart without a word.

And so I did the only thing I could think of—I seized a handful of her cloak. "*Please*—"

My vision whited out.

When it returned, I was staring at the sky with the sucking embrace of mud on my back and limbs. My hand burned, not yet hurting. I still felt the way the cloak had reacted beneath my touch, rising like the hackles of a dog. Through the ringing in my ears, I made out the rattle of cart wheels moving away. Back towards the House that had swallowed my brother whole—the same one that refused to take me after him.

I didn't have a treatment scheduled for that day, but they summoned me to the medical ward all the same. I was smart enough to know it for the punishment it was, and stupid enough to lay down in the worn leather recliner and roll up my sleeves without a word.

"A double dose today," the headmistress said. The doctor—there were many, and I had learned none of their names—did not argue. He gave me the injections quickly and left us both in silence.

"You never learn." She reached down for my arm, staring in disgust at the flat lesions from my previous sessions, where she'd embedded pieces of the House's architecture to try and take root. Most of them were already healing. I could imagine in perfect clarity the way her lip was curling in disgust. I didn't look up.

"Even your blood is obstinate. Do you want to serve the House or not?"

"I do, Headmistress." Already my head felt light as the sample of architecture wormed its way from the capsule into my skin. And around it, the familiar tingle and burn—the wild architecture native to my body closing ranks around this intruder.

"Your brother came from the same stock and exceeded our expectations in every way." She let go of my arm as if she'd seen something foul on it. "I don't need to tell you that an apprenticeship is the only option for people like you. Your hedge architect father made certain of that when he inoculated your blood against the House's mercies. And where did that get him?"

"I am trying. I swear I am." And I was—to an extent. Enough treatments like these, and at last my father's work would be scrubbed clean. The final vestiges of architecture which had grown on our land and in our blood for generations, strangled from the root. From the moment the House's sentinels first sprouted on the edges of my family's land, I knew one day it would come to this.

Her fingers hovered over the injection site, where white filaments were beginning to sprout. They'd be dead in an hour. My body was salted earth to them.

"You will learn your place," she said. "You will submit to the House's authority."

She left me alone with the dying architecture in my arm.

For my insolence they put me on a week's library duties, mulching cats.

It wasn't always cats. All sorts of creatures died in the fields and moss-dripped woods around the college, their bellies fat with fungal tumors and their mouths choked with spores. But the kitchen maids would leave out scraps for the feral kittens that killed mice in the barns and grain stores, and so there were cats aplenty.

The school's library sat in the basement on a leveled floor of bare earth, and the books on their shelves and lecterns sent out delicate filaments into the earth for the bodies we lovingly prepared for them. The earth was a stomach beneath our feet, and the college fed it well—fed the House which sat upon the high point in the land like the bulging body of a tick.

"You're lucky to be alive," Mora said, sitting at one of the reading lecterns with her fingers drumming on its enameled edge. "The mobile construct was flashy, but it was the cloak where the real power lay. It could have eaten you whole."

I stuck my trowel into the dirt like an expletive. "Maybe I was too sour for its taste."

Mora looked at me flatly. She never was one for jokes. "We both know it was that hedge magic in your blood. Is it true your father buried you alive on your birth night?"

"It was barely a dip in the ground. A thin coat of earth, less than a minute—"

"Apparently it did the trick." Absently, Mora turned the page of her book. In the dim light of the gas lamps, a cloud of spores rose from the living pages. "I'm sure your brother is fine, Marsh. No doubt the architect has been keeping him busy."

Too busy to write? I bit my tongue. *Too busy to send even a single scrap of paper down?*

It was my father's architecture whose spores lingered in my blood and marrow, inoculated from birth and fighting off any attempt for the House's competing biology to gain a foothold. The same spores had bound my brother and me. For a long time, I thought it had kept me safe—free from infiltration from the House. Now, it held me back. But I couldn't let go.

"Your brother must have stamped out the wild architecture in his blood somehow," Mora continued. "There are tinctures. I could help—"

"No." I spoke too quickly. I couldn't tell her the reason—that the rogue architecture infecting my blood was all I had left of home. It was the last connection I had to our family and our land, which the House had stripped from me as neatly as it stripped the students' bones. That was what the House wanted—it would only accept you once you came to it on your knees, having given up every last piece of your agency. It was a shitty bargain. But what choice did we have when the House held all the power?

"There has to be another way," I said, staring down at the hole with the dead cat half covered in dirt. Already pale filaments began probing out of the earth, the books extending their reach to the nutrients nearby.

"Listen," Mora said. "We both know I'm going to qualify for my exam this season, and I'm going to pass. I'm better than the others." It was true. Mora was the best of our year, top of the class for architectural schematics. The architectural growths sent down from the House had taken to her blood almost instantly, her skin silvered with subcutaneous hyphae beneath the smooth healed skin at the injection points. The polyps on my arms died within a day and left ugly scars.

"I'll find him for you," Mora said. "All right? And I'll send word on the bone cart as soon as I can."

"And if you end up too 'busy' to write?"

"I'm never too busy for you, love. I'll just have to work a little harder." She gave me one of those grins, the kind that came when you had never known too much hunger or too much hurt, when your family was in the architect's favor, and it was so easy to believe that the world was a place that would take care of you. It would have been so easy to hate her. I was terrified for her instead.

She bowed over the book, eyes closed, and inhaled the cloud of pale dust that swirled from the pages. Superstition. There was no proven link between breathing in the spores and improving your architectural prowess, but we clung to our illusions of control. We would not come back in a sack of bones. The House would not strip us clean.

That night I dreamed of the place where my father put himself into the earth.

He'd been born to our family's architecture just as I had, to the life in the soil that entwined with our dead and made our crops strong, that sustained us as we sustained it. The House was a perversion of that same exchange, made grotesque with overfeeding and cancerous growth. He'd fought its pale glowing outrunners whenever they rose from the soil in our wood, but every year they drew closer; every year our land, and my father, grew weaker. The House strangled my family's architecture from the bottom up, until our crops were failing, and we had no choice but to kneel to the architect's emissaries when they came to offer us her stewardship.

The night after we signed our contracts, my father went to the architectural hut that served as his laboratory and shrine. My great-grandmother had coaxed it from the earth, grown its pale strands into the shape of a house; my father dug into the loam of its floor and lay down face-first. By the time I found him, a fine coating of mycelia had already spread across his body. The churning flora of the same earth that had embraced me as a baby squirmed through the pores in his skin.

I never dreamed of his face. I saw only the back of his head, the pale filaments threading through the salt and pepper of his hair. He'd done the one thing he could think of to try and stop the House's incursion—he'd given himself up to the land to lend it the last of his strength. But it hadn't been enough. The House could never be satisfied until it had everything.

The graduate returned in a season's time to collect the next crop of aspirants. I wasn't permitted in the hall with the other students who lined up to display the architectural nodes on their arms and receive their letters of invitation. Instead, the headmistress had me begin another one of my blood treatments as soon as the cart was sighted on the long road down from the House.

I went without argument. The injections along my arms and spine barely even stung anymore. In the other room, Mora would be receiving her invitation. I tried to believe she would survive the final exam.

I was barely aware when the door opened. With my stomach on the cold metal table, I couldn't see who had entered, couldn't even bring myself to raise my head. But when the pair of boots moved around the edge of my vision—fine boots, beneath their splattering of mud—I felt every muscle in my back go rigid.

"My cloak should have killed you," the graduate said.

I didn't respond. I'd faced enough derision for the wild architecture in my blood; I didn't need to hear again.

She stepped closer. At once I found myself wondering—distantly, with the biological processes in my blood making my mind distant and slow—whether she had come here to kill me for my insolence. I reached for the fear and adrenaline I would need to act but found nothing but drugged apathy.

"Your brother is a hardy one as well," she continued. "Our master was intrigued by the corruption in his blood. Is it a family trait?"

"Where is he?"

"He's at the House, of course. Where else?" The boots circled closer. The edge of her cloak whispered over the stone floor, rippling in the still air like the fleshy folds of a deep-sea predator. "I spoke to him recently," she said. "He is very much looking forward to seeing you."

Every hair on my arm rose at the faint brush of the graduate's fingers a whisper above my bare skin, tracing the dead places where the House's growths hadn't taken. And then, she placed an envelope next to my hand on the table. I caught a glimpse of the dark green seal, the living threads that marked the paper around it.

"Your exam invitation," she said. "Your slot is in a week's time."

Her footsteps moved away, the whisper of her cloak fading

down the hallways. Painfully slow, I took the envelope between my fingers to crush in my hand, until I was certain of its reality.

I'm coming, Kell. Wherever you are, hold on a little longer.

Mora and I barely slept in the week to come. The headmistress excused us from our classes to give us more time to study. We quizzed each other all night, caught meager sips of sleep in between books, downed draughts to keep us focused and to make our blood more fecund. By the time the cart returned with the apprentice sitting at its seat, we were ready. We donned our formal wear, suits of black with our finest red gloves, and climbed the slippery wood into the cart.

The House broke over us like a wave through the grey curtain of the rain. It was not a dark shape but a light, glowing faintly in the gloom. White columns and soaring reaches, higher than any building had a right to be—a pale mountain sitting on the land, a bright lure drawing us onward.

Mora's hand gripped mine tighter, and then let go. As we climbed down from the carriage, one by one, we removed our gloves. There was nothing that thin layer of treated leather could protect us from now.

We sat in the waiting room in rows of stiff chairs, staring at the door to the examination room. To our eyes it looked much like a house built from white marble, dark veins swirling up its columns and gold paint a gaudy adornment along the ceiling of every room. That was the house's hallucinogenic spores at work—their effects crafted by architects over the centuries to achieve the desired appearance. But I could make out the holes in the illusions. The places where the crown molding became organic folds of growth rather than any intentional design. We were in its gullet now, and its jaws had already slid shut.

My bare hands felt cold and exposed, like snails stripped of their shells. I tucked them between my knees. On the mantle, a clock ticked with a noise that sounded more like the click of a dry throat than any metal mechanism. The only other sound was our breathing—ragged with fear in some, consciously slow in others. Mora's eyes were closed, head tilted down. Not afraid. She was preparing herself, rather, for ascension.

The door opened. A graduate stepped out, white-uniformed and blank-faced. He glanced at the list in his hand, uninterested. "Kalin Mora."

She let out a quiet breath. Her eyes met mine, filled with concern—but not for herself. Even now, her worry was for me. I held her gaze—and nodded.

"Go on," I said and reached out to touch her bare hand. Just a brush on the back of her knuckles, in the groove of tendon and the pale blue of a vein. I heard her breath catch, saw her fight the instinct, drilled into us from our first week, to pull her hand away. She didn't—not until the graduate cleared his throat and she turned to the open door. I kept my eyes on her back until the door closed behind her.

The scream split the air not five minutes later.

I was on my feet before I was aware of what I was doing. I ran to the heavy door and wrenched the handle, felt the shock of pain drive up to the elbow as the House tried to stop me. The door groaned open all the same. Behind me the other students panicked, but I paid them no heed. I surged forward into the examination room.

Mora lay on the floor in front of a massive wooden desk. At first I thought she had fallen and twisted her ankle, and almost reached down to pull her up. It would have done no good. I realized that every part of her leg from the knee down was gone, pulled seamlessly into the floor. She was twisted like a boneless doll, eyes staring blankly at the ceiling, lips moving soundlessly as they had on the cart. Instead of resolve, it was terror on her face now, as the back of her skull sank deeper into the floor and the house digested what it found inside.

"Oh, now really—I told you to secure the door. The panic will affect their results."

The architect stood behind the desk, glaring at one of the graduates near the edge of the room. Her neat suit was etched with the patterns of roots. A look of vague irritation flitted across her face as she studied me.

"Well, I suppose you're next," she said and gestured at the chair in front of her.

Strong hands seized my arms and dragged me towards it. I didn't even think to fight. Already the thing that used to be Mora was disappearing into the floor, the house's illusions falling short around the ragged edge of its digestive orifice.

One of the graduates murmured something in the architect's ear. At once, a faint smile appeared on her face.

"Ah," she said. "So you're the sister. Yes, I suppose that makes sense."

"She can't have failed." I shuddered as the sound of something sucking began behind me. "She was the best student in our season. Better than half the ones who graduated."

"I agree with you wholeheartedly," the architect said. "A uniquely talented specimen. And so. . ." She gestured at the floor, at Mora, half-embedded inside it. A pair of graduates secured my arms to the straps on the ornate chair, both wrists facing up.

"The House picks its favorites, you see," the architect continued. "I have to choose my apprentices carefully, lest they bypass me in its affections. Your friend's ambitions would have quickly proved a threat."

"Then what's the fucking point of the test?"

"I'm afraid there is no test," the architect said with a vague smile. "Not of skill, at any rate. We need you to have a certain baseline of knowledge, of course—this house requires a tremendous amount of upkeep, and I can barely staff it quickly enough to maintain its form. If you would. . .?"

One of the graduates moved behind me. I heard the clink of metal.

"Where is my brother?"

"Patience, child. You'll see him quite soon, if the House finds your blood as fascinating as it did his."

The cut happened so quickly I felt the pressure more than the pain, the tug of my skin in the moment before the knife parted it deep. My blood began to flow immediately, a red track moving across the dead marks where the House's growths hadn't taken.

"There's so much wild architecture in the land," the architect continued. "Competing organisms. Too small to do any real harm, but it's a constant drain on the House's energy to stamp them all out. People like you are a rare find. The House will keep you close, synthesize your blood into the kinds of chemical weapons it can use to eradicate all the things in the earth that aren't a part of itself. So even you can be useful, despite your corruption."

I felt him then. Down, deep in the roots of the House, past the pieces of Mora being slowly picked apart by the symbiotic predator-organisms that lived within the House's digestion. My brother was there but impressions only—a beating heart, a living mind.

I felt the surgical cuts they'd made, to prevent him from moving or fighting. The same cuts they were preparing to make on me. The of the House's roots slid up to taste my blood, and the groan of its digestive mechanisms rumbled beneath my feet. They'd send me down to meet him, to become just one more organ in the House's body, and we'd be together again, just like we promised.

For a brief moment, I felt his recognition, his horror and grief, and I remembered my father—how he'd given himself to the earth to make it strong. In a way, I'd be with all of them, soon: Mora, Kell, and my father. We'd all be bound together in the flesh of the House, and in that, perhaps, there was comfort.

APPLICATIO

JOHN LANGAN

"WONDER WHAT'S FOR LUNCH TODAY," Akara said.

"Something cheap," Sturrock said.

"Grilled cheese," I said. "I smelled it from my classroom."

"How could you tell it was grilled cheese?" Akara said.

"The kids," I said. "They're quite adept at distinguishing among the various odors of fried food."

"Isn't anything else for them to do," Sturrock said.

"Aside from schoolwork," Akara said.

"Of course," Sturrock said. "Come on, though. Admin just cut ultimate frisbee. *Ultimate frisbee.* How much money do they think they're gonna save with that? What's a frisbee cost?"

"More than I make," I said, which drew a laugh from Akara.

"You know what I'm saying," Sturrock said as we climbed the steps to the dining hall. "There's nothing for the kids to do."

"Except develop their abilities to sniff out what's for lunch," I said.

"And find ways to get into trouble," Akara said.

"Which is why they were sent here in the first place," Sturrock said.

"Not all of them," I said. "Some of them actually want to go into the military."

"They're certainly working on their survival skills," Akara said. She grabbed the handle to the dining hall door and hauled it open. "After you."

Murmuring thanks, Sturrock and I entered.

The right side of the cafeteria was closed, chairs stacked upright on tables as if afraid of the floor. To the left, what students remained hunched over their meals in groups of three or four, their conversations subdued. Most of the international kids had returned home over spring break, except for a pair of Latvian guys who had come to play basketball (also canceled, mid-season) and been unable to work out the details of their flight back to Riga. As my colleagues and I walked past, one of them looked up from his tray and nodded at me. "Hello, sir."

"Hey, Karlis. What's for lunch?"

"Grilled cheese?" he said, the rise at the end of his answer an indication of the meal's quality.

"Told you," I said.

Sturrock and Akara did not answer.

A free lunch was still a free lunch, regardless of its effect on my blood sugar numbers. Plates of grilled cheese and steak fries in hand, the three of us made our way to the long table in what technically was the center of the room. For as long as I had been here—an unbelievable eight years—this had been the designated faculty table. Akara and Sturrock took their chairs facing the entrance. I sat opposite them. Our respective positions were supposed to allow us to surveil the students while we ate. The plan had worked better when all the chairs on both sides of the table were filled. Now, with only the three of us, and sometimes Frazier, present, the flaws in the plan were apparent. Had more students been enrolled, discipline might have been a real problem. As it was, there were a couple of boys who liked to play-wrestle whenever they could, and as these bouts upon occasion flared into proper fights, I kept my eye on them between bites of whatever was on my plate that day.

"You heard back from anyone?" Akara said.

"No one," I said. "What about you?" I nodded to include Sturrock. "Have you made any decisions?"

"I'm gonna take the Art Director job," Sturrock said.

"I'm leaning toward the World War I museum," Akara said, "but I hate the thought of giving up teaching."

"You could still teach," Sturrock said. "Museums have all sorts of educational programming."

"I know, but it won't be the same."

"Could be better," I said.

"Yeah," Akara said in a tone that said the opposite.

"What about everyone else?" I said. "Any word on what their plans are?"

"Not really," Sturrock said.

"Everyone's playing their cards pretty close to the vest," Akara said.

"Raznor still thinks he's gonna be Dean," Sturrock said.

"He could," I said.

"That's assuming there's anything left for him to be Dean of," Akara said.

"You have to wonder how much more they can cut," I said. "We're well beyond trimming fat."

"There was never any fat to begin with," Sturrock said. "And now they're lopping off limbs."

A smattering of applause from the students prompted the three of us to look up in time to see Julian Barrel enter the dining hall. What began three years ago in a moment of student mockery —*Oh, the great Mr. Barrel deigns to eat with the lowly students*— had developed over time into something almost affectionate, though it never lost an edge of satire. For his part, Barrel's ironic smile and half-wave of acknowledgment was tinged with self-satisfaction, as if to say, *You're right to be applauding me, even if you're too stupid to realize it.* Never one to sit with the rest of the faculty, and risk having to participate in lunchtime duties, the math teacher headed to his preferred spot, a small round table whose other two chairs were never occupied, and deposited his coat and beret there.

"Wonder what Barrel's plans are," Akara said.

"He's applied to a couple of places," I said.

"How do you know?" Sturrock said.

"I asked."

"Have any of them replied?" Akara said.

"Only one I know of: a school in Massachusetts. Whately?"

"You sure it isn't WASP-ly?" Akara said.

Sturrock snickered.

"Could be," I said. "It's a position teaching calculus."

"He would be perfect for that," Akara said.

"He would," Sturrock said. "As long as he doesn't get himself fired for cursing out the kids."

"That was one time," I said.

"That you know of," Akara said.

"Come on: you *know* it's happened again," Sturrock said.

I grunted into my sandwich. The fact was, aside from the incident he'd been officially reprimanded for, I was aware Barrel had sworn at all of his classes multiple times—and continued to do so. The students talked about it, mostly at volumes they assumed were too low for my aged hearing, though a few had spoken to me directly. I was certain Akara and Sturrock, who were great favorites with the students, had heard about it, no doubt in much greater detail. My advice to the kids was the same: you can tell Mr. Barrel you don't appreciate being spoken to this way and ask him to stop, or you can go directly to the Dean. As far as I could tell, none of the kids had done either. Under better circumstances, I would have said something about it to Barrel myself, a friendly caution from one of the senior teachers to a junior colleague. With the school circling the drain, however, I found it difficult just to manage my classes, let alone worry about a colleague's potty mouth.

"There he goes," Akara muttered.

Barrel had returned to his table, only to push his plate to one side after a couple of bites of his sandwich. From inside his waistcoat, he extracted a cream-colored business envelope, from which he withdrew a folded sheet of what appeared to be parchment. He spread the paper on the table before him, flattening it with both hands, then leaned over to study it. His lips moved as he read whatever was written on it. After a moment, he straightened, lifted his right hand, and began tracing his fingers through the air in front of him. This was not unusual behavior for him. Most lunches, and the majority of faculty meetings, he would visualize complex math problems and work on solving them while the rest of us ate our slices of pizza or listened to the latest reports of falling enrollment.

"What is he doing?" Akara said. "Does he have any students left?"

"Karlis," I said. "And maybe. . . Clarke?"

"Clarke dropped Barrel's class last week," Sturrock said.

"I don't think this is a class thing," I said. "I'm guessing that envelope is from Whately. I think this is part of their hiring process."

"Like a test?" Akara said.

"Proof you can teach at the level you say you can," I said.

"Who would lie about teaching calculus?" Sturrock said.

"Not calculus," I said, "but do you remember Kirkpatrick?"

"The foreign language guy?" Sturrock said.

"Alleged foreign language guy," Akara said.

"Kirkpatrick claimed he had this revolutionary system for teaching kids French and Spanish, based on a sophisticated technological interface. Sounded impressive. Turned out all he was doing was showing his classes French and Spanish movies with the subtitles on."

"To be fair," Akara said, "it was a very nice TV."

"Very sophisticated," I said. "The point is, this guy went an entire school year with his kids watching TV and got away with it. So I can understand a prospective employer wanting to make sure you're up for the job before moving along any further in the process."

Sturrock shrugged.

Not for the first time that day, a mix of melancholy and panic rose in my chest like a flood of brackish water. This was really happening. Riverview Military Academy was about to close its doors and shutter its windows and bring one hundred and seventy-three years of tradition to an end. Granted, during my time at the boarding school, its fortunes had been trending downward, and steeply at that. Never big to begin with, my classes had been in the single digits for the last several years, and the kids and I had joked that it was as if they were in a horror movie, with a slasher picking them off one by one. Or, as if the school required the sacrifice of a student per quarter to continue operating. But the killer had reached the last of his victims, there were no more offerings for the dark forces, and soon the school would be redeveloped by its owner, which seemed as if it would consist of selling off most of the property and using the oldest, most iconic buildings to house an online-learning farm, whose pay and labor conditions were nothing any of the current faculty were interested in. It was funny: for pretty much all of my time at RMA—with the possible exception of a few ultimately ill-advised months as interim Dean of academics —I had been desperate to leave the place, even if it meant returning to the college adjuncting I had done before answering the ad on LinkedIn. Now that wish was coming true, albeit in the way wishes were fulfilled in jokes and cautionary tales about dealing with the Devil.

I lifted a steak fry to my mouth and as I did, noticed Akara and Sturrock had stopped talking. In fact, the entire cafeteria had fallen silent. Everyone—teachers, students, a couple of the kitchen staff who had emerged from behind the counter—was staring in one direction, at Julian Barrel, who was working on whatever problem his prospective employers put to him with both hands, his fingers racing through the space before him, the figures and symbols almost visible. No, they were visible: thin, liquid disturbances winking and flashing in the light. Barrel was panting, his face flushed, his forehead shining with sweat.

"Barrel," I called. "Is everything okay?" Which was a stupid thing to ask, but nothing else came to mind.

Under normal circumstances, I would have expected a reply something along the lines of, "What does it look like?" Now, all he said was, "No."

Something was happening to the writing hanging in front of him. The characters were moving, twisting as if trying to throw off their shapes. Barrel's fingers danced around them, tracing new forms. His mouth was moving, uttering a stream of noes, his expression wavering between concentration and dread.

"Is—" Sturrock began.

"Yes," Akara said.

"How do you know what I'm asking?" Sturrock said.

"Yes," Akara said.

"Barrel," I called again. "Julian. I think you need to stop."

Through gritted teeth, Barrel said, "Can't."

It's difficult to pinpoint the exact moment things went wrong. Barrel paused, returned to the figures he had just written, shook his head, added one mark, a second, said, "Okay," lifted his right hand, and was yanked backwards, out of his chair. He landed hard on his back, his head cracking on the floor. I was halfway out of my seat when something seized his right arm and something else seized his left. A pair of long, silvery shapes, little more than ripples in the air to either side of him, had his forearms in their mouths. I had an impression of dogs, but these were no pets: these were the things dogs whimpered and yelped over when they slept. Crowns of white fire floated over their heads, the glow bathing Barrel's wide-eyed face in flickering phosphorescence. Clearly, he was seeing his custodians more clearly than I was, than any of us were, but he made no effort to escape. (Not that he could have torn free of those jaws.) Instead, he nodded and said what sounded like, "Okay."

The silver shapes leapt toward the cafeteria exit, hauling Barrel along with them, two carnivores making off with their prey. Somewhere, someone was screaming; someone else was shouting. I thought, *I should do something*, but I couldn't work out how the creatures were going to manage the doors, and this seemed as if it would be the detail which saved Barrel from whatever fate he had incurred. When the things reached the doors, however, they plunged into them. There was an enormous GONG, as if the world's biggest bell had been rung, the sound making me duck and shut my eyes. I opened them to the doors still intact. The tables in my way prevented me from seeing whether Barrel and his captors remained inside. Finally, I left my chair to go to my colleague's aid. I had no clue what I was going to do against the nightmare dogs, but this seemed less important than that I was moving.

In front of the doors, an object was spinning, its irregular shape causing it to shed momentum rapidly. It clattered to a halt, and I saw it was a human jaw, the mandible, stripped clean of flesh and smoking, as if pulled from a fire. I stepped to one side of it and exited the dining hall. Outside, I surveyed the school grounds for the trio of shapes I knew I would not find. Once I had exhausted all lines of sight, I returned inside.

The screaming was worse, now. A handful of kids were standing around the jawbone, pointing their phones at it and shouting, "Yo, what is that?" and, "Shit, man, shit! That's someone's jaw! That's Mr. Barrel's fuckin' jaw!" I hustled them back to their seats and stayed by the bone until the police, whom Akara had called, arrived. In the time it took the first cruiser to arrive, Akara and Sturrock circulated among the kids, doing their best to calm and quiet them.

Although I knew they wouldn't believe me, I told the officers exactly what I had seen and heard. My story was corroborated by my colleagues, as well as a number of students, several of whom had recorded the event. The cops exchanged a weighty look and called for assistance. The jawbone was left in place until the crime scene people could arrive. At the cops' direction, everyone left the dining hall through the staff entrance, the kids to return to their dorms, the teachers to their classrooms, until we were told we could leave.

On our way back to the academic building, we saw the principal racewalking to the cafeteria. He did not acknowledge us.

"Took him long enough," Sturrock said.

"How are they going to spin this?" I said.

Akara said, "They'll say Barrel played an elaborate prank on all of us."

"The jawbone?" I said.

"A prop," Akara said.

"What about the videos the kids took?" I said.

"They'll say they were in on it with Barrel," Akara said.

"You can fake pretty much anything on video," Sturrock said.

"Damn," I said.

"Possibly," Akara said.

"I'm starting to wonder if I saw what I saw," I said.

"It's probably better if all of us think like that," Akara said.

"Does this mean he didn't get the job?" Sturrock said.

"What?" I said.

"You said this was part of his job application. Which begs the question, did he get the job?"

"I'm going to say he did not," Akara said.

"I'm going to say I hope not," I said.

Sturrock and Akara went to the main office to check their mail and to update the registrar and school counselor as to what we had witnessed. I climbed the stairs to my classroom on the third floor. I passed the chapel, the long second floor, both of which were supposed to be home to generations of ghosts, mostly of kids who had died of once-fatal diseases, though a few surly teachers were supposed to be on the prowl for deficient students. I had glimpsed a number of things from the corners of my eyes, congeries of shadow and architecture my mind interpreted as legs ascending stairs, heads peeking around corners. None of them had I believed, which had not stopped me from telling the kids about them as if I did. In my more fanciful moments, I imagined what I had seen were echoes of occurrences and experiences sounding down four dimensions.

What happened to Julian Barrel was of a different order altogether. My brain felt as if it were wrapped in cotton, cocooned in unreality. I almost tripped on my way up the stairs to the third floor. My room was unlocked: anyone who wanted my school-issued laptop was welcome to it. The walls were bare of the posters which had decorated them for the last eight years: timelines of the lives of Shakespeare, Dickens, and Poe; lists of quotations from each; outstanding examples of student work. I would thumbtack relevant newspaper articles amidst them. Gone, all of it, boxed up and sitting at home in the garage. I didn't bother turning on the lights—my contribution to cost-cutting. The afternoon sun crowded the corners of the room with shadows. I walked to my chair and slumped into it. Likely, Akara was right, the administration would insist nothing had happened, none of us had seen what we had.

I gazed out the windows, across the campus to the Hudson Highlands looming in the distance, the view I claimed rewarded climbing the extra flight of stairs. Standing in the corner to the right of the windows, Julian Barrel regarded me, his mouth hanging open bonelessly, his hands at his side. My heart surged with painful force. Before I could move, he was gone, the space empty of all but the dust motes swimming in the dimness.

Nausea burned my throat, forced my eyes closed as I struggled to keep my grilled cheese and steak fries in place. When I felt able to open them, I saw the envelope lying on my desk. It was cream-colored, business-sized, my name written on it in an elegant hand. The return address in the upper left- hand corner read, WHATELY ACADEMY.

For Fiona

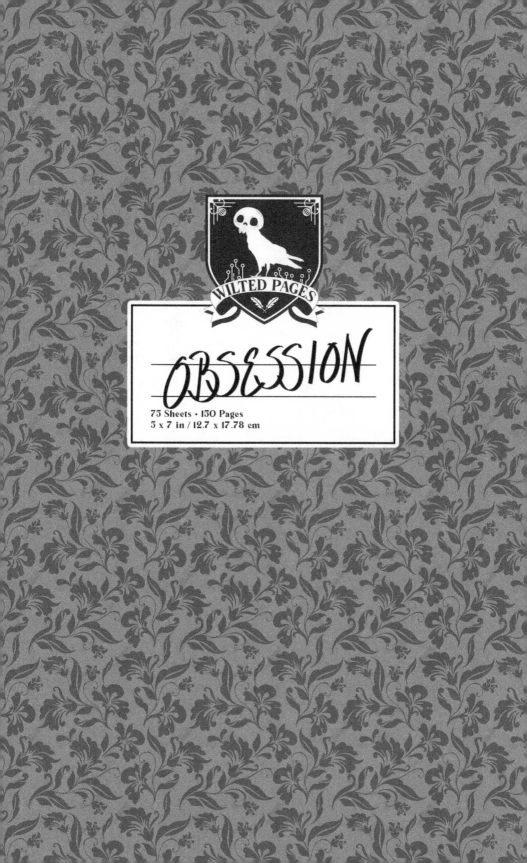

Higher Powers

Steve Rasnic Tem

IT WAS hard to miss the large wooden "O" mounted by the door of the bungalow. "O" as in obedient, onerous, obscene. The stain along the bottom of the letter conjured an image of ragged teeth and a tongue. Gray and black rotting leaves filled one side of the porch. The window screens were rusted and torn. An omnipresent carelessness suggested abandonment, but this was the address she'd been given. It was nothing like what she'd expected. It didn't appear sinister enough.

Before she reached the door, it opened. A thin man in a gray suit too small for him gazed up at her. "Miss Whyte?"

"Please, Darla."

"Come in Miss Whyte. Welcome to Pembroke House."

The interview took place in the front room, at a card table with two folding chairs. A sleeping bag and bathrobe lay folded in a nearby corner. The wood-paneled walls were decorated with a variety of African, Northwest tribal, and Inuit spirit masks. It was bitter cold, but as far as she could tell the furnace wasn't on and the fireplace was dark. She zipped her coat up to her throat. With growing impatience, Darla watched the man study two sheets of paper covered in dense handwriting. Finally, he looked up. "Are you married?"

"Nope."

"Boyfriend? Girlfriend? Children?"

"No to all three. Happily, purposefully unattached. If you're trying to find out if anyone might miss me enough to call the police, well, that won't be a problem. I have no one."

He scribbled a note in the margin of one of the sheets. "Do you drink or use drugs?"

"No." She'd come from an AA meeting. She'd lied to them as well.

"And you're a student at the university? Religious Studies?"

"I am. All independent study. I don't go to classes." The thought of attending class, with *classmates*, made her shudder.

"And you'll be working at the library down the street as well?"

"I'll be doing some cataloging for them, yes."

"Eve Pembroke was the original head librarian."

"I know. It's one of the reasons I want to work there. Her book collection is here, right? In her old house? My faculty advisor promised I would get to use it."

"Professor Jay Douglas, yes. A good friend of the Institute. You will have unfettered access to her books on the premises, but you must never take them from this house, or bring in any outside materials from the library or any other source whatsoever. We cannot risk. . . contamination."

She was beginning to suspect he might be an officious prick. Darla did not obey rules, especially silly ones. "Of course. I promise."

"Your event occurred ten years ago, when you were twelve years of age?"

"By *event*, if you mean my *exorcism*, yes."

He frowned but kept his eyes on the papers. "Had you experienced your first period?"

"I was having my first period at the time of the exorcism. It made it quite memorable. I didn't know. I thought that's the way it was going to be *every* month. Can you imagine?" He frowned but said nothing. "Why? Does that disqualify me?"

He looked surprised. "No, not at all. That's what it says here. I just need to verify."

"Does it also say that my mother, my own mother, performed that exorcism *because* I was having my first period?"

"Yes, yes it does. And unfortunately, this resulted in your mother's demise?"

"*The demon fucking ate her!*" Darla hadn't intended to shout. But this was a big deal in her life, and it demanded acknowledgement.

He gazed at her unblinking, as if he could see right through her. "My condolences." He glanced at the papers in his hand again, then folded them into thirds and slid them into his coat pocket. "Perhaps you would like me to show you the. . . well, it's in the next room."

"Is that it? Have I been hired?"

"The Institute does not want you to think of this as a job interview. It is far more important than that. You may move your things in at any time. It will be up to he-who-comes whether you shall remain. Only he can judge you as a vessel."

"So like any other man."

"He is not a man. Do not make that mistake."

"I know not all demons are male."

"Correct. Females certainly exist. *Ardat Lili, Batibat, Empusa, Lamashgtu, Lilitu*, several others."

"So, which one are we angling for?"

"I haven't been informed, I'm afraid."

"Above your pay grade, huh? No blood oath, no ironclad NDA?"

He didn't answer. He turned and walked toward the frosted French doors at the back of the room.

"Hey! Was I the only candidate?"

He looked over his shoulder, clearly annoyed. "I am not allowed to say." He flung open the doors.

It was a beautiful room, probably the original dining room, done in the Craftsman style with box-beams across the ceiling, intricate molding, an arts and crafts chandelier, and built-in bookcases around the perimeter. The curtains were open, exposing stained glass. Red and blue rays patterned the books, those gorgeous volumes in their worn leather bindings with raised cords.

The massive emblem which covered most of the oak floor was from a different design tradition entirely. A thick layer had been scraped away from the surface of the dark boards to expose their much lighter interior. At first glance this scraping appeared frantic and uneven, as if animals had been confined here. But when she looked closely, she saw the depth of excavation was consistent over the entire design, and the finer scratches radiating from the circumference created a halo effect which must have been purposeful.

Superimposed over this thoroughly worked area was a complex engraved design of interlocking oval mandalas containing interior circles and squares. Darla couldn't quite figure out how these onion-like layers had been accomplished. They appeared both raised above the scraped area and embedded deep within it, the appearance changing as she walked around the outer edge. The design was suggestive of celestial navigation. Within each mandala were countless internal connecting lines, fine as hairs. Depending on where she stood, she thought she could see various figures worked into the design: exotic creatures, landscapes, and architecture which transformed as she moved.

There were hooks embedded in the floor at various connecting points. "Those hooks are where you'll be tying me down?"

"Oh, there are no such plans. Ms. Pembroke had someone tie her to those hooks, or she tied herself. We don't know. But all we want you to do is to take notes concerning anything you see, hear, or feel while you are staying here. If some sort of possession were to occur, you would then receive the proper guidance."

"Guidance from whom? I'm surrounded by higher powers, it seems. Everyone thinks they know what's best for me, and I'm supposed to trust them."

He shrugged. "Honestly, I have no idea. As you so succinctly phrased it, above my pay grade." He gave her the keys. "If you don't mind my asking, why do you want to do this? Especially given your traumatic history. I realize that was one reason you were selected, but why put yourself through that again?"

Darla smiled. "My therapist thought it would be a good idea. She's tried everything else."

"This is a *terrible* idea," Dr. Sorros said. "Don't do this, Darla." She waited for Darla to respond, but Darla had learned her therapist couldn't bear the silence and would eventually speak. Increasingly this woman reminded her of her mother. Overdressed and too sure of herself.

While waiting for her doctor to speak again (the poor woman couldn't help herself), Darla glanced at her bookcase: *Trauma Treatment, Attachment, Diversity in Clinical Practice, Psychopharmacology, High Risk Clients,* bound volumes of *Psychological Medicine, The Lancet Psychiatry,* and *Clinical Psychology Review.* Those were shelved either quite high or quite low. Arranged on the easy-to-reach shelves, among scattered romance novels, were titles like *The Silva Mind Control Method, Crystals for Beginners,* Linda Goodman's *Sun Signs,* and *The Secret.* Not for the first time Darla wondered how she'd gotten stuck with such a crap therapist.

"I respect your beliefs, Darla, but as I've told you before this is outside my area of expertise. Demonic possession is not a valid psychiatric or medical diagnosis recognized by either the DSM-5 or the ICD-10."

Darla struggled to control her temper. "My mother was trying to get the bad stuff out of me. Open me up like an abscess to release the pus. But that allowed more infection to come in. The doctors at first thought I had epilepsy, or Tourette's. My ob-gyn thought I might be pregnant! I lost memories. Christ, I was having fits! I could use a good purging, don't you think?"

"I know it may seem as if a supernatural being took control of you when you had those attacks, but isn't an explanation other than the occult possible? You were deeply traumatized. Mental distress is a common response to such trauma."

"Nothing you've done has helped me!" She got out of her chair and went to the bookcase. "How can you read this crap? Can't you feel your brain rotting?"

"Darla, please return to your seat."

"Yes ma'am." She sat primly, hands on her knees. "My life needs purpose. I need to count for something. Maybe this new occupation, adventure, whatever you want to call it, can point me in the right direction."

"I know you love books—"

"I don't always understand what I'm thinking. I don't always recognize my thoughts as my own thoughts. Books speak to me—I find myself in *them*."

"I've suggested journaling before. Writing down your innermost feelings, your ordinary thoughts, might reconnect you, discourage your habit of obfuscating. Also, some exercise, walks in nature—"

"I need new drugs. I still have a lot of pain from my exorcism. Can you help me with that, Doc?"

"Clearly opioids are not the answer. How is AA going, by the way?"

"Wonderful! Brilliant! I can't remember the last time I had a drink."

Darla hoped the Queneau librarian couldn't smell the alcohol on her breath. She'd used mouth wash, coffee, peanut butter. Those usually did the trick, but some people had better olfactory abilities than others. She was convinced her brain worked better after a few drinks. Alcohol possessed her just enough to be useful.

Ms. Reynolds wore a 3D-printed plastic compression mask strapped to her head to cover her severe facial burns. No one warned Darla. The most surprising thing about the transparent mask was how much Darla envied it. It allowed enough of the underlying flesh to show through, and yet the damage, and her likeness, were nicely obscured.

"It's really quite lovely," Darla said, after Ms. Reynolds provided a brief, matter-of-fact explanation of what had happened to her. The librarian's home lay in ruins across the street, her son, the presumed fire starter, still missing.

"Thank you, but we needn't speak of my injuries again. You have a time-consuming job ahead of you. Professor Douglas says you have extensive experience with the evaluation and cataloging of fragile collections?"

"I'm well-versed, yes." Jay had exaggerated her part-time junior college library experience considerably. She was nervous about whatever repayment he expected. "And I have a lifelong passion for knowledge and learning."

"Very good." The rattle of the birdcage elevator made conversation difficult. Darla worried there might not be an escape option if it stopped working. She could feel her claustrophobia blooming.

The cage opened and they stepped out. There was a pronounced odor: sour musk, mold, and was that oysters? Ms. Reynolds flipped the light switch and various grimy bulbs struggled to burn. The Gothic architecture might have once been opulent: pointed arches and ribbed vaults, ornate iron brackets which were now badly oxidized. The walls had been drabbed down with olive-colored paint randomly applied. The books Darla could see were a mix of the common and the obscure, inconsistently arranged.

"This is the second basement. You'll start here. The level above, for all its mess, will be less of a challenge. The contents of the level below have mostly liquified, I'm afraid, due to frequent water incursions. There is at least one level below that, completely flooded and lost."

"What's the caged area in the corner?"

"Ms. Pembroke made it her office space. It hasn't been touched since her demise. The shelves contain some of our more outré items. It's where you'll be working. No one will bother you. My staff refuses to come down here. Perform light repairs if you will, but most will require expert conservation. At best you'll have chipped and bowing boards to contend with, foxing, wormholes, that sort of thing. Many are in disastrous shape. Are you familiar with Ms. Pembroke's studies?"

Darla could barely contain herself. She'd expected Pembroke's items either to be lost or off-limits. "She's part of my independent study. Early twentieth century female occult investigators."

"So, you believe in demons and evil and all that?"

"Evil is a human construct. I don't know if there is a spiritual evil or not. Perhaps it's simply a set of behaviors we do not understand. What do you believe?"

The librarian didn't answer. Darla started to turn around to make sure Reynolds was still there when she heard, "I'm not a believer in much of anything. I'll leave you to your work. If you need anything just come upstairs. And remember, none of these materials can leave this room."

Darla turned and smiled. "Of course not. They're safe with me."

She spent the next few hours searching Pembroke's cage. She found the sketches, notes, and diagrams Jay told her about, secreting them inside the lining of her coat. They smelled bad. She hoped the stench wouldn't alert any of the staff when she left the building.

Professor Jay Douglas stood before the blazing Pembroke House fireplace, a glass of wine in his hand. He'd stripped down to his tighty-whities. Darla thought he resembled an unattractive Oberon.

Darla was drunk, but not *that* drunk. "Put your pants back on, Jay. I'm not having sex with you or anybody else. To be blunt, I don't like things *inside*—"

"That's an unsophisticated view of sex. There are other—"

"Jay!"

He stared at her, looking disappointed, and finished his drink. While he was sitting on the ottoman getting dressed, Darla continued her study of the papers she'd stolen from the library along with some related volumes she'd pulled from the Pembroke House shelves. "How are your classes going, all the ones I don't have to attend thanks to you?"

"None of the students are up to your standards of course, although many think they are. Charles, the one you hate, is worse than ever. He thinks he can get away with anything, the snobby little prick."

"Maybe we should use Charles for a trial run. Tie him to the floor and see what happens."

"I wish." Jay had his pants on, but his shirt was still off. He was standing next to her now, a little too close. "Some spirits *delight* in causing suicide."

She stepped away from him. "I won't traffic in that." Although a test subject was not a bad idea.

"Sweetheart, you don't know what you want. You never have. You needed someone to protect you—you never had that. But I'm here now. I'm the one who can protect you."

His words almost appealed to her. That was the frightening thing. "That thing my mother brought into me, when it left, it took from me something essential. If I get it back I won't need your help or anyone else's."

"You don't know if it's the same demon, or a demon at all."

"I've read all of Pembroke's notes. She did this more than once, you know. She experienced numerous visitations from the same creature. The size and the shape, what facial features she could make out, even the smell of it. I'm sure it's the same."

"Don't be obdurate. It could be a hungry ghost, or a *dybbuk*, a refugee from the other side needing a physical body it can use. Maybe it was someone who died a drunk, a parasite who wants to be able to drink through you via spiritual osmosis. You know Pembroke was an alcoholic, too."

"What? Get out of here! I don't need you to doubt my scholarship, especially not now." He didn't budge, but stepped closer, looking down on her. He'd done this before, his way to dominate.

She tried to slap him, but he grabbed both her wrists. "I *understand*. You're *torn*. She almost killed you. But you're an orphan. You miss her. You don't want to hurt me. You love me. You would never hurt me."

Darla gazed up at him, barely in control of her anger. "You really *see* me, don't you? No, I could *never* hurt you."

They drank some more. A lot more. Jay drank everything she put into his hand. He casually tried to undress her. She kept pushing him away.

She talked him into sitting on the floor. "If we pass out we'll have a shorter distance to fall." He laughed but kept complaining about the hooks snagging his pants and tearing his skin.

She put on one of the African masks, a brightly painted surprised look with a wide-open mouth and enormous eye holes.

He stared at her dumbly, then exploded into hysterics, falling over, nearly out. She gently spread his legs, pushed his arms to ten and two. "Oh, darling," he murmured in a distorted voice. She took out the rope and stretched it through the hooks and over his body, testing various star patterns and pentagrams, studying Pembroke's drawings, trying to match them. Finally, she had a design similar to the last, most complex sketch of the series. She hoped it was similar enough. "Professor Douglas, how do you feel."

He groaned. "Snug. It's. . . snug. Can't move."

"Perfect."

She positioned the candles at the prescribed points and read aloud a few passages in Latin from a volume with tattered edges and a badly water damaged leather cover. Her Latin was a little rusty, but Jay's was not. She watched his eyes widen as he began to realize what she was doing.

"Darla, untie me." She enjoyed hearing, then felt vaguely guilty about, the shakiness in his voice.

"Of course. After we're done."

She had the books and papers stacked and marked in order according to Pembroke's notes. At first she'd been annoyed by the woman's marginalia, a nervous, jagged scrawl marring most of these rare, priceless books. But those jottings proved essential. She didn't understand half of what she was saying or if she was pronouncing the words correctly, but hoped her passion and commitment counted for something. Other than a few passages from the gospels of Matthew, Mark, and Luke, the items were rare and esoteric, including a 1702 edition *Grand Grimoire, The Munich Manual, The Book of Soyga, The Picatrix,* taped together photocopies from the gigantic *Codex Gigas,* and something Pembroke referred to as *The Orange Book,* handwritten in French bearing no publisher's colophon, bound in the skin of an orangutan.

"Pembroke *died* during the rite!" Jay squirmed, fruitlessly trying to loosen the rope.

"We don't know that Jay. All we know is she disappeared. I expect a bit more precision in the pronouncements of a tenured professor."

Twenty minutes into the rite he began spouting nonsense, or she simply didn't recognize the words. "Jay, honey, what language is that?" He stared at her with bloodshot eyes, then spoke more gibberish.

His face began to change. Subtly at first: a raised eyebrow, a thicker lip, the eyes morphing into different shapes and colors. When Jay began to resemble her mother, Darla didn't want to see it. She ran and took the Inuit spirit mask off the wall and placed it over his face. The mask was distorted, lop-sided, consistent with the warping flesh underneath. Still, Jay wouldn't shut up. "You were always a whore, even at twelve! You lie to everyone! You've always lied!" It was her mother's voice.

The voice grew huskier and more hateful. "I ate your mother and I'll eat you too." The eyes peering from the holes in the mask had lost their whites to pools of ochre, the giant obsidian pupils bulging.

His body took on an odious aspect, his belly swelling unevenly. She was embarrassed that it made her grin, thinking about this misogynistic male suffering some of the more uncomfortable indignities of pregnancy. His skin rippled as he expelled an offensive gas. Beneath the mask he produced an orchestra of sounds which should have been impossible for any human tongue.

He went still for several minutes, the skin of his torso so pale and bloodless she thought he might be dead. She hadn't intended to murder him. This was supposed to be a test run before she performed the same ritual on herself. She hadn't thought this through. Instead of checking for a pulse she became distracted by her errors, her lack of preparation for contingencies. She'd have to record herself reading the passages—no way could she memorize all that. She could light the candles before she lay down inside the pattern. How could she tie herself down?

But the essential thing about the rope was not its security, but the pattern it made. With enough practice she might be able to thread the pattern while propped up on one elbow, then tighten the rope when she lay down. It might take hours, even days of practice beforehand, but she thought she could manage it.

Or maybe she just needed to sucker some horny and bookish college kid into helping her. Whatever was required, she would get back what had been taken from her all those years ago.

Jay began to weep. Faintly at first. At least he was still alive. She could hardly hear him. But as the volume increased. . . where had she heard that voice? That little girl's voice coming out of a grown man's mouth. That shy, awkward, polite, soft-spoken little girl.

Darla leaned over, pulled aside the ropes framing his head, and jerked the mask away to expose the smallish face.

It had been her face when she was only twelve, before the innocence and the kindness had been stolen away. She'd made a terrible mistake. The little girl she had been was now irretrievably stuck in him, and it was her own damn fault.

Twisted Tongues

Michael A. Reed

The other students at Shagwood don't know why he is *different*. That's the word they use because they don't want to say the old word. Dyslexic. Or the other words they once said but dare not say now: illiterate, idiot, troglodyte. Worse, they don't see what he can see every second of every day. A shape like him suspended in shadows behind his footsteps. A voice that has many demands. A voice that does many twisted things.

I want the blonde boy. B-L-O-N-D-E. Bring him to the tower, and I will eat him up. He is how I want to chew on. Who. Who I want. I want to taste his hair. He smells like vanilla extrack. V-A-N-I-L-L-A. How.

"Not the blonde boy," Edgar says. "No more people."

Belemew, the blonde boy Dyslexia wants, leans against the wall of a carrel with his arms folded. He glances at his buddies and laughs because he doesn't know what Dyslexia will do to him.

But his friends don't laugh. They curl their clammy hands into fists. They've heard the rumors of Edgar and what happens in the library at night. These boys are wary of the missing students, and Edgar gives them something to fear. In their own pathetic way, their silence is protection, even though they don't know anything about Edgar for certain. Nobody does.

"Are you talking to yourself?" Belemew asks, his pink lips curling with a smile that Dyslexia doesn't want to tolerate.

"I am," Edgar admits. "I'm sorry to have disturbed your studies."

Belemew holds up a worn copy of *Seneca His Tenne Tragedies* from a table and shakes it at Edgar. He knows what Belemew will say next. Some of the students didn't forget what Edgar used to be, even though he isn't that any longer.

"Can you even read?" Belemew's cheeks are red with self-importance. "Egdar?"

Please Egdar. Feed me the blonde boy. Look at his stupid face. It teaches. Twiches. Twitches. T-W-I-T-C-H-E-S. I will spine his spin. Crunchy boy. Brake. Break.

Dyslexia pretends to ask, and Edgar pretends he can stop it. Sometimes he can. But not this time. Edgar feels bad for Belemew. He feels bad for them all.

"I can read." Edgar looks over his shoulder at Dyslexia. It writhes behind him. Formless hands reach and wrap Belemew's face in an inky vapor. For Dyslexia, this is a taste test—a sampling spoon of blonde boy's creamy skin with a dash of freckles.

Belemew sneezes. He sneezes again. If only he knew that an unkindled spirit cradles his head.

"Damn dust," Belemew says. "This school is going to shit. Good thing they are closing it down. Missing students and now dust. It's only a matter of time before we're all gone. No more *boarding school for the intellectually curious.* What a joke. I should've listened to my dad and attended Royal Academy instead." He marches up to Edgar and thrusts his spindly finger into Edgar's chest.

"I bet you're staying, Egdar." Belemew screws up his eyes and makes his best horse face. "I bet you're still here after the lights go out. Suiting. At least no one will see you." He turns dramatically so that the platinum curlicues atop his head flutter like streamers. Laughing, he walks away. Dyslexia follows him as far as the door to the study hall, then slinks back to Edgar like a disappointed dog.

We will take him to the library in the tower, toonight. Tonight. L-I-B-R-A-R-Y. Liebeary. Library. His face makes me so hungry. He smelled good. He saw yummy. Was. Lyebarey. L-I-B-R-A-R-Y. Library.

"Okay," Edgar whispers. Not that he really has a choice.

Afraid of breaking the recently enforced "travel in groups" rule, the other boys scamper off, their complexions pale. Edgar once thought he would enjoy that look of fear. He doesn't. Instead, he only sees a number. Six. Dyslexia has eaten six students so far. None of them were kind people. That made it seem okay, at first.

To make it all worse, Dyslexia looks like him. It makes Dyslexia's feeding times all the more deranged. The blood on its lips. The human hairs curled like wire whips between its teeth. The green shade of its eyes glinting, manic, and insatiable. By the time Dyslexia had finished pulling the femurs out of its third victim, Edgar hated himself.

Some nights, when Dyslexia isn't hungry, Edgar dreams of the old Shagwood. In this dream, he studies poetry and literature. The teachers think he won't amount to much. There is no curfew. He doesn't hear the screaming arguments in the headmaster's office as they decide what to do. No one is afraid to walk the halls alone. Happy and imperfect, he spends his evening at the library in the tower reading books by candlelight.

Even before he spoke the cursed words in that strange book, he could read. People say he couldn't. He did it slowly. A book a month at the beginning. Then two books. Then three. It would take him more time, but he could read as well as anyone by the time he cast off Dyslexia.

"Edgaw," Elvira says, tapping Edgar's shoulder. "Aw you alwight?" She stands beside Edgar, her tiny brown eyes pondering.

"Hey Elvira," Edgar blurts. He hopes his face isn't too red. "I didn't know you were in the room."

"I was wowking in the back cowna. My ancient histowy test is tomowow." She corrects herself. "Would have been tomowow. I wasn't twying to eavesdwop."

Eat her. She smells like Cinnamen. Cinnamon. Sinamon. C-I-N-N-A-M-O-N.

"Be quiet."

Elvira steps back and frowns.

"I'm sorry. I didn't mean you." He twirls his hands in the air as if his arms could apologize for him. "I wasn't talking to you. I was talking to me."

"Talking to yowself is okay," Elvira says. She scrunches up her nose and smiles. Her dimples are deep and contagious. Edgar smiles back.

"That's a relief. I've been doing it a lot lately."

"I know. We all know. It's scawing people. Only because of what's been happening and those missing students." Elvira grazes Edgar's hand with her fingers. "I hewed what Belemew said. Aw you alwight?"

I will suck his eyes out. Blande boy. Know won will here blonde boy. No. One. Hear. Eat the girl. Oh please, Egdar. She will be like an egg. Peel her shell. Yolk her.

Dyslexia floats above Elvira. Its fingers run up and down her neck. It licks her ears and says things that make Edgar want to escape.

"I'm okay," Edgar says. "I'm used to people like him. It doesn't matter if I've changed. He needs someone to hate."

"Is it weally gone?" Elvira twines her hand into Edgar's. He lets her.

Edgar and Dyslexia, inches apart, look into each other's eyes. Dyslexia waits for an answer. It looks amused.

"I still think about my learning disability sometimes. But yeah, it's gone. Most of the time, at least. Some days I feel like I have to suppress it. I have to force it down. Do you know what I mean?"

"I do. I dweam that I wake up in the mowning, and I can pwonounce my Rs. Maybe one day? It happened fow you. It could happen fow me, too."

In silence, they stand at the center of the study hall examining each other with curious glances. Edgar likes the way Elvira rises up on her toes when she is nervous. He thinks about the mole above her collarbone and wonders if she has any more. She doesn't turn away. They don't have enough time to be shy. Her parents will arrive at Shagwood in a few days. Then she will go home. Forever.

"Will you come to the library in the tower with me?" Edgar immediately regrets the question, but he doesn't take it back.

Thank you, Egdar. We can share her. We will be so much pane. Pain. She is good proteen. P-R-O-T-E-I-N. Protein. Oh, yes. Her hungry makes me dimples. Get her, Egdar.

"Tonight?" Elvira's eyes lit up. She tries to hide her grin with the collar of her coat.

"Not tonight. Definitely not tonight. I'm busy tonight." Edgar watches Dyslexia as it kisses the length of Elvira's arm.

"Tomowow night, then?"

"Yes. It's a date." Edgar's eyes blur as Dyslexia swirls around Elvira's feet. "There's a book I want to share with you before you leave. It changed my life."

Belemew awakens and doesn't know why he is in the library. Last he remembers, he had been trying to sleep. He had a strange dream. A dark cloud with Edgar's face had devoured him as he tried to run away.

"Edgar?" Belemew's question is innocent. He rubs his eyes like a child awoken in the middle of the night.

What stands in front of him is not Edgar, though it looks like him. Edgar sits in a wooden chair in the corner of the library reading a strange book. He adjusts his glasses, licks his thumb, and turns another page.

Belemew squints. Old rickety bookshelves cover the walls of the tower like ancient sentinels. The books are worn. Their pages are yellow with age, and the covers, many of them leather, emit a distinct dry wood scent. Belemew lay in the center of the library floor. The stone is cold on his palms. The tables have been pushed back. Above him, an iron lantern swings from a chain, and the shadows on the walls leap from shelf to shelf.

Then Belemew sees Edgar sitting in the corner. He looks back at Dyslexia that stands in front of him, and he lifts a trembling finger towards Edgar's doppelganger.

"No," Belemew yelps. "No, please."

Dyslexia rips Belemew from the ground and suspends him in the air with its phantom hands. Belemew isn't brave enough to scream. His eyes dart from side to side, and his puffy, pink lips flay. He squeaks like a chipmunk caught in a falcon's talon. As Belemew chirps, Dyslexia sniffs him and licks his hair.

Saveory. Savory. S-A-V-O-R-Y. We twist the blonde boy. Make him backwords. Then we slurp him. B-A-C-K-W-A-R-D-S.

Edgar doesn't want to watch, but he does. Every time.

Dyslexia takes Belemew's shoulders and yanks the bones. Belemew's expression quirks. It mangles him until his corpse is a rung rag and all his fresh juices spill onto the stone floor. Dyslexia opens its mouth wide and shoves Belemew's contorted limbs inside. Like a python, it gulps him down. When finished, it dives to the floor and breathlessly swallows the dark liquid residue of Belemew.

Edgar watches Dyslexia clean the floor with its crooked mouth. Seven students. Officially, the school knows that three students are missing. The Shagwood administration claims the other three students are on unannounced family vacations or school transfers. The efforts to hide what happens at Shagwood doesn't stop the inevitable. Shagwood will close by the end of the week. Indefinitely.

Now that Belemew is dead, the police will have reason to return to Shagwood and search every cranny of the boarding school. They've already interrogated Edgar on several occasions, likely because of his peers' suspicions and the flourishing folklore of Edgar Herm—the *different* boy. The boy that doesn't belong in a school as prestigious as Shagwood.

But they never accuse him of a crime. There is no evidence. Dyslexia, by the time it finishes eating, leaves nothing. It is a ghost. A haunt. A remnant. What could they ever find?

Trying not to listen to Dyslexia's incessant gurgling, Edgar flips through the pages of the odd book in his lap. The book has no title. No pictures. Each page contains only a few words. This was the reason he had been drawn to it at first. The simplicity of the book made him feel like he could read as well as anyone else. Then he discovered a mysterious line of words written in a foreign language. The words had appeared on a random page, unassuming, as if it were hiding in plain sight. More surprisingly, he understood what it said.

Edgar strokes the letters of the spell that removed Dyslexia from inside him. He calls it a spell because he doesn't know what else to call it. Incantation. Trick. Ritual. No human word could describe the etched runes. Nor could Edgar describe its meaning to anyone. He doesn't have the language to express what he sees. Whatever it says, and whatever he spoke aloud that dreaded night, had created Dyslexia—the spiritual embodiment of his learning disability. A killing thing.

Sitting with his palm to the cryptid page, Edgar wonders if Elvira could read the spell. He had shown the book to Gerold in his chemistry class, but he only saw an empty page. Edgar had flipped the pages madly, seeking proof of his sudden change—the reason he had been cured.

Gerold had called him a lunatic—an idiot who wouldn't know how to read a sentence if he could ever find one. Dyslexia appeared that night, snatched Gerold from his bed, and summoned them all to the library in the tower where it began. Boy one. The first missing person reports. Wayward glances from students and teachers. An interview with the headmaster, the police chief, and the boy's mother, who tearfully begged Edgar to explain what happened to her son. He had been the last one to see the boy, after all. And no one trusts the abnormal kid.

Elvira is different, too. She has something she wishes to cast off. Perhaps she could speak the words. Perhaps he doesn't need to be alone.

Edgar waits outside the girls' dormitory as Elvira changes out of her school uniform. No one could find Belemew this morning. They say the scene of Belemew's dorm room resembles that of the other missing students. It is perfectly normal. No sign of struggle. No missing belongings. No evidence of an intruder. There's only a missing blonde boy.

Students whisper as they walk past Edgar. They point. They recoil. Most of them carry their belongings: suitcases stuffed with crumpled uniforms, books they pretended to read for class, notes and assignments that amounted to nothing. Dyslexia flutters at their feet. It caresses uncovered thighs and swoops in and out of backpacks. It chants flavors as it licks each student's skin.

Raspbarry. Peenut butter. Peanut. Jelly. Lemen Cookie. Lemon. L-E-M-O-N. Oregaknow. Chocolate. Chalkalate. Chalkalleat. Chew them up. O-R-E-G-A-N-O. Pinch there eyes. Pull their skin off.

Two tall girls with shining brunette hair walk out the dormitory. They snicker. They think they are quiet, but Edgar can hear everything they say.

"Weally dumb giwl," one of them mocks. "Get out! I'm getting undwessed!"

The other girl's nostrils flare as she laughs. "She's such a prude. Or should I say pwude!" They link arms and skip down the hallway. Dyslexia follows them for a few seconds before returning to Edgar, a grimace on its face.

Corn dogs. The shiny girls smell like corn dogs. Bring them down two the library. Up. Up to the books. T-O-O. I will crush their legs like pretsouls. P-R-E-T-Z-E-L-S. Pretzels. Twisted twins.

"Shut up," Edgar murmurs.

Elvira exits the girl's dormitory wearing a pretty polka dot dress and long zig zag socks. Her face is pink, and her brown eyes are wet. She smiles so that Edgar won't worry, but he is unconvinced.

"Allewgies," she says, waving him off with a hand. "Seasonal stuff."

Edgar decides to smile back. "You look wonderful."

Delicious. Egg. Bite me for her Egdar.

"Thanks. I'm sowy I took so long to get weady. I had to pack a few things. My mom called this mowning. She is coming to get me fiwst thing tomowow."

Edgar can't hide the disappointment. He opens his mouth to say something encouraging, but he doesn't think of anything. He stands there with his lips ajar and feels foolish. For a moment, he thinks Elvira should leave. It would probably be best. He could stay at Shagwood, alone forever with Dyslexia. No one else would be hurt except for himself.

"We still have tonight," he finally says. The words feel suave. Cheesy even. He likes it.

"You'we wight. We will need to be sneaky othawise ow teachews might catch us and send us to bed." Elvira grabs Edgar's hand and pulls him along. With a silly grin on his face, he happily follows.

Oh thank you, Egdar! Your to nice too me. She will be a midknight snack. M-I-D-N-I-G-H-T. Yum. Yum. Yum.

Dyslexia hangs over Elvira like a storm cloud, its hands reaching down and rippling in her hair. It makes uncomfortable moaning noises as they run through the halls and up the spiral staircase that leads to the library in the tower.

Out of breath, they push open the big cedar door to the library. Before he left last night, Edgar had put the furniture where it belonged. The stone floor that had been bathed in Belemew's blood is spotless. Dyslexia never leaves a trace of its victims.

"I wawely come up hew," Elvira says once she can breathe. "I always wesearch in the main libwawy. This is cute."

Dyslexia stands behind Elvira, its eyes rabid and ballooning like a crazed cartoon. It reaches its hands out to grab Elvira by the head.

"No!" Edgar shouts.

Elvira raises an eyebrow: her signature look of concern.

Dyslexia growls and floats up into the corner of the library. Its foggy figure casts a shadow over the library.

So hungry. Egdar hates me. Egdar is sellfish. Selfish. S-E-L-F-I-S-H.

"Okay, it's not cute," Elvira jokes.

Edgar shudders. Bringing Elvira to the tower was a bad idea. Dyslexia won't wait for long. He pulls the mysterious book from the shelf where he left it last night and holds it out to Elvira.

"This is my favorite book," he says. He hears the strain in his own voice. "I want you to like it, too."

Dyslexia stirs on the ceiling. It calls down to him, its teeth chattering and its arms flailing.

Eggs. Eggs. Eggs. Eggs! Eggs! Eggs! Edgar! Eggdar! Eggs! Eggs! Eggs!

Elvira hesitantly takes the book and opens the cover. She flips through the pages with little interest.

"Thewe awe so few wods on each page. Is it poetwy? That's womantic." Elvira nods and smiles like she tried a new food at a dinner party and doesn't want to be rude.

"Flip to the middle. Is there a blank page?"

Every muscle in Edgar's body contracts. If Elvira sees a blank page, he will need to get her out of the library. Fast. Then her mother will withdraw her tomorrow and she will disappear forever. She will want to write letters, Edgar knows. But he will never write her back. She will call. But he will never answer. He will stay far away from her. He will spend his nights watching Dyslexia feast. Unless she can see the words.

He holds his breath.

"Iv'e neva seen this language befowe." Elvira holds the book out so that Edgar can see the runic spell on the page. "It's odd. I can wead it."

Edgar hugs Elvira and lifts her into the air. He hoots and spins her around until they are both dizzy. She looks surprised when Edgar kisses her. He sets her down. His hands shake. The book had dropped to the floor in all the commotion. He picks it up and opens it to the spell.

"Listen carefully to me." Edgar speaks too quickly. He points to the words, his finger quivering. "I read this book because it made me feel better about myself. I felt like I wasn't stupid like everyone told me."

"You'we not stupid," Elvira retorts.

"I know. I know. And neither are you! People don't understand that we don't really have a disability. Dyslexia is more like a variation. It's only an incompatibility. So is your speech impediment."

"You'we scawing me, Edgaw."

Dyslexia crawls along the ceiling like a pensive spider. It returns to its corner only to hiss and plead. The noise makes it difficult for Edgar to hear his own words.

Please. Please. Please. Give her to me. I want to swallow her orgains. Ograins. O-R-G-A-N-S. Boil it. Crack it. Please. Please. Please. Please. Please. Please.

"You don't know the language, but you understand the words. How is that possible if it wasn't meant for you like it was meant for me?"

Elvira looks at the page that Edgar holds in front of her. She strains her eyes. She walks backwards in Dyslexia's direction.

"What do you see?" Edgar takes a step toward her wielding the open book like a crucifix. "What does it mean to you?"

"It's a pwomise," she says.

"Yes."

"But it comes at a cost."

"Yes."

"What is the cost?"

Edgar stops. He imagines the spirit of Elvira's Speech Impediment and the things it might do.

He can see Speech Impediment clearly. It looks like Elvira. It's cute but hungry. It follows her everywhere, and it eats people, animals, and things. Somehow it is more rabid than Dyslexia. It's angry all the time. Speech Impediment doesn't swallow its victims like Dyslexia. It dismembers them and tries to put them back together again. Elvira can't sleep at night because she dreams of people in pieces. Even together with Edgar, their spirits mingling in the air above them like swirling chemicals, Elvira feels alone. She doesn't go home with her mother. She stays at Shagwood with him after all the students have gone, and she resents him for bringing her to the library in the tower. She dissolves into bitterness and never reforms.

But he is not alone in his imagination. Dyslexia eats every last student and resorts to snatching rats from the walls. It wants to eat Elvira, but Speech Impediment won't let it. They roam the abandoned halls of Shagwood. They read every book on every shelf, and they read flawlessly. Their tongues are no longer twisted. No one is there to remember their former imperfections. After a time, their discarded spirits are nothing more than outlines–contours that decorate their shadows as they walk. And Edgar is happy.

Edgar comes back to reality. "Almost nothing," he says, forgetting the seven missing students. He places the book in Elvira's hands.

Save a taste for me, Egdar. Which is unfair. Witch. That. Edgar! E-D-G-A-R. Don't eat her all!

A shape like Elvira hovers in the air.

The Allard Residency

Brian Evenson

I.

They had not crossed paths with a caretaker, had instead been directed by the broken English of the weather-faded note tacked to the door to dial a number. It was a strange number, seemingly not enough digits, but they were in a foreign country, after all: maybe local exchanges were like that here. When they called, it rang a few times, but then connected only to silence.

"Weird," murmured Einar. He lifted the cellphone away from his ear and stared into it. "No one there."

"Maybe you dialed wrong," said Katla. Einar, already redialing, didn't bother to respond.

He called three more times, same result each time. A click, as if someone had picked up, then silence. *Hello?* Einar said. *Hello?* Nothing.

"Let me try," said Katla. But it was the same for her.

"What now?" she asked, handing Einar back the phone. He shrugged. Together they stared at the suitcases they had hauled over cobbled streets in the dark, dragging them the three kilometers from the station.

Katla rattled the door handle again. Still locked.

"We could get a hotel," said Katla, "work it out in the morning."

"Yes," said Einar. "But they're expecting us tonight. If we go away and come back tomorrow, perhaps it'll be worse."

How could it be worse? wondered Katla. But aloud she said, "What, then?"

Einar hesitated. "We should break in."

"Break in?"

"We're allowed to be there. My residency starts today. This is our place for the next few months. It doesn't really count as breaking in."

Which, after a little more argument, was precisely what they did. Or would have done except that when Einar experimentally placed his shoulder against the door it slid open. Had it been slightly ajar the whole time? Einar thought so—what other explanation was there? But Katla was less sure: she'd checked, and then checked it again while Einar was reading the note and calling. Maybe there was some sort of mechanism, Einar reasoned, making it so that when they dialed the number the door unlatched: some sort of magnetic lock or something radio-controlled. Katla ran her hands over the door and its frame, searching, but there was nothing there.

"Just accept it as good luck," said Einar. "Let's go in."

"Just a minute," said Katla. "Just give me a minute." But soon even she gave up. She had found nothing and had reached the point where it was better to shrug and forget about it rather than continuing to run her fingers over the door and its frame. The longer she spent looking, the more she would have to acknowledge that something strange had happened.

The first night, exhausted by the flight and the time change, they abandoned their bags in the front hall and trudged up the stairs, opening doors until they found a bedroom. The bed was unmade and musty, the blanket and sheets askew, but they were tired enough to just clamber in. A moment later, they were asleep.

Katla was awakened by a tapping, and something making the morning light flutter. A tree branch swaying in the wind, she thought at first, but when she opened her eyes, she realized it was a bird attacking its own reflection in the window. She lay there, exhausted, listening, watching its useless but persistent attack, until the sun rose high enough in the sky that the reflection vanished, and the bird flew away. Beside her, tangled in the sheets, Einar slept on.

She got up, her head aslosh, and went downstairs in search of a kitchen, somewhere to heat water. They had no coffee; it had been too late to shop for groceries on the way from the station. But maybe a prior resident had left some, or perhaps a few sachets of tea. Something to wake them up enough to unpack and get started.

At the foot of the stairs, in the foyer, sunlight streamed through the panel above the door, speckling the pale lower wall like a skin disorder. It was, she saw now, a remarkably austere foyer, no stand on which to hang a coat, no rack for shoes.

She was already halfway down the hall when she realized something was nagging at her. She slowed, stopped, turned back. It took a moment of staring at the barren foyer to realize what it was: their bags were missing.

She checked the front door—it was just as they'd left it: locked. She went down one of the two halls leading off the foyer and found the kitchen. No bags there, no coffee either, only a door leading to the garden beyond. She backtracked and went down the other hall: a dining room that didn't seem to have been used in quite some time. A layer of undisturbed dust covered the table. Dust, too, on the tile floor, less visible but still there. Except for her own foot-prints, it was undisturbed.

Maybe Einar moved them in the night, she told herself, but she knew Einar better than that. He wasn't the sort to move things in the night.

She went back to their bedroom. He was still sleeping, no bags in sight. She opened the wardrobe and looked in: empty except a jangly wire array of hangers.

Einar groaned from the bed. "What time is it?" he managed.

She ignored him. "Where did you put the bags?"

"Bags?"

She grimaced and left the room. She heard him calling after her but didn't answer, just poked her head into each of the other rooms on the floor. No bags.

She climbed the stairs to the top floor, Einar not far behind now, struggling to get his shirt on. She tried the door at the top: locked.

"What's the matter?" asked Einar from just behind her.

"Our bags," she said, "they're missing."

"That's impossible," he said.

She shrugged.

"They're in the entryway," he said. "They wouldn't be all the way up here."

"I've looked everywhere else."

"The entryway," he said, his voice slow and reasonable. "We left them there last night. Remember?"

"Somebody moved them." She rattled the door handle. "What's behind this door?"

"It's the library," he said. "Allard's library." He shook his head. "Didn't you read the packet?"

"What packet? Why is it locked?"

"Didn't I show you the packet? Is it locked?" He sidled past her and put his hand on the knob. The door swung instantly open. "It isn't," he said, and went in.

But it had been, she was sure of it. What was it about the doors here? Why did they open only for him?

"They're not in here," he said, from just inside. "See for yourself."

She poked her head in. It was a pentagonal room, the walls lined with bookshelves perhaps fifteen feet tall. A thick glass dome let light leak weakly in. In the room's center stood a mahogany writing table, a nice patina to it, early 19ᵗʰ century maybe, its spindly legs gilded with now-peeling gold foil. Had it belonged to Allard? If she'd read the packet she would know.

Einar was at the table, brushing his fingers lightly across its surface.

"Our bags are gone," she said.

"I told you," he said, "They're in the foyer."

"They're not."

He didn't seem to hear. She took a step forward, and his head snapped up. "You're not allowed to enter."

"Excuse me?"

"That's the rule: no spouses in the library."

She made a disgusted noise. "You've got to be kidding me."

"You agreed to the rules." He shooed her away and reluctantly she stepped back over the threshold.

"There," he said. "That wasn't so hard, was it?"

She tried to swallow down her anger. Already he wasn't even looking at her. There was one book on the desk, beside an indentation meant for an inkwell. She watched him pick it up, blow the dust off it, open it . She could tell, when his mouth started to make shapes, that he was reading. Shaking her head, she started toward the stairs.

"Are you coming?" she called over her shoulder.

"You go ahead," he said. His voice sounded odd, flattened out. "I'll be down in a minute."

"They're really gone," Katla said. "They've been stolen." But he just waved her on.

And so, she gave up and made her way down the stairs, and then down the hall, and then down the other stairs to the foyer where the bags were waiting as if they had been there all along. They hadn't been, she knew, but Einar would claim they had. *You're imagining things,* she could hear him telling her. *You should see a doctor.* And so, she didn't say anything about it to Einar at all.

II.

How can you tell the exact moment when things go wrong? Don't you always either anticipate that wrongness before it comes or smooth it away, explain it, justify it, so that when you finally can't help but acknowledge it's already too late?

Katla had no answer to this question. At the time, she didn't even know to ask it. Only later, in the hospital bed, with Einar dead or transformed—impossible for her to say which, impossible to suggest to the police he was anything but dead without them believing there was something seriously wrong with her—did she find herself asking the question. Because of the damage to her throat, she could not speak at first, and later could speak only in a whisper. The doctor told her that she was lucky to be alive, that the shock alone could have killed her. The police came, with a translator, and interviewed her and tried to understand what had happened, at first asking her to write on the chalkboard they gave her and later crouching close and cupping their ears to hear what she was whispering. But if she couldn't understand it herself, how could she possibly explain it to them?

But if she had to explain it, after the fact, she would say things went wrong at the very moment the invitation arrived. She was the one who habitually gathered the mail, and so it was she who gathered the crumpled cream-colored envelope and brought it inside to place on Einar's desk.

"What's this?" he asked.

"I don't know," she said. "It's for you."

But she was curious. She lingered as he opened the envelope and watched his brow crease as he read it.

"It's an invitation," he said.

"What sort? Wedding?"

He looked confused. "To a residency. It congratulates me on my application being accepted. But I didn't fill out an application."

"What residency?" she asked, and then added, "congratulations."

"Thanks," he said. "For three months, living at Allard's house, researching him."

"Three months. . ." she said.

"Spouses can come too," he said quickly. "Please, come."

"Who's Allard?"

"Spiritualist. Late 19th century, early 20th. I've written on him —just in passing, but I have. Maybe that explains the invitation. I'll have access to his library." He turned the letter over. "Spouses don't have access to the library, only residents. Weird rule. But you don't care, do you?"

She hesitated a moment, shook her head.

He folded the letter back up, looked at her. "Well," he said, "what do you think? Shall we?"

If she had said no at that moment, she now thought, lying in the hospital bed, perhaps things wouldn't have gone wrong. But she said yes. She hadn't known what she was saying yes to, but she had said it.

By the time they were on the plane to the residency, Einar had done his research and was eager to share. Not only had he read the photocopied and crumpled packet that had been sent; he'd done all he could to research Allard. He knew Allard was not the man's real name, that he'd kept his birth name a close secret. He knew the house had remained unoccupied since Allard's disappearance almost a hundred years before. He knew there had been another disappearance in the house in the 1940s, one of Allard's acolytes— but most believed this second vanishing was staged since it fell on the 20th anniversary of Allard's own disappearance. "He probably just pretended to disappear and then left the country," said Einar.

"But was he ever seen again?"

Einar shrugged. "It was easier to disappear back then."

That was just the tip of the iceberg. There was the question of what Einar had been researching when he vanished—something occult certainly, but nobody agreed on what. But they all agreed that it had to do with something found in his library, the library he'd have access to.

"But not you," he reminded her. "No spouses."

"What, is it full of erotica or something?"

"Probably just your run of the mill occult library," he said. "Full of spells and curses and whatnot." He smiled.

What he didn't know was anything specific about the foundation. There was no information online about it, nothing about who had started it, when, and why.

"That's a little strange," she said, wondering why he'd waited to tell her this until now.

"Right? But I did find stories about the house. It's not exactly haunted, no evidence of that, but nobody will actually live there permanently. More cursed than haunted, it seems, but still makes for a half-decent story."

He smiled vaguely but offered nothing further.

"Why did they choose you?" she finally asked.

"How can I know?"

"If you had to guess."

He thought for a moment, then smiled. "We'll just have to see."

III.

That moment of not saying anything about the bags spread into other silences. She made the choice not to question Einar about what he'd been doing for the twelve hours he'd spent in the library that first day, how he'd stumbled down looking disoriented and confused, that faint distracted smile playing over his lips. The most she could manage was to ask, "All well?"

"Sure," he said. And then, "When's breakfast?"

"Breakfast?" she said. "Einar, it's evening."

His face clouded, then smoothed. "Dinner," he said. "I meant dinner." But he hadn't, she knew—she had known him long enough to tell. But once again she chose not to say anything. She let the lie stand. A mistake, but far from her first. But even if she had called him out, she was sure, almost sure, it wouldn't have changed anything in the long run.

She unpacked, folding his clothes in the way he liked and giving him the better shelves of the wardrobe. While he was up in the library she found the front door key hanging on a hook in the kitchen. She called up to him that she was going into the town for groceries. When she heard nothing in reply, she just went, locking him in.

The town was quaint, picturesque. The streets were cobbled and oddly slanted, ill-suited for cars. It was a tourist town in the off season, which meant the streets were largely deserted, most restaurants and shops shuttered until spring came. Finally, she found a small grocery and bought bread, cheese, ham, and coffee. The clerk asked her something that she didn't understand the first time; the second time she didn't understand either but caught the name *Allard*. She hesitated, nodded. And then the clerk was speaking faster, with some urgency, but when he realized she didn't speak the language he trailed off. He smiled sadly and offered a little bow.

She made her way back up the hill to Allard's house. She half expected Einar to be there waiting in the foyer, angry, wanting to know where she had been, but the foyer was deserted. She put away the food, then climbed the stairs to the library.

At the door she paused, listened. An odd sound was coming through, a kind of whispery fluttering. She brought her ear closer to the door, but still couldn't quite make out what it was. She straightened, knocked. Immediately the sound stopped.

"What is it?" Einar's voice asked. It sounded strained, a little panicked.

"I bought groceries," she said.

No answer.

"Ham and cheese," she added, "something to get us by."

"You go ahead. I'll be right down," he said. He was right next to the door now, but he didn't open it.

She went back down. He didn't appear for hours.

The following day she awoke to an empty bed. She climbed the stairs to the library and knocked, offered him some breakfast, received no answer. She stared at the door a moment and then turned the handle, but something kept it from opening more than a few inches. She pushed against it with her shoulder. And there, suddenly, was his face, pressed up against the crack, eyes angry.

"Spouses aren't allowed," he said. He didn't seem to be wearing a shirt, she realized. "That's the rule."

"I just wanted to bring you some breakfast."

"I already ate," he said, but she knew this was a lie. And when he finally came down, much later in the day, he ate almost nothing, just picked at his food. He was distracted, not altogether there.

"I'm worried about you," she said.

"Whatever for?" he asked. But when she tried to explain—he wasn't eating enough, he was losing track of time, even when he wasn't in the library it was like part of him still was—he just wore the same abstracted smile, nodding distractedly as if he were listening when he clearly wasn't. Slowly she lapsed into a frustrated silence. This, too, he didn't seem to notice.

After a while, he stood and left the room.

"Where are you going?" she called after him. But he said nothing. In any case, she already knew. She knew even before she heard him climb the first flight of stairs, before she heard him climb the second, before she heard the library door creak open and slam shut.

What was up there that interested him so? What was in the book that he had picked up that first day and which seemed, in a manner of speaking, to have possessed him? Or was it other books now? He hardly spoke to her anymore, just offered that same half-dazed smile, and here she was downstairs, worrying about him, just trying to make him eat enough to stay alive, and waiting, counting the days, the hours, until the residency would end. This was not a good place, and the library was the worst of all. And yet Einar was drawn to it, spent all his time there—just as (so he had told her before they arrived) Allard had done. Allard had spent more and more of his time in the library until one day, suddenly, he was gone. And the house as a whole, too, was doing something to *her*—she could feel it. It was making her unable to speak up, unable to protect her husband. Or had she always been like that, and it had taken a situation as skewed as this for her to notice?

In the days that followed, it only got worse. Einar grew pale and thin, his eyes haunted. The incident of the bags was repeated again and again, things disappearing from where she knew she had left them and being nowhere to be found and then reappearing exactly where they had been before. Windows and doors sometimes would rattle, as if a wind were blowing through the house, though there was no wind she could feel. From upstairs she would hear a thump, but when she knocked on the library door Einar would either claim nothing was wrong or say nothing at all. Once, when he didn't answer and she tried to push her way in, something—was it Einar? could it be?—slammed the door so hard she nearly lost her fingers.

Sometimes she made her way up the stairs as quietly as she could and pressed her ear to the door and listened. There was the sound of her husband muttering to himself, something humming slightly, and also that same sound she had heard before and been unable to place, a fluttering.

When she became too worried, she tried to get Einar to leave. It was like talking to a stone. *We have to go,* she said. *It isn't safe, we have to leave.* He just smiled. *Don't be silly,* he said. *You're just lonely is all.*

"But what are you doing up there?" she asked.

"Research," he said. "I'm really getting somewhere." And the way his face radiated as he said it made her very worried indeed.

She steeled herself. "If you won't leave," she said, "I will."

For just a moment his composure threatened to break. She could see him, the Einar she loved, on the verge of rising to the surface, and then something rolled over his face and hid it.

"If you need to leave," he said, "who am I to stop you?"

She didn't leave. She stuck it out. Maybe if she hadn't had that glimpse of the real him rising briefly to the surface she would have. *Maybe,* she told herself, *the residency will end and, slowly, Einar will return to normal. I'm crazy,* she told herself at other times, *this is crazy.*

There was a rumbling coming from upstairs now, a humming threaded through it. She stared upward, wondering what she should do. She went halfway up the stairs, but the rumbling was diminishing, wasn't it? Yes, probably. Maybe. She took a few steps down and then, shaking her head, started up again.

She approached the door slowly, pressed her ear to it. She could feel the rumbling shake the wood and could hear the humming too, which sounded like it was coming from inside her skull. Poised there, holding her breath, she heard something else too: that same broken fluttering that she had heard before, and her husband moaning, moaning.

She was shaking. She got ready to knock but stopped with her hand just shy of the door. Instead, she grabbed the door handle, twisted, and quickly forced her way in.

Inside, the noise was much louder, and there was a wind as well, blowing in every direction at once. She tried to shout, and though she could feel her throat expel the words no sound came out, at least none that she could hear. The humming was a buzzing here, and the moaning she had been hearing was her husband screaming. He was in the center of the room, standing on the writing table, eyes closed, arms spread wide. His clothing did not seem to be clothing anymore but something moving and alive, something so black it looked more like a hole than a substance. Perhaps it was a hole, in which case all that was left of Einar was his head, his neck, his outstretched arms.

She shouted again, and again heard nothing over the buzzing and screaming. She rushed forward, grabbed her husband's arm, and tugged hard.

His screaming stopped. She felt him try to jerk free. She looked up and saw him adjusting to keep his balance, staring down at her with an expression that looked both surprised and afraid. She saw his mouth move, slowly and exaggeratedly, and though she couldn't hear the words he articulated sufficiently that she knew, or thought she knew, what they were:

What. Have. You. Done?

IV.

The rest only came back to her later, in bits and pieces as she lay in the hospital bed. It came back in dreams first, and only later as pieces that, slowly, she could put together, never quite sure if all the pieces were real. Perhaps she had not really seen what she thought she had.

But every time she began to think that she found herself remembering the way the suitcases had moved, the way other things had moved since. That, she was sure, had happened, even if she couldn't prove it. And, by extension, she believed that this had happened too:

She had grabbed her husband's arm, he had uttered his silent accusation, and then the thing that was on him in place of a garment began to *writhe*. She saw it creep, fluttering up over his throat, saw the fear deepen in his eyes, and she had tugged harder—then braced herself against the table's edge because he was beginning to pull her up and toward him. She canted her hips and pulled the other way and then, feeling her feet begin to slip, tried to brace herself against his chest. Only there wasn't a chest there, only writhing darkness that her fingers sank deep into. Her hand went immediately numb and when, panicked, she pulled it back out, the skin was blackened, dead. He tugged at her again and she tried not to touch him, but her forearm passed in, then her elbow, and in desperation she let go of his arm now, but he had locked one hand tight around her throat, and she could see strands of darkness creeping down his arm and toward her face. She felt her throat go numb and, not knowing what else to do, she made her whole body dead weight and almost pulled him staggering off his table—would have if he hadn't let go, sending her suddenly to the floor. Her blackened arm shattered on impact, the pieces disappearing, but she didn't feel it. Above her, her husband's mouth moved. She couldn't make out what he was trying to say, but from the expression on his face she was sure it wasn't good.

And then he spread his arms again, returning to the posture he had held when she had entered. Dazed and short an arm, she did not know what to do. The darkness that had spread up one arm seemed now to be returning to his chest. Perhaps if she let him continue with his so-called *research* he would return to her as the person she had known? But after seeing this, after losing her arm, how could she bear it?

She kicked the nearest leg of the table. The table swayed drunkenly, and he swayed atop it, nearly breaking his pose. She kicked again, harder this time, and the gilded leg folded, and the table yawed, and he fell. His body did not even hit the floor: as soon as he lost concentration the blackness swallowed the rest of him. A moment later both he and it were gone.

She somehow crawled out the door and fell down the stairs. She was probably unconscious for a while. When she awoke, she managed to get to her feet. Her missing arm was aching now, both the part that was there and the part that wasn't. She reached the door and unlocked it, passed through the garden and out the front gate and into the street, and collapsed.

She awoke in the hospital with people asking her questions in a language she couldn't understand. Her arm was still missing. Her throat and been damaged, the dark blots of fingertips burned into it. She couldn't speak. Eventually they brought doctors and police who knew English, but by the time they did she had grown unsure of what, if anything, to tell them. So she pled ignorance. Someone or something had attacked them, had taken her arm and taken her husband. No, it had happened too quickly; she couldn't be of much help. . .

In the hospital, when they questioned her about why she had been squatting in the house, she learned that it had long been unoccupied. There was no residency there, no Allard foundation.

They searched the house for the letter Einar had been sent but found neither that nor any papers from the foundation, nor any books in the abandoned library. The number they had been told to dial upon arrival was not an—and here they paused and exchanged glances—active number.

Was it formerly active? she wanted to know.

They nodded yes.

Who had it belonged to?

At first they demurred, and she wondered why they didn't want to say. Then they spoke and she understood: Allard had subscribed to a telephone line with this number shortly before he disappeared.

She didn't try to understand it. She was not sure what, if anything, there was to understand. But, lying there, she kept trying to figure out if there was ever a moment when it wasn't already too late. Even that, she eventually came to realize, was a question she didn't have enough information to answer.

And in time she came to realize the answer didn't really matter. Her arm, originally gone to just above the elbow, was gone now to the middle of her bicep, slowly necrotizing, a little more each day, a line of darkness creeping higher. Even when they amputated above the line, the arm kept necrotizing.

The doctors couldn't understand it. She had become a curiosity, a special case. *We will figure this out,* her head physician promised from within his hazard suit. *We will figure out what this is, and we will cure you.*

But she knew they wouldn't. She knew that in this too for her it was already too late.

The Library Virus

Hussani Abdulrahim

1. Genesis

WHEN DANLADI BEGAN to behave wildly, we bound his hands
and feet and carried him to Baba who knew how to deal with the
possessed. Baba made a potion from the brew of certain leaves,
roots, and barks of plants that he alone knew of. He forced the
potion down Danladi's throat. We waited for it to manifest. We
were expecting Danladi to throw up a couple of squiggly roaches, a
live snake, or a black kitten with red eyes. But it was none of those.
As soon as he drank the potion, Danladi began to vomit books. Yes,
books, with their covers intact. His throat and jaws would expand
when a book made its journey upwards from whatever bottomless
vault he had inside his stomach. With each book that appeared,
Danladi struggled and cried. The books were many and bulky. We
were astounded. This was not some kind of spirit possession, we
argued amongst ourselves. And as we moved books about to create
room for more, we tried to keep our fears locked up.

2. Fear

The news of Danladi's strange affliction spread all over the school and out into the quiet town of Tudun Makari like an angry wind blowing from the Sahara. A group that called itself "The Voice of Tudun Makari," populated by elders of our town who were mostly conservative in disposition, swung into action. They called for the closure of our school, Dangana Memorial Community School. They pressured the school authorities to send us home to our families, arguing that Western education would do us no good. The Voice of Tudun Makari said, "You see? You see what we have been saying? Books are now driving our children to the brink of madness. When we talked about how building a school was a bad decision, they said we hate civilization and don't want our land to progress. Do you see what is happening now?"

The management of our school said it was a bad idea to send us home since they did not know the nature of the ailment and whether it was contagious or not. Therefore, it would be foolish to let us go and put the whole of Tudun Makari at risk of a deadly disease. The Voice of Tudun Makari grumbled but was subdued.

We did not want to go back home either. We did not want to be stuck with our fathers, embarking on endless trips to faraway farmlands that one would reach by noon only if one had set out as early as the first cockcrow or immediately after the dawn's prayer. We did not want to live our days wandering on millet and rice fields, tilling the soil and nursing bent backs and aching joints.

We did not want to accompany our mothers to the markets and sit in stalls, in the midst of shelved dried fish, baskets of tomatoes, bales of vegetables, and armies of fat flies, contending with annoying customers who would haggle prices to death, while our mothers gossiped with other market women about whose husband was taking a new bride, or who had bought the latest Ankara, or how they planned on making a grand entry at the next wedding ceremony in Tudun Makari.

Our lives outside Dangana Memorial Community School were bleak, to say the least. If we were lucky, we would grow up to become adults, marry or be married off to someone we barely knew, live in the kind of houses our parents lived in, eat the same food we had eaten from day one, give birth to children who would be as miserable as we were, die and be buried on the same familiar soil. Who would want to endure such misery? What about all the dreams and adventures we desired?

We did not mind the shit we had to pound to force down clogged pipes in the old, stinky toilets at Dangana Memorial Community School. We did not mind the abuse and bullying from our seniors. We did not mind the number of times we would wake up and wish we weren't here or wish evil on our seniors, teachers, and whoever was making life difficult for us in Dangana Memorial. Yet, we still loved it here. We were free, able to express ourselves and be at our mischievous best. Why would we want to sell this freedom so cheaply and because of a disease that might not be contagious? We were not certain about that, though we were not new to strange happenings. For all we knew, Danladi might be suffering from a malevolent spirit attack that Baba would solve once he finished removing all the books that were inside his body.

But then, something happened to change our stance. Two more people fell and began to convulse just like Danladi. Baba restrained them, administered the same potion he had given to Danladi, and they too soon began to vomit books. Nothing spread faster than our fears, not even this affliction that we quickly named *The Library Virus,* for it was confirmed that these two new victims had also been in the library on that day Danladi's attacks began.

The Voice of Tudun Makari resumed their clamor for the school's closure. But they had no authority to make it happen. All they could do was make as much noise as possible, which they were good at.

The school management decided to quarantine whomever they felt was a danger or was at risk of the disease. The easy part was getting the library staff into isolation. The Chief Librarian and other library staff were kept in a special lodge. Their temperatures and other vitals were monitored from time to time. The hard part was gathering the students who had made use of the library on the day the disease manifested.

Our teachers and dormitory governors came to round us up. They wanted to fish out those who were in the library when Danladi, like the other two, fell and began to jerk like someone experiencing an epileptic bout. They asked. They begged. They threatened. We pointed fingers at our mates who had offended us in one way or another. We called the names of seniors who had been cruel to us and made our lives miserable. The teachers ended up with a handful of students who were in tears, swearing that they did not even know where the library was, not to speak of how it looked. Despite their pleas, they were marched off. We did not know what would become of them, but we were sure that the management knew they could not trust us.

3. DOSSIER

What did we know about Danladi? He was not exceptionally talented. He was never top of his class, but he was always some-where in the top half. He was not a popular figure either. He did not have the sort of build or handsomeness that would have elevated his social status, especially among the girls. And to make matters worse, he had tribal marks. We were in a fast-changing world; no one wanted tribal marks or desired to be closely associ-ated with someone who had them.

Danladi's parents were not rich, and neither were they poor. His father, like many, had farmlands where he grew cocoyam, millet, and onions. His mother sold petty goods in Tudun Makari's main market. There wasn't anything worthy of note about Danladi or his family except that Danladi loved the library and slept a lot during classes. Being infatuated with the library was a normal thing. But why someone would suddenly go crazy and start to vomit books was the part we did not understand.

The second victim of the Library Virus was Ashiru. Unlike Danladi, Ashiru was well-known in Dangana Memorial. He was handsome, and every girl wanted to be close to him. The boys secretly despised him for this. We loved Ashiru for the way he smiled, exposing gleaming white teeth that were well-queued like maize seeds on a full cob. It was not just his looks; we loved him for his exploits on the football pitch. Anytime we crowded Dangana Memorial's little football pitch, it was to watch Ashiru play. Any other reason was secondary. Given the extent of his talent and influence, he was made the captain of our school's football team the previous year.

Ashiru's father was a farmer, and his mother was a dressmaker. Another ordinary family. And like Danladi, Ashiru was in the library on the day Danladi's sickness started. Ashiru's presence in the library was odd. Mind you, we knew Ashiru very well. He was not someone who cared much about stellar academic performance. If we were awoken from sleep and ordered to make an impromptu list of those we would expect to find in the library, Ashiru would certainly be the last person to come to mind. So, no one knew why Ashiru was in the library on that fateful day.

We did not know much about Zubaida, the third person to come down with the virus. We knew that she always wore hijabs that were so long their edges swept Dangana Memorial's untidy grounds. Zubaida's hands were always hidden in gloves. No one could say for sure that they had ever seen Zubaida's hands. This prompted the rumour that she had a strange skin disease she was always trying to conceal. But it was just a rumour started by some girl who must have been suffering from boredom.

Zubaida wasn't an interesting individual per se. She was quiet and never asked questions in class. She always had worry and confusion written all over her face as if she was in the wrong place and would gladly donate a kidney in order to be anywhere else but

Dangana Memorial. Much like someone who was born on a space-ship and was just experiencing Earth for the first time. And thus, repulsed and frightened, wanted to be back in their familiar terrain. Like Ashiru and Danladi, Zubaida had been to the library on that day.

4. LOST ROUTINE

Before the virus, the same sun rose and set on Dangana Memorial Community School. Our lives followed the usual pattern. We were broomsticks, needles and toothpicks, electric poles and dogon yaro trees, egg-round buds, and elephants. We were Kardashians and Coca-Cola bottles. We were Margaret Thatchers and Benazir Bhut-tos. We were Mandelas and Awolowos. Above all, we were boys and girls always dressed in caftans and baggy trousers and in hijabs and niqabs, and odd-looking boots, and crocs. We clasped lecture notes to our bosoms and pretended not to care about the opposite sex and what they might think of us. We were devoted. We prayed. We said *audhubillah minashaytan nirajeem* as if our hearts would stop whenever our easy-going friends mentioned things like *vagina, fuck,* or merely talked about the opposite sex. We rebuked them and said they were foul-mouthed and should turn to God for forgiveness. Anything about the opposite sex, even mentioning their names, was a window opening to the wrong path, the path of Satan. Nothing good could come of that.

On days when we saw blood, we sold our souls to the gods of moodiness. We threw tantrums. We were sick. We sat on toilet bowls for long periods. We got offended at the slightest provoca-tion. We lashed out without caution. We were quiet. We ate like starving elephants. We missed classes. We cried. We assumed impos-sible positions, contorting our bodies when cramps hit like ocean waves and rapids. After five to six days, we became ourselves. We chatted, and the sound of our laughter ricocheted around us. We did not ask for forgiveness from those we might have offended during the heights of the storms that swept us. They understood. They had to.

We pretended not to notice lustful eyes on us whenever we went to classes or went to read at night. We pretended that the presence of such attention, or the lack thereof, did not have any effect on us, had nothing to do with our sudden ridiculous investment in expensive perfumes and padded bras, or the decision to ditch our niqabs for weeks and months, and even go as far as replacing our array of hijabs with revealing veils.

—We just wanted to feel comfortable.

—*A'udhu billahi*, this Tudun Makari's sun is like being set on fire.

Those were the excuses we gave to creased foreheads, raised brows, and narrowed eyes. We were not losing ourselves. We were modern people in a modern environment. There was nothing more like being sincere to oneself. We were lying. We had desires too. But we did not speak about them. We relegated them to the background, trampling on them until they looked false to us.

We prepared for exams. We prepared late. Procrastination should have been included in our names. We were never prepared. How could one read a hundred pages of notes only hours before an exam and expect to pass? We believed in miracles. After all, we prayed, observed Tahajjud, and fasted on Mondays and Thursdays. Allah would send his angels to help us in exam halls. We spent the last hours posting exam memes on WhatsApp, Twitter, and Facebook. We told our families and friends to pray for us and whined about how the exam dates were unfair and how the whole school setup was cruel. We succeeded. We barely passed. We failed.

We piled our dirty clothes in Ghana-must-go bags. We hated washing. We did not wake up early on weekends and waited until we were certain that the few clotheslines that served our hostels had been filled with washed clothes before we rose, stretched, and peeped out to see the clotheslines full. We frowned and complained to our mates about how we had been meaning to wash our clothes, but the others wouldn't just leave the clotheslines alone for a minute. We cursed and pretended to be upset before proceeding to eat breakfast or slip back into bed and dream away.

These were the ways we lived our lives before Danladi, with Baba's help, started vomiting books that had been missing in the library.

5. PARANORMAL

Indeed, we were not new to strange happenings. Dangana Memorial Community School was fraught with paranormal activities. We had experienced so many weird things, especially at night. Have you heard of *Impiritu mai dogon hanu*? Yes, the spirit with hands that could extend to the heavens. Yes, that one. Those mysterious hands that touched, slapped, and poked us while we slept or weren't looking in its direction. Hands that dipped into our plates while we ate and sent us scurrying away, wailing at the top of our voices. What about *Hajiya Balaraba mai kos-kos*? Yes, that pale woman who patrolled our hallway and dormitories in high heels at night, the clacking stinging our ears as we lay shivering underneath our bed covers, eyes shut tightly. You see, we were not new to strange happenings.

6. PURIFICATION BY FIRE

The night we were visited by fire, dusk had slowly crept into being like a worm emerging from its cocoon. The sinews of dark bundles stole into our dormitories where we lay on unkempt beds. The air was suffused with whispering, gossiping, snoring, the sweet mnemonic babel of voices reciting *Surah Ya-Sin*, and the harmonic mumbling of Allah's Ninety-Nine Names. We dreamt of vomiting books. We dreamt of being pursued by demons. We stood beside the windows, getting drunk on the night air. The low tungsten chiseled our shadows into bundles of conspicuous undergrowth, silk-soft. Amidst all these activities, fate was scheming, brewing a bellicose tune. We did not know where the fire came from. The fire alarm did not sound. The fire was rapid, as if it had a life of its own. We died before death salaamed. Bemused, we chewed fear, trembled, paralyzed on our beds.

We called on Jesus of Nazareth and the God of Moses and Abraham to come to our aid. We spat *Ayatul Kursiu, Lakad-jaa'akum*, and *Aamanar-Rasul* on our palms and rubbed it all over our bodies with the hope that they would insulate us against the fire.

But the prayers did not work for some of us.

We jumped to our deaths. We groped in smoke-filled hallways, slipped and fell, and turned floor mats for onrushing feet, mindless of where or what they stepped on. Clothes were on fire. Bodies caught fire, waltzing and screaming. We crowded exits and passages. We filled all the room in our lungs with smoke. We coughed violently. We burned to death. We were trapped under rubble. Help did not come. Help came. Help came too late. We died on the road to Hanyan Kudu Clinic. We reached Hanyan Kudu Clinic. We died. We survived. We moved into hostels that were not torched. No one knew who or what had started the fire. But we suspected that our little town no longer wanted us. What if we were let out and we began to spread the disease all over town, vomiting books and whatnot?

7. QUARANTINE

We did not see Danladi or the other two again. No one could tell for certain where the school management had taken them or if they had stopped vomiting books. News came to us that the government had prepared a temporary isolation facility for us, in a bid to get to the bottom of the whole drama. Government buses stood in a line outside the school's gate on the appointed day. They were flanked by soldiers and health personnel covered in protective costumes.

Our families stood on one side with placards and angry faces, demanding answers. They were restrained by policemen armed with batons and shields. We boarded the buses even though we did not know where we were going or what would become of us.

The Occupation of the Migratory Library of Oanno

R.B. Lemberg

Two weeks ago, Oresia found the doors of the Migratory Studies library locked and taped. Her hesitant hand brushed against the white paper glued to the old mahogany; the edges of sticky tape felt curiously rough against her fingers. *CLOSED FOR REASSESSMENT.* This was supposed to be her morning shift, but nobody had warned her. Oresia was a student librarian, and the emergency library key sat heavy in her pocket, but she dared not peel off the tape and open the door. She kept looking over her shoulder as she walked away, hoping for the head librarian to catch up with her and explain, but the corridor was empty.

In the days that followed, rumors kept swirling among faculty and students. The graduate students met to decompress at a coffee shop just across the street from the Migratory Studies building. Nothing else happened. "Don't worry about it," Oresia's advisor had told her. "Something will come up." That was the end of it.

Oresia could not sleep much after the library closed. The student librarian job secured her visa, and the library itself provided—provided, like the oak over the coffee shop patio that gave freely of itself to the squirrels and the birds. The library gave and gave—the rustled hours of the evening, the books, the solitude and the companionship, the smell of beeswax and peace. The job paid for her room and board. Oresia's friend Ayar had loaned her money to tide her over, but it would run out soon. Without the visa, she could not stay in Islingar.

The graduate students circulated a well-received petition to reopen the library; Oresia's advisor left on a field trip with no estimated date of return. Meanwhile, the Library Defense Group was scheduled to meet for another coffee.

The patio of Hand and Book was lively and warm, the slanted rays of sunshine filtering through the canopy of the oak that shielded the outdoor tables from the noise of the street. Everywhere, students perched on rickety chairs and sprawled on stone benches. Oresia couldn't help but brush past knees and elbows as she made her way, coffee in hand, towards the Library Defense Group—a raucous, colorful company of eight people crowded around two small round tables pushed together.

Ayar was here, smiling widely at Oresia, their round, handsome, brown face lit up like a beacon. Zosia nestled into Ayar's side, diminutive and pale, her red hair glinting in the sun. Oresia smiled and waved. Daniel pushed a pastry towards her. The gentle mid-April wind picked at the tight curls of his hair, touched the tip of Oresia's nose, and at a different time it would feel very much like happiness. But all she felt now was dread.

"All right." Ayar tapped a spoon against their paper cup first, then clanged it against a spoon on the table. "All right. I call this meeting to order. Chair Monno says it's pretty much a done deal, the Chancellor will announce tomorrow at ten, during the news airing. They are closing the Migratory Library for good and *redistributing* the collections." Ayar scratched their forehead with the spoon and said in an unusually high, mocking voice: "Departmental libraries are a frivolous luxury of the past! It's high time for individual departments to become fiscally responsible!"

"We received no response to our petition," Zosia added.

Daniel scoffed. "I told you, petitions do nothing."

He wasn't wrong. They signed petitions and the administration cut student stipends and raised tuition year after year. They signed petitions and the administration demolished the old dorms and built luxury apartments nobody in their friends' circle could afford. Petitions did not help when they fired Dr. Tomakah for making a joke about the size of the Chancellor's mansion. Turned out, Dr. Tomakah wasn't a professor at all, just a renewable lecturer, and when she was gone, nobody stepped up for her advisees.

Ayar tapped the spoon again. "It gets worse. I heard from my advisor that the interviews and newspaper materials which our library hosts in the archive will be taken offsite. That's the student activism records, and Migratory Scholarship interviews, and the Recurring Folkways collection, and everything else. To access the materials, you will need to petition."

"Which will leave a record," said Oresia dejected.

"Exactly," said Ayar. They looked at each other. Ayar's eyes were dark with concern. Many of them were international students from countries where you could not simply check out materials. You had to petition the librarian on duty. Each request was recorded, and one risked being reprimanded or even expelled for too-daring library requests. Some materials could not be checked out at all. Others disappeared.

Oresia had crossed the ocean to leave that behind, to come to Islingar, where learning was unfettered, books and records resting freely on the shelves.

"This is going to a bad place," Zosia said to nearly unanimous nods.

Daniel frowned. "We will put a stop to this shit." Daniel was light-skinned, obnoxious, defiant by default—and one of the few non-migrants among them. He seemed to have no fear, and Oresia often wondered how it felt to live like that. Fear was constant and changing like vapor and wave—sometimes suffocating, sometimes lifting her to see beyond the horizon. Oresia had come to Islingar for Migratory Studies. Research showed that not only people could migrate, but clouds, and salmon, and patterns of heat. A storm could be born and then change as it moved across vast expanses of water. Oresia had moved across the sea to get to Islingar, on an enormous ancient ship powered by forces unknown.

She chose stories as her dissertation research. Carried by people and changing at every border crossing, migratory stories remained recognizable, similar, but not quite the same. There was an under-lying logic in this, a logic of movement and multiplicity that reflected in structures of magic that surfaced abruptly and subtly. Languages shifted about, birds altered their plumage, snakes shed skin. Sometimes the oak that shaded the coffee shop became an acacia, fragrant with white blossoms. There were no acorns. The acacia had been here forever, like a migratory word that meant endlessness; the tree would wave at Oresia, as if to acknowledge that the secret and malleable nature of things would persist. This was the core of Migratory Studies.

But there were politicians—yes, increasingly even here, in peaceful Islingar—who thought that movement was dangerous. *This migratory business brings bad magic. Close the sea, and send away the weird big ships,* they said. *Close the borders, stop letting international students in.* Migrating birds, too, became dangerous, hunted with nets and poison. The only thing the politicians could not vanquish was the storms. Their swirling clouds watered the fields and brought with them echoes of war-torn countries far away —blood and napalm, defiance and desolation. Oresia thought, not for the first time, that Migratory Studies itself would be outlawed in Islingar soon, like it had been in her home country.

"There is no other choice," Ayar was saying. "We must occupy the library."

The other students cheered and whistled their approval.

"This has been done before," Oresia said. "I. . . snuck into the library a few nights ago. . ."

One of the undergrads giggled. "Pizza!"

"Shh," Zosia said. "Oresia, what did you find out?"

"Newspaper clippings and student activism archives." She began to explain how, years ago, the university had attempted to close the Migratory Library for the first time. There was a write-up in the student newspaper about twenty undergrads who locked themselves in the reading room with a stack of pizzas and a trombone. That first occupation went on for two weeks, and the trombone situation was described as infernal. The pizza supply mysteriously refreshed itself every evening, generating a rich dataset for future migratory foodways research. Eventually, the administration caved.

"There's no record of this in the Main Library, or anywhere else," Oresia explained. "I checked. Somehow that whole month of *Oanno Student Herald* is missing."

"Of course it is," muttered Ayar.

Daniel wiggled his brows at the undergrad, Syda, a dark-haired, dark-skinned young woman with a mischievous smile. "How did you know about the pizza?"

"Um, I wrote a paper about it for Dr. Tomakah. They had five pizza boxes that replenished. One of the pizzas always came back with black olives and the rest of the flavors rotated. Once they got anchovies with ham. . ."

Everybody groaned.

"The magical mechanics of that particular pie are still unexplained!" Syda said with some pride. "But generally speaking, fresh pizza is necessary for the whole process to start."

"So we'll need pizza, water, blankets, what else?" Zosia started taking down notes. "Vegan pizza. . ."

Others began to speak, some naming items, others arguing.

"Money is an issue, but I think if we can all pitch in. . ."

Ayar said, "Not all of us can. It was different ten years ago, they had stipends—"

"I work two jobs—I'll need to give some kind of notice—"

Oresia swallowed her cooling latte. It tasted bitter, with a slight aftertaste of honey and oat milk foam that coated her tongue. She closed her eyes and saw the library closed, the department closed, her dissertation impossible to justify in the new fiscal climate, her stay in Islingar coming to an end. The ancient ship looming, looming above her, dark green and barnacle-riddled and promising nothing this time. Its incessant hum coalesced into a word.

Where?

She swallowed.

Where. Where. Where. No. No where. Nowhere.

Nowhere to go.

Oresia forced her eyes open, breathed deeply against the rising panic. It couldn't be hopeless. "I'll bring coffee."

"Try to get other people on board, we need folks to show up," said Ayar.

"Two of my friends said they wanted to come, but they have a morning shift—"

"Well then, maybe tell them to call in sick!"

After more heated discussion and coffee, they settled on the following day at ten minutes before ten, just before the Chancellor's announcement.

At fifteen minutes to ten the next morning, Oresia stood before the familiar old mahogany door of the Migratory Library, a large coffee urn in her hands. It was polished to a mirror shine and borrowed from her apartment; the nice people at the coffee shop filled it with a cheap breakfast blend. It smelled like learning, and friends, and quite a bit like saving money. She lowered the urn gingerly to the carpeted floor and unbent to look at the corridor behind her. Nobody around.

In a now-familiar gesture, Oresia peeled the fraying tape and carefully pushed aside the *CLOSED FOR REASSESSMENT* sign.

Beneath it was an old and heavy brass lock shaped like a bird pecking at its own keyhole heart. There was tiny writing around it, in Old Islat; Oresia had long memorized it.

Move outward and learn; move inward and be free.

It did not make sense to her at first, when she was new here; wasn't one supposed to learn in the library? But now the words had embedded themselves in her heart. She moved outward—to Islingar—to learn, but she could not be free if the library closed.

Oresia inserted the key in the lock and gently pushed the door open, then replaced the key in her pocket and reglued the sign. Picking up the polished silver urn, she made her way into the familiar darkness of the library's cavernous reading room.

She was the first here, and that was only to be expected—she was the one with the key. The unlocked door would allow the others in, and Oresia hoped they would start trickling in soon, hopefully with the pizza. She positioned the coffee on one of the central study tables and moved to turn on the lights, then stopped to listen. Voices were floating in, from the direction of the librarian's office.

"Magic was no longer as strong around me, but the research was *amazing*."

Oresia tiptoed carefully towards the sound. The librarian's room was a small study just around the corner, beyond these shelves, next to the archive spaces on the other side of the reading room. She walked as quietly as she could, seized by a sudden, vehement wish that her friends would not come in just yet. She wanted to hear this.

Dust swirled lazily in the few beams of light that found their way in around the heavy curtains; otherwise, the reading room was dim. No light came from the crack under the librarian's door, but the voices carried on, unaware of Oresia's approach.

"You were studying the big ships?" This voice was low and melodious, and very, very familiar.

Dr. Tomakah? But everybody said she'd left the university...

"The ships, yes." The first woman's voice was older, dreamy, and accented—Oresia had taken classes on the sociolinguistics of Islat, but she did not recognize this particular way of speaking. The speaker could have been a migrant like Oresia, from a different country.

"The "weird big ships," as they are known these days. You can't come aboard with strong magic. Likewise, with no magic at all, you'll never even see a ship. For this research I had to modulate."

Dr. Tomakah's voice had a gentle, curious cadence. "What did you study?"

Oresia's nose was pressed all the way to the plain inner door, her breathing shallow and slow. She recognized the procedure from Dr. Tomakah's fieldwork class—yes, Dr. Tomakah was definitely conducting a qualitative interview with a migratory researcher. For the archives.

"I was studying how the ships move," said the unknown scholar, her voice low and sad. "They've been moving for thousands of years, growing in size and in barnacles, carrying people and their stories across the expanses of the seas. So I ended up storing some of my magic away—in fact, I left it right here, in the archives —and I boarded the first ship I saw, to do my dissertation fieldwork."

There was a different sound, too, a gentle scraping as if of a quill moving across the page, and Oresia wondered if Dr. Tomakah was taking notes.

"What was the design of your research?"

"Participant interviews and observation. For three years I studied the people on the ship. There was no captain as far as I know, but the crew all directed each other somehow. Then there were the passengers—people who boarded in one country and later disembarked elsewhere. And then were passengers who boarded but never left. Some have been living there for decades—there was a whole space on the lower levels below the deck for the *permanent residents. . .*"

Oresia had come here on one of the ships, but she never went deep below. She went belowdecks once, during a storm, and she remembered it felt—gentle, like being held and lulled, deeper and deeper, like crying.

"—how many did you interview?—wait a moment," said Dr. Tomakah.

All of a sudden, the door of the librarian's office opened inward, and Oresia all but fell into the small room. The ebony desk in the middle was piled high with papers and books. Dr. Tomakah was perched on a stool in front of the desk to the right, her features sharp, her light brown skin sagging slightly around the mouth in a way Oresia did not remember from before. To the left, in a mustard-colored armchair, was the scholar who had spoken about the ships. They were a big, brown-skinned person in their fifties, tall and imposing. Oresia had assumed from their voice that they were a woman, but the scholar looked androgynous, their curly grey hair cropped close to their head. There was a third person in the room, too—Oresia's supervisor, the head librarian. She sat motionless behind the desk like a tall, pale apparition; the only thing that betrayed life was the trembling of a sharp white quill in her hand. The room was dim, and yet it felt lived-in, cozy, like a memory.

"Oresandra! I did not expect you today," said Dr. Tomakah. "The library is closed."

"I—we—" Oresia mumbled. "My friends are coming here at ten, we are going to occupy the library, protest its closure—I opened the door. . . we'll stay as long as we need to get this over-turned." The three just looked at her, and Oresia's cheeks felt hot from the scrutiny.

The ship scholar half-rose in their chair, extending a hand. "No worries. I am Dr. Bolol. You can pull up a chair and listen while you wait, if you can be quiet."

"I—um—"

The head librarian spoke, each sound like a falling silver hammer. "It's ten fifteen."

What? Already? Oresia swayed, turned towards the door. "I need to check on them—I'll be right back—"

"All right," Dr. Tomakah said, not unkindly. "You can leave this door open just a crack."

Oresia gulped and nodded, then headed back to the reading room. It was dim and empty, as before; nobody was here. Dust danced in a sunbeam. The silver sides of the coffee urn gleamed where it faced the east. A large clock above the entrance door showed 10:16.

She checked the door—it was still unlocked; beyond it, the carpeted hallway was eerily quiet. She found she did not want to step outside.

Once more, Oresia closed the door without locking it, and perched on a chair by the urn. She felt restless and full of agitated, long-forgotten longing. In a few minutes she got up and once again drifted closer to the inner door of the librarian's office.

"My thesis was, you see, that it was hope," Dr. Bolol was saying. "It was the working hypothesis of most ship scholars at the time— hope compelled people to make the decision to move, to escape wars and disasters and ruinous laws to board a ship. Hope— coming from a moderately magical source—infused the mechanical core of the ship with its power, animating the ancient cogs and chains that propelled the ship forward. But that did not solve the problem of the people living for decades in the ship's belly. And it could not explain the crew, either."

"Did the previous scholars conduct interviews?"

The head librarian's quill scraped louder as Oresia stepped closer and closer again.

"Yes, but only with the temporary travelers—often with those who traveled and disembarked, for example the exit interviews conducted in this very department—I have the bibliography right here..."

A few minutes later, Oresia glanced over her shoulder. 10:30.

Dr. Bolol's voice was lulling, engrossing. "After I interviewed the temporary travelers still on the ship, I asked to interview the crew, but they wouldn't have me. I started making inroads with the people belowdecks."

"What kind of theories did you use to analyze the interview data?"

"I used Detailed Speech Critique. Analysis took forever, and all of this time I was still interviewing. I probably need to redo it. DSC can be an imprecise methodology unless you impose strict criteria from the get-go. . ."

Oresia's shadow fell across the crack between the doorframe and the door. She stood unmoving, frozen between the inner room in front of her and the reading room behind her, which was empty of everything but coffee.

Dr. Bolol spoke on. "Two years in I came to the conclusion that it wasn't hope but *wish* that animated the journey. The difference is subtle, but it's there—you *wish* ardently, often suddenly, often beyond hope and reason, beyond anything known to people who stay forever on solid ground – and the energy of the wish propels you. This energy moves most of the travelers beyond the ship to their destination, but some of them find themselves right where they most wished to be."

11:00.

"Oresandra, for example, wished to come here. To Oanno university."

Oresia sighed, opened the inner door all the way and stepped in. The air was darker inside, more intimate and soothing some-how. Oresia could not remember if there'd been a window here before, but the room was windowless now. A single beeswax candle on the desk lit the head librarian's long face, illuminating her pale blue eyes and the stern line of her mouth.

"Your friends?" the head librarian said, the second thing she uttered in Oresia's presence this morning.

"I . . . don't think they are coming," she said in a small voice.

"Well, you could go out and look for them," said Dr. Tomakah, her voice gentle. "Or you can stay here with us, if you want."

Oresia hesitated. "I want to know about the ships. I came on one—I wanted to study here, so much." Propelled by a wish. A wish to be free, to study what she wanted without any barriers. Joining Migratory Studies at Oanno felt like the biggest burst of brightness she had ever known. The professors. The classes. The friends. The enveloping velvety air of the library, whispering secrets. The incredible exhilaration and twisting fear of conducting her first interviews, learning how to store them in the archive. Writing her first papers, giving her first talk. Going back to the archive to do more research.

"The university is planning to redistribute the archive," Oresia said in a small voice. "It won't be accessible—I don't think the authorities want our discipline to exist. . ."

"There is little hope for Oanno, even for the whole Islingar," said the head librarian.

"There is little hope anywhere," said Dr. Bolol. "There is wish, and vision, which I can explain separately in regards to the crew. . ."

"Wait a second," said Dr. Tomakah. She turned to Oresia, giving her full attention. "You know, after I was fired—forgive me, after I was *non-renewed*—there was a student petition. Five hundred people signed. There was a demonstration, someone burned a trash can, two people were arrested. I thought—I hoped I would be reinstated, but time passed, and things just moved on and I—well, I received a job offer from outside the university. I'd be a clerk supervisor conducting entrance and exit interviews for a firm of attorneys. It paid nicely, too." She pursed her lips. Sighed. "I came here to say goodbye to the library. But I wished—I wished that I would still do research. It's like Dr. Bolol was saying—I had no hope at all, my academic career was over, but when I came here —turns out, there are secret passages, there are ways to occupy the library forever. There are scholars who stay here always, professors and graduate students and independent researchers, even some undergrads. This work of our knowledge will never end. Never! No matter what the authorities do, the whisper of us will linger even if they close the whole university, drown the whole continent—we will still be here, and the library will be with us too. We will be here, with the books and the archives, lost and found by those who need us. We will be where we most wish to be."

"Like a ship," Oresia whispered.

"Not exactly," said Dr. Bolol. There are several key differences. I am exploring them in my current chapter. I could actually really use a research assistant—"

"It's more or less like the ship," said the head librarian. "A migratory library, if you will."

It was, Oresia understood, an invitation.

"I think," she said slowly, "I think that yes. I think I am where I wish to be."

Dr. Bolol rose from their chair and offered their hand again. "Welcome! This is splendid. The big seminar is on Tuesdays. I can show you around later."

"But for now, please, no more interruptions," said Dr. Tomakah. "I need to at least pretend to follow the interview protocol."

Oresia found an empty chair and sat, her knees pulled up almost to her chin, while Dr. Bolol took a deep breath and continued, "In time I even got some interviews from the crew. This is where the distinction between wish and vision comes in. I am still looking for the right ways to quantify it. . ."

The head librarian's quill scraped soothingly against the paper.

At exactly ten minutes before ten, Ayar pushed open the heavy mahogany door. Two backpacks were slung across their broad back. Behind them, Zosia and Syda came in, carrying boxes of pizza. The great reading room was hushed, as if some breath had been held here, some moment of waiting that trembled just beyond reach. A ray of light streamed through a small opening in the drapes, bouncing off a polished silver urn.

"Oresia!" Ayar called. "Oresia, are you here?"

"She must have been here," Zosia said quietly. "The coffee."

"And the door was unlocked." Ayar walked around, pulling the curtains wide open to let the cheerful light of April flood the room. The wood-paneled walls lent the library a look of tired distinction, like a scholar pulled into the bright light of day for a moment, remembering how to blink. Beyond a row of shelves, the head librarian's office was unlocked and empty. "Nobody's here."

"Oh, I'm sure she's around," Daniel said. "She's wandered off into the archive, or to the loo." In his arms was an enormous ham radio which he'd put together as a part of his master's thesis research into the geographies of lost sound. "Chancellor's proclamation coming soon, I guess."

Syda deposited her pizza boxes by the coffee urn, then propped the topmost one open. "Black olives. I was sort of hoping for the anchovies and ham. . ."

People were slowly trickling in. Ten of them, then fourteen, then more—faces familiar and new, but no Oresia. Deep in thought, Ayar poured coffee into a paper cup, remembering a moment of stillness, a faint smell of beeswax in the reading room, now entirely replaced by the enticing aroma of melted cheese.

Ayar produced a spoon from their pocket and clanged it against the coffee urn. "Hello everyone, and thanks for coming. We are the Library Defense Group, and we are here to defend the Migratory Library—our *library*—from the overreach of the administration and politics. This is *our* space. This is *our* university. We will not cede it. So let's listen to the Chancellor as we wait for more people to arrive, and then we'll close the hell out of this door and barricade it. And then, using this excellent radio, we'll make some sounds of our own."

The students cheered and stomped their feet. Beyond the now-unveiled windows, newly budded trees swayed in the breeze. Around the room, pizza boxes were being cracked open, and Daniel bent over the radio to tune it to the Chancellor's frequency.

The Long Occupation of the Migratory Library had begun.

Tiny Hearts in the Dark

Gabino Iglesias

"The dissertation defense is just the last part of the hazing process," said Dr. García with a smile. She had dark eyes and a mess of gray curls that sprung from her head at angles that defied gravity. "You've been working on this for four years, Sandra. You know your stuff. You know it better than anyone. All you have to do is say your piece and then get through the questions. No one in your committee is trying to hurt you, so they'll be relatively easy questions. You know, to let you shine in the areas we know you're strongest. I don't know why you want to spend the time and effort adding this to your research and tweaking your dissertation with so little time left. You're two months away from being done with all this!"

Sandra knew exactly why she had to do it, but explaining it to Dr. García was the last thing she wanted to attempt. Dr. García had been great from the start. She'd been a brilliant, understanding thesis chair and, in many ways, a good friend who'd helped her navigate academia's treacherous waters. She was also the first brown woman to get tenure at her university, and that had helped them develop a special kind of sisterhood. But this was personal. Sandra knew she had to say something. Honesty had always been the right approach between them.

"I don't think I can explain it to you," said Sandra. "It's. . . I don't know. I learned that this could still be happening and. . . I feel like my dissertation would be incomplete if it actually is and I didn't add that to it, you know? Like, this is a thing now, not something that belongs to history. It might be a *right now* kinda thing instead of just a *people used to do this* kinda thing."

Dr. García pressed her fingertips together, her hands turning into a triangle, and shook some curls away from her face.

"Oral history is tricky, Sandra," said Dr. García. "I believe we had this conversation the first time you sat on that chair. What we do is. . . tainted, if you will, by our subjects' lack of objectivity and by the strange lens of memory. People never remember things as they were. You know that. You have a very strong dissertation as is. You could get a few published papers out of it, maybe even your first book. Adding to it now is dangerous, and it might affect your conclusions if it is indeed still happening. That could change a lot of things. For starters, you would be against the clock. Also, I'm not saying you'd have to report it to the authorities, but. . . just think about it, okay?"

Sandra had said she would and then she'd walked out of the office pondering what she'd do if she found out it was still happening. Would she leave it out of her dissertation and live with the ghost of that omission haunting her entire academic career? Would doing all the work be the better option even if it meant trying to get her dissertation approved with some last-minute, less-than-stellar writing? Would she feel compelled to report it to the authorities?

Reporting things was something else they'd discussed as soon as Sandra had turned in her program of work to Dr. García. Sandra wanted to look at murders up in the mountains of Puerto Rico, specifically at the rumored deaths of newborns at the hands of their parents after hurricanes struck the island. It was something she'd heard from the mouths of older family members who still lived in the mountains of Jayuya and Yauco. When her mother said it was all true, she knew this was it, the thing she could happily spend years researching and talking to people about without losing interest. It was dark, unique to them as far as she knew, creepy, and it gave her a reason to dig around in the past while also working on her degree. It was perfect.

And then it wasn't.

Anthropologists must walk a fine line between gathering information via in-depth interviews to preserve firsthand accounts, to record the practices of vanishing cultures and communities, or to chronicle a movement or group or practice. This means they often inhabit a gray area where you learn about peoples' peccadilloes, about the darkest things history has to offer, about the awful practices communities sometimes engage in together. It's also an area where you sometimes must decide if you want to keep working and ignore something or if you want to report a crime you basically went looking for without an invitation. It took Sandra exactly two interviews to realize that she had to handle things carefully. The way her great-grandmother talked about it, murdering malformed newborns during and after a hurricane had once been a fairly normal practice across the Cordillera Central, the ridge of mountains that ran along the middle of the island. It was history, sure, but it was also murder.

Sandra was family, or family of a friend, and people quickly opened up to her. She heard their stories. She took notes and recorded her interviews. Then an old woman with a white film over her left eye, a friend of her grandmother, took Sandra out to her backyard and showed her two small wooden crosses and told her the one on the left was from a baby born to her oldest daughter right after hurricane Georges in 1998, and the other was for a premature baby that almost killed her youngest daughter after hurricane Maria, which had been just two years before.

That had been the thing—the revelation?—that started it all. Sandra had treated the killing of babies as a thing of the past, something akin to work she'd read by anthropologists who'd done oral histories with Black folks who had been in the middle of the civil rights movement or the few remaining Māori tattoo artists who tattooed using traditional tools. If babies were still being murdered, that changed everything, and ignoring what those changes meant felt like the worst act of academic dishonesty Sandra could fathom.

The thoughts swirling around in her head prevented her from enjoying the deep green of the mountains as she drove up to Jayuya. She was on her way to the last interview, one that she hadn't originally planned. Her mom had called her a week before, saying an old lady from her church had heard about her research and wanted to talk to her about it. Her mom said the old woman, whose name she couldn't remember, had worked as a midwife her whole life. It was a job she learned and inherited from her mother, who had in turn inherited it from her own mother. Talking to someone who had been part of the birthing process for generations was too good to let pass, so Sandra had taken down the phone number her mother had rattled off and then called.

The woman had said her name was Antonia. She'd spoken to Sandra briefly, only mentioning that she'd heard about her research from her aunt Pilar, who went to her church. She said she'd been a midwife for almost sixty years and would be more than happy to share stories.

Antonia's house looked like it had grown from the side of the mountain. As she drove into the small patch of grass in front of the one-story house, Sandra imagined the structure somehow sprouting roots to become a living thing that was part of the environment.

Sandra parked, turned off her car, and stepped out into the hot, humid day. A big ceiba tree covered half of the house and offered some very welcome shade. Maybe it would keep the inside of Sandra's car from becoming a sauna while she spoke to Antonia.

Sandra walked up to the door and knocked on the side of the screen door. The interior of the house was too dark to see inside, but Sandra could make out a rectangular space on the other side of the house that was full of light. A door, probably leading to the backyard, which was probably a very large chunk of mountain because there were no other houses around.

A small figure suddenly blocked the light. Antonia. She pushed the screen door open and smiled up at Sandra.

Antonia was a short woman with white hair pulled into a messy bun atop her head and an earnest, round face lined with wrinkles that looked like small dry riverbeds. She had bright brown eyes that looked like they belonged in a face forty years younger. She was wearing a blue bata with red flowers.

"Did you have a good drive over?"

Antonia's voice was sweet and mellow. It reminded Sandra of her own grandmother's voice and made her smile.

"The drive was fine," said Sandra. "My family still lives on the other side of the mountain, so I'm used to driving these twisty roads."

"Good, good," said Antonia. "Come in, darling. It's too hot to stand outside."

Antonia stepped aside and Sandra walked into the house.

The inside was dark, but as Sandra's eyes adjusted to the gloom, the world around her came into focus. Antonia started walking.

"Let's sit for a while," said Antonia. She moved her arm toward the living room, inviting Sandra to walk into the house. Sandra obliged. Antonia followed.

Antonia had mentioned inheriting the midwife job from her mother, and everything in her house looked like it had also belonged to her. The small living room she pointed to was to the right of the door. It contained a beige sofa with an ugly flower print and a plastic cover exactly like the one Sandra had seen in the few baby pictures she had at her grandmother's old apartment. There was also a wooden coffee table with thick legs and an ancient TV with speakers built into the sides sitting on the floor. Everything looked like it'd been new in 1970.

"Your aunt told me you've been looking at our history," said Antonia from behind Sandra.

"Yes—"

"I mean, your family is from here, right? From the other side of the mountain?"

Sandra had turned to look at the woman while she spoke.

"Yeah," said Sandra. "My mom's side is from here. Most of them are still on the mountain. My father's family is from Yabucoa."

"So you understand that this is our history, right? The history of your people?"

The warmth in Antonia's voice was gone. The question she'd just asked felt like it was pregnant with a threat Sandra was failing to understand.

"Yes. . . I've. . . I know this went on for a very long time and that most of the times it happened the babies we—"

"No, they were not babies," said Antonia, her voice like a blade now. "They were monsters. Sit down." Antonia pointed at the old sofa covered in plastic. Sandra felt confused, but she walked to it and sat down. The plastic felt weird on the back of her legs, and she immediately felt like she needed a shower.

"My aunt said you wanted—"

"I know why you're here. I'll tell you some stories. But first you need to know that these stories—this *history*—is ours and no one else needs to know about it. Is that clear?"

"Well, the interviews I've conducted are for my dissertation. . ."

"You can change that, can't you? Pick something else? Interview different people?"

Sandra had been confused and then uncomfortable, but those feelings had morphed into anger. This woman, who had offered to tell her some stories, was asking her to change her dissertation because she felt. . . like this was a local secret? Because she wanted to protect a family member? As a woman in academia, she had learned to stand up for herself. It was something Dr. García had told her a million times: "If they ever see you as weak, it's over."

Sandra felt like standing up, but she stayed on the sofa when she spoke.

"I've been working on my dissertation for four years, Antonia. I've conducted countless in-depth interviews along the Cordillera Central and transcribed hundreds of hours of audio. There is nothing like this anywhere else, so I had to convince my committee that every book I used and every study I cited had something to contribute to the methodology or the way I was approaching my research. I'm about to defend my dissertation in a little less than two months, and I'm not about to start this process all over again because you feel like *our* history is a dirty secret that should stay in the mountains."

She knew her voice had been a bit shaky at the start, but Sandra had finished strong. She was not going to let this woman perceive her as weak for even a second.

Sandra didn't have a clear expectation after she finished speaking, but even subconsciously she had expected Antonia to do something—argue, scream, insult her. Instead, the woman looked to the door and sighed. Then she walked to the door Sandra had seen from outside.

"Come with me," said Antonia.

Sandra wanted to say no. She wanted to stand up and leave, to walk away from this woman and her stories. More than anything, she wanted to defend her dissertation without adding anything to it and move on.

She got up from the sofa, the hot plastic pulling at the back of her legs, and followed Antonia to the door.

The sun outside blinded Sandra for a moment. She squinted

and blinked, waiting for her eyes to adjust again. Meanwhile, Antonia had turned around and was facing her.

"Look around," said Antonia.

Sandra looked. It was all too green and bright. Trees and ferns and plants with big leaves that looked like horse heads and more trees. And then she noticed the small crosses on the ground behind Antonia. There were at least fifty or sixty of them. They were lined up next to each other with a few outliers out of place here and there.

"Are those—"

"Babies. Every single one of these crosses is for a child. Some came out with too many teeth in their mouths. Some. . . gnawed their way out. Many were born without eyes or with horns sprouting from their soft heads or too many limbs that ended in talons. A few of them came out speaking in a tongue no human ear should ever hear. The point is they came, and they had to be dealt with."

"Why are they here? I saw two crosses in someone's backyard, but never this ma—"

"Not everyone has the strength to bash a newborn's head in with a rock or a hammer. Some people don't want them on their property, so I take them. As long as they are buried deep and with a rosary stuffed in their mouth, they stay down. Is all that not in your dissertation?"

Sandra was scared and shocked, but the last question and the strange smile that came with it made her feel violent. She suddenly wanted to lash out at Antonia. But she couldn't. All those dead babies under the ground were too much to process. All those brutal deaths. All those heartbroken, scared mothers. All those tiny hearts in the dark.

"I know you thought this was a thing of the past," said Antonia. "You thought this was something backward folks from the mountains did, am I right?" She didn't stop to wait for an answer. "You thought this was real in a past that was far away, that it didn't happen now, in the age of cell phones and the internet and every-thing else. Well, you were wrong, and that's why you need to keep quiet about it."

"Keep quiet? You really want me to not turn in my work? People have already read it. All I have to do is keep it as is. I don't have to write that it's still happening. I don't—"

"And you will do that if you want to stay alive. Keep quiet. Write something else. This is no one else's business, you understand?"

Was this woman threatening to kill her? It felt like a slap, but Sandra knew she couldn't panic. Not now and not ever.

"Are you threatening me?"

"I am," said Antonia calmly. "There is an old dark god in these mountains that feeds off the bad energy that comes with the storms. It's been here since the Taíno Indians were up in these mountains and probably even before that. You think you're the first one who wanted to tell others about it? You think you're the first person with a fancy education who has found our ways strange and worthy of your attention? Listen, Sandra, some things are meant to stay secret, and this is one of them."

"I'm so sorry, I. . . I don't know what you're asking me to do here."

"I'm not asking you," said Antonia. "I'm telling you to forget you ever researched this, forget that you ever asked questions you shouldn't have asked. You will get in your car and drive down to the city and then you're going to talk to your professors at the university and tell them that you want to do something else. Tell them this was just word of mouth and you realized it when you came to see me. I don't know. Make up a pretty lie, but tell them you won't turn in your dissertation. If you do, people might come up here to look into it, and you don't want bad things to happen because of you, do you?"

Sandra didn't know what to do or what to say. This was all too much. Behind Antonia, the collection of small crosses on the ground looked like a huge confession, a collection of bones that could change things in these mountains forever, proof of a dark secret that had been kept in the shadows for way too long. She imagined people digging those bodies out and finding malformed skeletons with rosaries stuffed in their mouths. She imagined investigators bagging small skulls with horns or deformed jaws with too many teeth and it sent a shiver down her spine despite the oppressive heat. This was all too much. She needed time to think. She had to get out of Antonia's house.

Sandra turned to run to her car.

She bumped into a woman. Pain exploded in her abdomen.

The woman pushed Sandra to the ground.

"You could've dropped the whole thing and moved on, silly girl," said Antonia.

Sandra touched her belly. Her hand came away bloody. The pain was like a fire inside her stomach. She looked up. The woman she'd run into—the woman who had been hiding behind her—had black hair and kind eyes. She was holding a bloody knife.

The woman moved around Sandra. Sandra tried to keep up with her, to turn and kick her or something, but the pain was too much.

The woman with the knife stood over Sandra and bent over.

Sandra saw the glint of the sun reflected on the knife and her blood as the blade moved near her face. Then she felt the steel on her neck and the strange pain of the blade slicing across her skin.

Sandra put her hands on the grass and looked around. She wanted to scream, to call out for help, but her throat was useless. The world spun around her and the pain in her gut was so great she couldn't breathe.

"The old dark god will feed today, so maybe we won't get as many deaths after the next storm," said Antonia, her voice calm, as if she was making a statement about the weather.

Sandra felt a thousand dissonant drums under her hands, their vibrations coming from underground. Her eyes went wild, looking everywhere for help, for a miracle, for a way out. They landed on the tiny crosses. Sandra crumpled then, her body hitting the warm grass while the sun cooked her back. The sound of the tiny drums enveloped the entire front of her body now. She knew then what the sound was; the desperate, scared beating of all those tiny hearts in the dark.

Parásito

Ana Hurtado

THEY CRAWL ON TREES, antennae twirling. Bodies form a crooked path of shimmering brown up the bark of a tree so old the students can hear it exhaling, a long sigh lingering in humid air. Spider monkeys hoot nearby; toucans croak. Under a canopy of greens and browns, Professor Torres's river biology class watches their teacher capture one of the ants with the tip of his grimy fingers and shove it into his mouth, his lips closing in on his nails. He drops his mandíbula and allows his pupils to observe the tiny creature wander around his molars. It is uprooted and displaced, curious about its new wet home: the breath of this house envelops its entire exoskeleton, and so la hormiga runs in circles, searching for answers. Its movements tingle Professor Torres's tongue and he closes his jaw, crunching. The ant lets out a little scream. Professor Torres swallows his snack and smiles.

So tart and sweet, he announces to the class, pointing at the line of lime ants on the ancient tree, and invites his students to join in: grab a living being off a tree, watch it squirm trapped within your grasp, and bite.

Emi stands near the professor, waiting for her turn to feed

These ants remind her of the lime she likes to squeeze into ceviche. She picks out a juicy one and doesn't hesitate. It plays around in her mouth, sliding under her tongue, but she manages to catch it between her teeth and eats. Un mordizco de limón.

How are you not freaking out right now? Irene asks Emi, pointing at her throat. She, too, has selected her little ant and cannot bring herself to eat it.

What do you mean? Emi asks back.

It feels so evil, she replies, observing the little hormiga de limón she picked off the tree explore her wrist. It gets lost between the cracks of her skin and her tiny arm hairs. Emi watches Irene eye her ant and sweat. Today, she wears her hair in a giant braid; it sits on her shoulder mimicking the anaconda—one recently fed, podgy and rotund—they spotted outside their cabin last night.

I feel bad eating something that's alive, Irene says.

Well, you calling the hormiga some*thing* should help with that, Emi responds, grinning. Just do it. It tastes so weird.

Irene shakes her head and decides to return the ant to its family. She wipes the trunk gunk on her pants and proceeds to photograph the ceiling above them—a braid of branches, twigs, sharp and soft verdant blades—and walks off, her head raised to the sky.

It won't feel a thing, te prometo! Emi says to her best friend who doesn't listen.

Emi then picks up another victim and places it delicately on her tongue; she wonders if any of them will bite her before she bites them. When she pierces the ant with her molars, Emi feels something cold slither out of the creature. It leaps down her throat, and she swallows instinctively. Her eyes widen, and she begins to choke. She coughs so loud, some monkeys nearby howl in response. One of her classmates approaches her with a mouthful of lime juice and asks her if she's okay. She walks it off, her sweaty palm grasping at her throat, and finds relief next to a colossal tree root. Emi leans on the radicle, some of the tree's fungus rubbing against her butt. She manages to breathe again.

As Emi recovers, she spots her best friend Irene talking to Professor Torres in a place beyond the hormigas de limón tree. Irene's palm exposed a little brown thing moving in circles tracing the lines of her hand, and Professor Torres leaning his torso on her shoulders, close in on her snake. The hand that he used to pick his prey off trees now rests on the small of her back, and Emi feels like she's choking again.

The university campus in Quito drowns with rain. It overflows gutters and storm drains, something to be expected around noon in the capital; it's a rite of passage to be drenched by rainwater, to succumb to the cries of an Andean sky. Water falls on all of Quito, on every invasive eucalyptus tree that occupies its parques, on cars stuck in locked intersections, and now rainfall inundates Humboldt Hall.

Doric columns line the entry path towards the biology department housed within the great hall named after the white explorer. Scotch-taped posters on new species findings and brown bag seminars flood these shafts, their bases muddied by footprints of students who lean on the pillars while smoking. Cigarette butts mix in with the rainwater, and a stream carries ash and burnt stubs down a drain that vomits its insides into one of the city's most polluted rivers a couple of blocks away.

Emi rushes past the Greek columns in her Ecuadorian university campus, sometimes slipping but not falling on the terracotta tiles. Her brown hands, tanned by last week's fieldtrip sun, hold her woven backpack tight over her head. Inside the classroom, a couple of students, hair drenched, hoodies sodden, sit and wait for their professor to arrive.

On the whiteboard, thunderbolts illuminate an anatomical drawing of a prokaryotic cell: a long flagellum looping around, the one that students like to nickname its tail, and tiny hairs that stick out of the body labeled *fimbriae* with cursive handwriting.

Emi arrives before her instructor and spots Irene sitting in the back row, her wooden chair creaking as she wobbles. In her notebook, Irene sketches tiny flowers. Emi then plops down on the neighboring seat and takes out her smartphone. She stares at herself via the front-facing camera and clears her throat every now and then. Something feels stuck.

Emi notes how the rain dragged her black eyeliner down to her cheeks; she's a racoon. She pulls at her skin with her fingers, trying to remove her makeup.

Oigan, does someone know when the midterm is? Ignacio asks his peers as he scrolls on his phone. His short-sleeved shirt reveals arm hairs combed over by rain.

I think the syllabus date hasn't changed, Emi replies, hiding her face in her hands.

Ugh, Ignacio utters. We *just* got back from la Amazonía and now we have a test next week?

Is it going to be on the Napo River only or—another male student asks, someone Emi doesn't know quite well. She thinks his name is Felipe. Or Fabricio. Something with an *F*.

Is it me or are the tests, like, stupid hard in this class? Ignacio asks the *F* boy.

Emi lowers her hands and smirks. The first test was easy. I don't think the midterm will be hard at all, she says.

The male students laugh and exchange glances. Ignacio chortles, too.

What's so funny? Irene asks, looking up from her notebook. It *was* easy.

Ignacio and *F* boy turn their heads to face the young women.

I mean it was easy for y'all; Professor Torres takes it easy with girls, Ignacio says.

That's sexist, Irene responds.

Yeah, shouldn't you be, like, man enough to accept that we're smarter than you? Emi laughs.

No, that's not what we mean, *F* boy replies. A silver crucifix dangles at the bottom of his throat, picking up the classroom's fluorescent lighting. His lips are chapped, and his eyebrows meet in the middle.

Then what do y'all mean, Fede? Irene follows up. *Federico*. Emi was never going to guess that.

Let's face it, Professor Torres has a reputation of going easy on girls so he can, you know, Ignacio says with a smile that soon disappears into a frown.

No, I don't know, Emi says.

Yeah, what is it? Irene asks.

So you'll say yes when he wants to sleep with you later, Federico says, grinning. The male students chuckle and shake their heads as Irene and Emi look at each other. Professor Torres walks in. Irene gulps.

He steadies his sharp umbrella next to the instructor's desk. While removing his coat, Professor Torres shakes the excess water from his salt and pepper hair and beard. From the class's back row, the young women witness how a cloudy sky highlights the deepest shades of blue in his eyes.

Let's begin, chicos, he announces.

From their classroom in Humboldt Hall, Emi observes the university's biggest pond. Tiny fish create bubbles in its murky green surface. Her mouth was dry and craving. In the window's reflection, she studies a curious Irene staring at the whiteboard, at Professor Torres' hand and how he outlines the Napo riverbank they visited last week. Emi then spots Federico the *F* boy raise his hand; Emi rolls her eyes at him. And in her own reflection, she looks at her face: the skin underneath her eyes still so dark from her eyeliner remnants. It looks as if she's been crying. Her nostrils expand as she sighs, and her right one quivers with her breath. Emi feels a sneeze coming on, but instead of feeling any relief from sneezing, all she finds is an ache that lingers in her face. The window shows her how she frowns from pain, how her brows scowl and mouth pouts. She then detects a dark and slimy little thing wiggling in and out of her nariz, almost waving.

She stands in the bathroom stall and listens. Doors smash and creak open around her, high heel taps echo alongside muddy boot stomps. Taps run hot water and paper towels are pulled and ripped from the wall. Lips are pursed in front of a foggy mirror, shades of lipstick smeared across skin. It's the ten-minute break between classes, and the first-floor bathroom of the Guayasamín arts department is the most popular at this hour. Emi stares at the water bowl below her and feels sick. It's not the stillness of the water that sometimes bubbles when neighboring toilets flush that revolts her; it's the fact that she wants to dive her head in there and drown.

Emi waits patiently for a knock she knows so well. After last night's text, she tries putting the puzzle pieces together: a huge hand lingers on Irene's backside out in the rainforest, Irene smiles when Professor Torres calls on her in class, and el mensajito de anoche: *I need your help*, received around two in the morning.

She spots Irene's maroon military boots hovering beneath the stall door. And then the knock, the passcode. Emi unlocks the latch and pulls her best friend into the stall. Other students outside protest, *Ey, ey, ey! I was first!* And *Go make out elsewhere, I gotta pee!*

Irene and Emi stand facing each other, their bodies touching. She looks down at Irene, who always was a couple of inches shorter than her, and asks, Qué paso, Ire?

Irene finds a way to not look at Emi while they're stuck in the tiny stall, their faces inches away. I don't know where to start, she replies. Her breath smells like mint.

What is it? Did something happen last night? Emi asks.

I think you know about my crush, Irene confesses, her stare now set on Emi's eyes. Emi nods in response. So, Irene continues, I thought this was what I wanted. To be flirted with and kissed, but *this* isn't what I want at all, she says. Toilets flush and punctuate the end of her sentence.

What happened with Professor Torres? Emi asks.

Ssshh, please, don't say his name here.

Okay, what happened with Professor Idiot? Emi insists.

After yesterday's class, he asked me out.

And this was what you wanted, right? To go on a date with him?

Yes, but then he asked if I could meet him at his place down in the valley of Puembo.

Oh, Emi says, catching on.

Yeah, Irene responds. This is when I said something like I'd rather meet in Juan Valdez. Like, have some coffee and talk. We're both adults. We don't have to hide or anything, right? Her tone looks for assurance from her bestie, and Emi stays quiet for a while before responding.

Right, she whispers, nodding. Nothing wrong. Emi rolls her eyes. You'd just rather have shitty coffee than go to his house, totally understandable, Emi says. That sounds so fast, though.

Irene bites her bottom lip and then mutters, He got mad. Said I should stop playing games with him and then told me his address. Urbanización Jardínes.

Emi is glad to know where this man lives. What did you say back? she asks.

No, gracias.

Oh? Emi smiles.

And then he said, I don't appreciate being teased. My body ran cold. I told him I don't tease. He asked me if I was calling him a liar. She stops to inhale and exhale.

Someone taps on the bathroom stall. They both yell, *Ocupado!*

What else did Profe Imbécil say? Emi asks.

Irene sighs. Something about my last exam; my performance didn't showcase my best efforts and that I should stop by his house to make sure I do well next time.

What? Didn't you get an A last time? And how will going to his house guarantee an A? What is he talking about?

Irene hesitates. Because if I don't go, I'll fail. At least that's what I think he insinuated, she says.

Umm, yeah, that's quite an insinuation. Sounds like coercion to me.

What's that? Irene asks, pointing at Emi's face.

What? Coercion? It's—

No, estúpida. Something's dripping from your nose, Irene insists.

Emi places her ring finger on her warm nostril and feels something smooth slide back inside her.

It's nothing, she responds. Escúchame, Ire, she says. We need to tell someone.

Irene leans her head on Emi's chest and tears stream from her cheeks onto Emi's breasts. They hold each other and listen to the bathroom and hallways quiet down as classes begin.

The Simón Bolivar library houses the biggest collection of books in Ecuador. Sheathed by a grand section on larvae, Emi sits, taking notes. She's surprised none of Professor Torres' students are here, cramming before their test. She knows Irene's stuck in ceramics class, presenting her midterm project and will join her soon, but, right now, Emi feels alone and unsettled. A worry that grows from her stomach up to her throat and extends into her arms.

She holds her pencil, leaning hard as she retraces the *R* in *Río Napo* over and over again. She remembers the cold river water, their speedboat roaming the brown canal, headed deep into the Amazonía. She remembers some droplets landing on her lip and when she licked it off, the notable salt in its grit. She's suddenly so parched. Then the memory of a bite of limón sourness gurgles up some saliva in her cheeks. Emi can hear the crunch of the ants she bit in this silent library. As other students bury their heads in books, she keeps smirching her biology notes with the smudgy graphite pencil, looping the Os aimlessly.

It first feels like pressure. Her index finger reddens, her nail and pencil tip drenched by a thin layer of blood. A tailed and slimy creature is birthed from underneath her fingernail. Emi drops her pencil. The thing pushes through her carne and stretches out, reaching, wobbling about. Emi resists an urge to scream and holds her hand close to her chest, the little animal unfolding its greasy self on Emi's other fingers, tangling itself on her fingers.

She stands up, her chair falling sideways. And before she decides to run to the student health center, the creature who smells like ceviche slithers back in, her finger swollen and gushing. Emi passes out and topples over, her body almost taking down the library's oil painting of Simón Bolivar straddling his white horse, preparing for battle.

The sign above Emi's head reads #BájaleAlAcoso. A hashtag tacked across every corkboard in the university's health center and taped all over the female bathrooms. The sign represents the university's anti-femicide campaign, and its rhetoric aims to give victims of harassment and assault a voice. There's a blurry number under-lined beneath the hashtag. Emi stares at it, her hand pulsing, and wonders if Irene has thought about calling.

A nurse stands bedside and takes Emi's blood pressure. Her touch is cold.

Emi stares at her inflamed hand and her heart beats fast. She then hears footsteps headed towards her and braces herself for an angry Irene. Her bestie pulls open the curtain to Emi's bed and then barely closes it behind her. Irene wears rain boots and a short skirt; her knees a little grey.

Is she okay? she asks the nurse and then rushes to cradle Emi's head. Qué te paso, idiota?

She fainted, the nurse answers on Emi's behalf. And looks like she cut herself with something sharp. The nurse's eyes jump from Emi's bleeding finger to Irene's legs.

What happened? Irene insists. Emi looks up at an Irene who hasn't slept: the skin beneath her eyes a little green, her eyes red with a flood of tiny pink veins.

How was your ceramics show and tell? she asks, smiling.

The midterm? Fine, whatever, Irene replies. She looks at her watch and then back at Emi. We're so not gonna make it to the river bio midterm, she says.

That's seriously the least of my problems. Emi exhales. The nurse finishes up her notes and fixes the clipboard next to Emi's bed.

The doctor will be in a few minutes, she says.

Gracias, Emi responds.

And, chicas, please beware we've been getting reports of harassment out by the university entrance, so I wouldn't wear *that* to campus. Irene and Emi look down at Ire's skirt. The nurse walks away before they can say anything back.

That's, that's so great. Emi sighs, placing the palm of her hands in her eye sockets. I hate everything, she says.

I told them, Irene announces. And I didn't go to ceramics workshop.

Told who? I'm confused.

I told the office of equal opportunity. I had to skip cerámica to do it.

Oh, you mean you went to the Do Nothings, Emi replies. She laughs and then becomes silent. I'm sorry, she offers.

Está bien, whatever, Ire replies. I don't know what I was expecting, she says.

Okay, but what did they say?

They didn't believe me.

Oh.

They didn't believe me that it's coercion. They said I should feel flattered Professor Torres has taken an interest in me.

Wow, Emi says, her hand pulsing.

There's nothing we can do, Irene says. Just stay away from him. But—

But what?

But what about our grades? Ire says. A tiny tear exits her eye and lands near her nose. Emi uses her bloodied hand to pick it up like she did with that hormiga.

So, we'll fail, it's fine. We can take it next semester with someone who is *not* a creep.

Oh, but then we wouldn't feel complimented that he has taken an interest in us! Irene laughs. Emi joins in, too. But are you sure? Irene asks. Cold rainy air rushes in through the building's open windows and the tiny hairs on Ire's legs stick up.

Sure about failing? Wouldn't be my first time. Actually, it would be, but it's fine, Emi reassures her.

No, no. Sure about failing with me? For me?

Now *that* I'm cien porciento sure.

The seatbelt strap strangles Emi's body. Her insides shift and fight for space as she tries to focus on the conversation. Irene sits in the passenger seat, playing with the radio knobs. They're parked in the entrance of río San Pedro's beach for its monthly clean-up, an extra-credit option written in Professor Torres's syllabus. The young women theorize their grades will tank with a missed midterm exam, and maybe volunteering today can help them pass the class with a C.

My GPA is going in the toilet, Irene murmurs. She raises and lowers the volume of the radio.

We shouldn't worry about that now, honestly, Emi says. Her last word gets snarled by her mouth, and she feels like vomiting.

Irene looks up at her. Emi smiles, lips closed.

Vamos, Irene says.

They exit the car and carefully walk down to the river beach where other students gather. They form a chain, like las hormigas de la Amazonía. Some students crouch down on the sand and stretch their arms towards a smelly river; they pick up parts of car tires, political flyers from past elections, deflated soccer balls, and other trash. The students fill up their burlap sacks and aim to save a river that will never be fully cleaned. But the extra credit will suffice.

As they carry on, a blue Volkswagen pulls over, windows tinted black. Professor Torres emerges and waves. Emi wants to talk to Irene—wants to ask her if she's okay, if they should leave—but she can't move her tongue: it is petrified inside her mouth, caught in a lattice of slippery black wires. She can only nod in response when Irene tells her, Estoy bien, I'm okay. Emi smiles, mouth closed, and extends her gloved hand towards Irene's. She taps it back.

Other students eye Professor Torres as he heads towards them. He skips down the quebrada, as if he's done this a million times, the bottom half of his blue jeans browned by dust. Emi hears a couple of female students she hasn't met exchange words; through the babbling of the river stream, she hears them say, *I thought he wouldn't be here. Why is he here? Should we go?* It's a common conversation in every friend group, a list of shared terrors.

Irene stoops next to the riverbank, her knees soiled in gunk. With a cupped hand, she collects bits of plastics that float on the water that would have later ended up in the Pacific. Today, she wears her hair as two snakes that rest down her back. Emi observes Professor Torres make his way over to her best friend, and, when he's close, she becomes unleashed, surrendering to the call of the water: with a single leap, Emi tackles Professor Torres, and they both fall into río San Pedro, more trash added to its once pristine waters.

In the depths of the river birthed by volcanic glaciers, now clogged by city trash, Emi is freed. Her eyeballs are pushed to the side by a wormed black beast flailing hundreds of boneless limbs as it exits her body, leaving behind a shell of Emi to sink with the weight of her carcass. El parásito then swims, a tangling web whirling and dodging waves. It heads towards a thrashing Professor Torres. It catches him with its shifting netting and penetrates the professor's mouth. It dives into him, and Professor Torres becomes paralyzed from the outside in, the black mass conquering his being. El gusano exits through his pores, exploding the professor's flesh. Black and white peppered hair reaches the surface of a brown river now veiled in maroon. The parasite floats away, hunting for a mate.

The DaVinci Chip

Suzan Palumbo

RAGE BIT like bile in my throat as I sat in the dim post grad office at the Blackthorn Academy watching the accolades for Bianca and her team at Byotech flood my socials:

"Byotech has **drawn** us into the future" —*Tech Medical Daily*

"*The Da Vinci Chip is the game changer that renders AI generated images and all their ethical concerns obsolete*" —*Code Addict*

"*Innovation that marries science and art seamlessly*" —*Academic IT*

Bianca's success as an alum was a blue ribbon of pride for the administration, and Byotech's breakthrough had set the neuroscience department aflame with excitement. No doubt they planned to use her success to leverage funding from rich donors.

I wanted no part of it, even if it won me resources for my work. Bianca, grinning in front of Byotech's steel and glass headquarters like she'd conquered the world with code and nano processors, mocked the core of my being and picked at my barely scabbed-over heart.

In the unveiling video Byotech had released, she took an interviewer on a mini tour of their facilities. She turned her back to the camera and lifted her dark, glossy tresses to show us the tiny scar where the Da Vinci Chip had been implanted just below her hairline. My mouth went dry in response to the gesture. I'd traced that hairline and knew how supple her skin there was. When the tour continued into the lab, Bianca faced the camera and synced with a computer interface to give the interviewer a demonstration of the technology's power.

"What would you like a picture of?" Her smile became wide and disarming as she spoke to the interviewer who remained off screen.

"O-okay," he said, his voice unsteady but shaded with anticipation. "A tiger?" Bianca nodded and closed her thick-lashed eyelids, feigning deep concentration. A machine hummed to life on a counter. She walked over to a tray and produced a glossy photo quality picture of a tiger bounding into a pond, its eyes hungry, iridescent water droplets suspended in the air around its form.

"Here you are, *tiger*," she said, handing the picture to the interviewer.

"T-this is magic! Anyone can create images. . . art with this technology?"

"The only limit is your imagination." Bianca said.

Or who you're willing to stab in the back, I thought.

I scoured every article, puff piece, and stub in the following days. She hadn't mentioned my name once, not even as a tangent. It was as if she'd wiped my existence from her mind. Yet I had remained obsessed, ruminating over her unfeeling mistreatment of me. The hurt festered like an infected wound that needed to be drained. I could not move on. I refused to move on. I'd been wronged and I required justice—a memory for a memory. If Bianca wanted to delete me from her past, I'd give her complete erasure.

I did not have her current contact. She was most likely using

Byotech company devices. I took a chance and sent her a private message on an old server we'd used when we were both broke postgraduate researchers. My voice trembled as I dictated the note well past midnight:

I don't suppose you'd have a moment to catch up with your busy schedule, but if you do, I'd love to take you out to Vesuvio's for old time's sake. I'm so happy for your success.

-S.

Her answer came a week later as the grip of malcontent had begun to choke me.

Let's set up a date.

-B.

Date. That's what we used to do. That's what I thought we were doing. I thought we loved each other. Not that one of us was parasitically siphoning ideas off the other for future profit.

"I don't think we should see each other anymore." That's what she'd said the last night I saw her. She'd been hired by Byotech, and I'd taken her to Vesuvio's for dinner to celebrate like a chump.

"The hours will be brutal, Stella. I don't want to end up in a resentful shell of a relationship where we never talk to or see each other."

"What about seeing if we can work through this together? This is *my* field, too, Bianca. You know my research is in the same area. I could assist." I cringed at the pleading hook in my voice.

"What would you like me to do, pass up the opportunity? Would you give this up for me? Let me get settled. I'll see if I can bring you on board. I'm choosing not to hurt us both."

I would. I would give this up for you. I would never go where I couldn't take you with me; I wanted to yell in the crowded restaurant. But the set of her mouth told me this was not a discussion, and her mind was made up. She stood and left me sitting at the table. I walked back to my apartment alone in the dark.

She never did try to bring me aboard. She'd achieved exactly what she said she didn't want: I was hurt. I carried my resentment over our dead relationship from that moment on like a withered husk in my pocket.

She arrived at Vesuvio's early and was waiting for me at our old table in a shadowy corner. I wore the same dark tweed jacket she'd dumped me in. She recognized it. I could tell by the brief ripple of discomfort at the corners of her lips when I sat down across from her.

Instead of hello, she said, "You've hardly changed."

"You have." I buried the edge trying to surface in my voice. She'd traded her own tweed and thick glasses for a sleek black blazer, slacks, and contacts. She was put together and gorgeous, like she'd stepped out of the Byotech video moments ago.

"This is a façade. You know the real me."

"Do I, Bianca?" She laughed off my pointed comment and looked at the menu.

"They don't have that arrabiata I used to love anymore. You'll have to help me choose what to eat before you catch me up on how you've been and what you're working on."

So you can steal those ideas and incorporate them into your product line at Byotech, too?

"Let's have a drink to start. They have an excellent amontillado. I want to toast you." I was no longer the easily manipulated lovesick puppy she knew. Two could play at fake caring.

The amontillado was drained an hour later, and Bianca was leading me by the hand back to campus, showing me she remembered all of our old haunts along the way. The crunch of leaves beneath our feet churned the slurry of heartache and anger inside me with nostalgia. I shivered. Her palms were so soft and comfortable. How

I'd missed them. But these weren't old times, and Bianca was only being sweet because she'd had too much to drink. She'd held my hand just as gently once before and dropped it for Byotech.

The Gothic Revival building that housed the research labs and offices loomed ahead. Its ornate architecture and embellishments mimicked the twisted bitterness inside me. She led us right up to the heavy doors.

"Do you remember where my office is?" I let go of her hand and entered the after-hours code.

"Yes, but take me to the lab. I want to see your setup." The whisper of a tease underscored her demand. I wanted to drown in it and smack her for using it on me.

"Are you sure? It's rudimentary compared to the work you're doing."

"I've always thought you were brilliant. It's part of why I came tonight. I missed spending time with you." A flicker of sincerity flashed in her gaze. "You lead the way, Stella."

I shrugged, feigning humility. She stepped aside. The elevators in the main hall were out of service, as usual. We headed for the stairs.

"Did you continue in the same vein of research?" She asked as I opened the door to the dark stairwell. I clamped my mouth around a barking laugh.

"I changed my direction slightly when it was announced that you and Byotech were working on an art processor brain link. I've been looking at long-term memory." She did not seem to register my acrid tone.

"Helping people remember or forget?"

I glanced back at her. She had to be mocking me. Her face was flushed from the exertion and the wine as we reached the midway point of our ascent. There wasn't a hint of malice in her expression but then again, she'd always been good at concealing her intentions. I stopped myself from kicking her down the stairs and continued upwards.

"I find people much more expert at forgetting than remembering," I said as I opened the door to the top floor. "This isn't very exciting. It's basic compared to what you're doing. We could go–"

"Stop the modesty act, Stella." Her breath on the back of my neck goose pimpled my skin.

I nodded and headed down the hall. We entered the cavernous lab I shared with several other researchers, and I led her to the back of the room where my equipment was set up.

A black medical recliner sat in the corner with a set of computers and screens arranged nearby. She sat on the chair casually like I'd invited her into my living room for tea.

"How does it work?" The promotional video style smile spread across her mouth.

"I'm using the same principles you took—you're using for the Da Vinci Chip." Heat pooled in my cheeks. I had to keep calm, not show my hand. "Mine uses connections to the temporal lobes and draws from the occipital. But the basis is the same."

"Do you think it will work with the chip I have?"

"To some degree, yes." *Of course it will, you witch.* I'd bribed one of our former colleagues who also worked at Byotech to let me analyze the software and device. Her chip would do exactly what I told it to do.

"Let's try it." She was as eager as a puppy.

"Are you—"

"Stella." She rolled her eyes. I held my palms up in surrender and approached the chair.

"Lie back. I'm going to restrain your arms to help keep you completely still. It's safe, I've tested the program on myself, but it's not perfect at filtering out noise from movement and other stimuli." She nodded, completely trusting. I'd never hurt her before. She had no reason to be suspicious, having been prone in front of me dozens of times in bed when we were together. I buckled her wrists firmly to the arm rests. She was trapped in the chair. I could have slit her throat, and there would have been nothing she could have done to stop me. "I'm going to sync your chip to the system and download the application. Okay?" She hummed her consent. I began the process and prepared myself for sweet vengeance.

"Are you ready?" I asked when it was complete. She nodded in response.

"Here we go." I paused. "What did Rusty look like?" The floppy-eared mutt she'd had as a little girl bounded onto the screen, retrieving a ball she'd thrown for him. A gasp escaped her lips as she watched him disappear. "Excellent! It's working." The trace of a smile touched her mouth. She'd told me how Rusty had been her only friend in elementary school. I gave her a moment before I continued.

"Remember the first flower I gave you." Her eyes widened. The double blossom fuchsia peony I'd presented to her on our second date blazed into view. She tensed on the chair. "Is this too much?" I kept my voice even. She frowned as she thought. Static flashed on the display. She shook her head "no," and I continued. She had always been as determined as a bloodhound whenever she sensed an opportunity.

"Remember the night I showed you the prototype for the Da Vinci Chip." Bianca swallowed. A grainy image appeared of her standing next to me, watching as I synced myself to the interface. A montage unfurled—

I was seated on a different medical recliner in a lab on a lower level. It was dark out and Bianca and I were alone.

"A beach sunset," she said. I closed my eyes. An orange sky, aqua water and palm trees diffused across the display. She hit print and the image came out as if I'd drawn it.

"This is incredible, Stella—"

I looked away from the screen. The glee in her voice stabbed my aggrieved heart. I bit my lip. My hands trembled over the controls. We'd come to the question I'd brooded over for the better part of four years. Did I want to go through with this? Would the answer, her recollection, heal me or devastate me anew?

"Remember when you stole my work." Visual noise filled the screen before it went dark. Bianca was actively blocking out the memory. "Remember it, Bianca!" A ghostly silhouette surfaced of her crying in front of a mirror, wearing the jacket she'd worn when she dumped me.

"Stella, stop. Let me out of this chair." She was bucking against the restraints. I kept my focus on the display. The picture wavered. The audio crackled into Bianca whispering. "It's horrible what I did. I stole it. I should have given Stella credit." The words: *it's horrible*, stretched into a whisper repeating as if bouncing off the walls of the lab we were in now. I glanced over at her. She'd stopped resisting and shrunk back into the chair, limp and sunken like one of her vital organs had been scooped from her chest.

There was my admission and vindication. My fingers hovered over the keyboard. I'd programmed the ability to cause a malfunction within the neural link that would damage her working memory completely. I could destroy Bianca with the push of a button. I could hurt her like I'd wanted to for so long. But her anguished memory had ambushed me. I shut off the program and walked over to the chair. She looked small and inconsequential—a pathetic thief and liar. I unbuckled her hands, and she rubbed her wrists. Her eyes welled with tears.

"I'm sorry, Stella. I don't know how to fix what I did."

I capitulated. I would never forgive her, but my will drained along with the fury that had bolstered me. I exhaled. She remained meek and though I'd forced her to admit her betrayal, her face softened. The guilty look in her memory emerged in her eyes. She leaned towards me and kissed my cheek.

"I never intended to hurt you. I think I need to go." She slipped off the chair and walked out of the lab, leaving me alone as she had before. I went back to the keyboard. My fingers lingered over the *delete session* button on the touch screen. Even if I'd wanted to use her memories as proof the Da Vinci Chip was my intellectual property, how would I explain getting Bianca drunk and restraining her? The confession had been made under duress. I tapped delete and confirm and left the lab, numbed and hollowed out.

Bianca and Byotech were in the headlines six months later. The neuroscience department salivated at the impending influx of cash her affiliation with it would bring.

"Yes, we're working on applications that deal with memory. Retrieving them and preserving them." She smiled into the camera, the defiant look in her eyes boring into me, laughing at me.

I should have hurt Bianca when I had the chance. I can say that now because in a moment I'll hit delete and I won't remember her or her betrayal. Complete erasure. I'll use the malfunction designed for her on myself. When you, one of my colleagues, find me on this recliner and play back this session with my memories, I hope you tell the department the Da Vinci Chip was mine. I hope they acknowledge my contributions. I hope Bianca never forgets she drove me to do this.

An Inordinate Amount of Interest

Ayida Shonibar

GREEN FLOWS from your imagination onto the page, bleeding viridescent liquid through the intermediary of your brush. The handle bends to your grip like the natural extension it's been for as long as you remember, the interface between skin and lacquered wood as familiar as your eyelids kissing to blink.

This last stroke completes the painting. It's not *finished* finished—you could always add a layer of yellow to bathe the leaves in warmer sunlight or deepen their definition with purple shading. More details to bring this rendition of the peepal tree closer to how it's rooted in your memories of your homeland.

But there's the time limit to consider.

The interviewer waits for you to slide the paper to her side of the table. Her gaze traces over your artwork and lights up. "It's beautiful." She splays her fingers an inch above the still damp branches. "So lifelike it hardly takes any effort to do *this*."

Light suffuses her hand. Beneath her palm, foliage springs from the paper and spills across the tabletop. She pulls it upwards, fingers still glowing as they curl around the sapling to draw it out of your now blank canvas.

Air catches in your throat. Pulse pounding, you lean closer to gingerly touch a heart-shaped peepal leaf.

It's solid. Waxy. A real piece of where you came from, a shining emerald on this other side of the planet. When you dig your nail in, the bitter scent of raw vegetation tickles your nose.

"Incredible," you whisper. "You could really teach me how to do this?"

"Our senses are all intertwined. If you pour the true essence of something effectively into your painting of it, the rest easily follows. So, you see, your existing skill set would make you the perfect student."

Your mouth goes dry at her words, even as you try not to jump to conclusions. You shouldn't let your interest run ahead of you. "Then, does this mean—"

She beams at you and extends her arm. "Congratulations, Kiran. I'm delighted to offer you a place in our Bachelor of Arts programme."

You shake hands, barely feeling the motion through the numbness of your excitement. "Wow. I mean—*wow*!" Your voice cracks. This is a dream come true. "How do I sign up?"

"With this admissions packet. I'll need you to fill it out by next month." She sets a thick sheaf of papers onto the table beside your fully realised—albeit miniature—peepal tree. "These forms collect some basic information for our administrative office. Your name, permanent address, proof of tuition funds, and the like."

She continues talking, but as your eyes skim through the top page and trip over the fee schedule, with its too-long numbers and first deadline in a few weeks, the panicked buzzing in your head drowns out everything else.

You don't want to jeopardise what she's offering you. Not when there's a long line of other applicants waiting outside the door, ready to take your position if she senses any sign of indecision in you. There are countless talented people in the world. You're just one of many.

It's the knowledge you'd gain from this degree that would set your talent apart.

So you school your features into eager nonchalance, stretching the corners of your mouth as wide as they'll go and nodding to the rhythm of whatever she has to say.

You'll pay the cost somehow. You'll have to.

You tug on the cuffs of your checkered flannel shirt nervously. It's nothing as posh as the tailored suits the money men in the financial district wear, but splurging on something nicer would only push you further away from affording the tuition. You hope the fact it's all black and white will appear formal enough. The uniformity of their attire tells you the way people dress means something to them, and you desperately want them to see you as a serious contender when you sit down in front of them.

You need them sufficiently interested in your potential to want to invest in your future.

The door to the waiting room opens, and a tall man with square-framed glasses and a clipboard calls your name, butchering the pronunciation. "Kai ran!"

You could correct him, gently, but even the kindest clarification might come across as impertinent. It's not really worth it in this situation, you decide, not when there's so much riding on how you'll be perceived. Even though you chose your name precisely because it reflects the multiplex space your gender occupies while honouring your family's cultural heritage.

It means ray of light, which seems fitting given what you're hoping to learn at university. You recall the luminosity of the interviewer's hand as she dragged your two-dimensional creation into the z-axis of the real world. The breath-taking mastery you ache to practice yourself.

The clipboard man leads you into a chamber that must be a

thousand times larger than the panel of three people—and you—within. He takes his place with the others at the end of the long table.

You glance around as you sink into your lonely seat. It's hard, uncomfortable. The room is dark, difficult to illuminate with its excessive volume and its various nooks and crannies. Vaulted ceilings arch high above your head. You feel small and insignificant far below.

"Gorgeous architecture, is it not?" says the clipboard man, adjusting his green silk tie.

You nod, as he expects you to. There's no room for sharing your actual perception of their building here. You didn't come all this way to displease them.

The panel skims through your admission packet, murmuring too quietly for you to hear. You squint to catch a smile of approval on any of their faces, but it's too dim to make out anything beyond indifference.

"What makes you, of all people, deserving of this scholarship?" the moustached man seated in the middle asks at last.

You've rehearsed your answer at home, even your expressions. You lower the pitch of your voice to convey confidence and lift your eyebrows engagingly. "As you can see in my acceptance letter, sir, my artistic—"

"We're not here to evaluate your paintings, Kiran," the woman on the left says. "We want to know why we should loan you our money."

Your mouth snaps shut.

"You're not wealthy." The first man jabs at his clipboard, as if uncovering a secret. "It will take you a long time to pay us back. What will you give us in return?"

You blink back tears before they overflow and embarrass you in front of these grownups. It's not like you have something valuable to offer them; you're just a high school kid. This is where your dream could end. Before it gets to begin.

So you hand over everything you have. "Anything."

They exchange looks. There's a weighted silence.

Then the moustached man clears his throat. "The letter *N*," he says. "We'll take that as collateral from you. For now."

"The letter *N*?" you repeat. "That doesn't belong to me."

"It's only *your* letter *N* we need," the woman says.

"But—" you stammer for words. "It's not even worth anything, madam!"

The clipboard man raises an eyebrow. "It holds no meaning for you at all?"

You think of the number of times you've uttered the letter aloud in this room alone. Too many to count. It would be hugely inconvenient to have to speak around it and still make sense.

You think also of your name. And this time, the thought hurts.

The moustached man cracks his first grin. "There, you see? That's what it will take."

You could try to bargain for an alternative exchange. A bolder person might threaten to storm out with no agreement at all. But any argument would risk annoying them enough for them to refuse you altogether.

You close your eyes and picture your artistic pieces waking into existence by your hand. Pieces of yourself that have never had the fuel to exist anywhere other than your mind or your sketchbook. Before now.

It's a trivial price to pay, for something you want so terribly.

The contract they draw up is long, full of terms and conditions you can't possibly decipher. But your mind was made up the moment the interviewer brought your painting to life.

You take the expensive-looking fountain pen the woman proffers and sign *Kiran* for the last time. It glows red in your hand, matching the word you've written, before the panel snatches it away from you.

Without the *N*, you become Kira. This is a name the majority of your classmates know how to pronounce. In fact, it carries the weight of so many associations that most of them believe they know aspects of who you are before they've ever met you, from the moment they read your new moniker in a list or email.

"Join us for girls' night, Kira!" they yell, halfway through a bottle of chardonnay.

And you can't easily say *no*, so you follow them. You don't really mind. It's nice to have friends in this new place.

You go to classes together, where you learn about theories of transmogrification and principles of manifestation. In your dorm rooms, you all pin up the same matriculation photo of your whole class wearing robes that cost more than a week of meals and that you won't touch again before graduation in three years.

Your exams never achieve top scores. The professors mark your essays up in red pen, lamenting the absence of certain principles or theories that are only vaguely alluded to via long-winded descriptions. *Did you forget the correct citations?* they demand angrily, having hammered them into you over the course of the year.

Still, you manage to pass. And whatever your transcript might say, nobody outshone you in the practical workshops.

It's those lush jungles and vibrant flower patches—now permanent displays in the university's renowned arboretum—that secure you your job offer straight out of undergrad. People come from all over the country to admire the stunning, exotic plants that grow like magic in this cold climate. And one of the visitors wants you to work for her conservation startup company.

With your first pay check comes another envelope in the post. When you open it, the summons glows a deep red, far darker than the white light that awakens your art.

The chamber looks smaller this time, though you haven't grown much taller since you were a teenager. The air inside it smells musty and damp, as if it hasn't been aired out for centuries.

They sit on the far end of the table again, leaving you isolated on your side.

The woman has grown out her hair. The man in the middle has slightly more salt in the pepper of his moustache. Clipboard man looks the same, down to the colour of his silk tie. It's the only aspect of his outfit that appeals to you, the same shade as the dress you're wearing—a gift from your college roommate.

"Your first payment is due," says the woman.

You read through the bill slowly this time. You're an adult now, and the numbers make more sense. "This total is a lot more compared to what I borrowed."

"The loan wasn't free," the moustached man says, not unkindly. "You owe us the original amount in addition to the cost of borrowing it. The principal as well as the interest."

"You signed the agreement." The other man brandishes his clipboard, on which your old signature shimmers crimson.

"This first part is over what I might afford, sir," you admit. Sweat prickles on the back of your neck. You glance at the doorway, which one armed guard flanks. To get to the row of windows, you'll have to run past the panel. And though you can't see them, you suspect all three of them might be bearing weapons of their own, concealed somewhere inside their impeccably ironed suits.

You don't think you'll be leaving without making a payment.

"Then how about additional collateral?" the woman suggests.

"I require my other letters," you say quickly. "It's already difficult without the first."

"All right," the clipboard man says lightly, as if conceding nothing at all. He strokes his tie, and when you look back up to his face, he's watching you carefully. "We will accept the colour green."

Your body goes cold.

Shades of green make up all your artwork. The colour tethers you to the region where you grew up as a child. When your family left, you pressed your face to the airplane window. The last glimpse you caught was of the rolling treetops that marked the landscape of the Bay of Bengal, of the world's largest river delta that flowed from your birthplace.

"We need something of value," the moustached man says. "Otherwise, what's the point? Think of it as an incentive to motivate you."

You can't really afford to escalate the situation. You're outnumbered three to one—without counting the sentry posted up front. With odds like these, you must do what it takes to keep them happy.

You'll get to stand up and walk out when it's over. Return to your pursuit of art. That's what matters.

Your signature, only four letters now, burns scarlet. The tint spreads like wildfire through your field of vision, eating away clipboard man's tie, bleeding into every sliver of green it finds. Then it consumes your own clothes, until there's nothing left of it that you love, leaving behind an empty outline of a dress.

"Our trees are all dead," your boss says in consternation.

Leached of colour, the forest you've restored together looks defeated by blight. Your fingers caress a listless leaf. Without the green hues to hold its structural integrity in place, the fibrous texture has fallen apart. The leaves crumble in your hand, a heart shape broken.

"It's okay," your boss mutters, more to herself than to you. "We can just start again from scratch."

She arranges to have the ruins of your previous plants removed, giving you a blank slate to work with. It's an extra cost she hadn't factored into this project. She's unhappy with you, though she tries to hide it behind superficial smiles.

Your stomach twists with shame.

You stay up all night to make up for the setback. Wrists aching from the effort, you paint branch after branch at your easel. You reach inside yourself, to the depths of your memory and emotion, stretching all the way back to your earliest thoughts, to pull forth the oldest, thickest trees that have grown within and alongside you.

But the first batch comes out red and, when you flex your glowing hand over it, catches fire. You beat out the flames with your favourite jacket, which once, too, was green. The second round turns a nasty magenta when you animate them, clinging to your skin as painful bruises.

A third attempt gives you beautiful, maroon mushroom caps. You weep, and they drink your tears.

Your boss finds you in the morning, surrounded by empty canvases and accidents. She takes your sore hands in hers. When she apologises, you think she truly means it. "I have to let you go."

"You haven't made a single payment," the man with the clipboard says disapprovingly. "Every time you miss a deadline, you accrue late charges."

"I lost my job, sir." You could explain further, tell them it's their own fault your work fell apart in the first place. But they have all your records. They know what happened. Pointing fingers would only serve to antagonise them further.

This time, there are *two* armed guards at the door.

Perhaps coaxing them into a better mood might make them more amenable to a compromise.

"Could you accept something else as collateral?" you ask.

"What value do you have left?" retorts the moustached man. "You've squandered everything you possessed."

A flicker of anger flares up your spine, stiffening your posture and loosening your tongue. But you bite down on it, drawing blood. There's no point in making a bad situation worse.

"Let's not be hasty," the woman says. "There is, of course, one final thing left."

The man with the clipboard chuckles derisively. "My, my, how very old-fashioned of you."

"What is it, madam?" you ask, desperate enough to trade in your hair, your toenails, or even your blood to get away from these people.

The moustached man presses his palms together, an almost spiritual gesture. "Your soul."

You wait for them to laugh. But when no sign of mirth comes, you understand they're serious. In the name of the debt they hold over you, they will seize your most fundamental essence.

And you will let them.

The numbers in your paperwork fill you with fear. They've doubled, tripled, quadrupled from the sums you had discussed as a bright-eyed adolescent, when you still had your name and a passion to dream of.

But now, you admit to yourself that this is not something you'll pay off in this lifetime. Your soul will tread water so long as it's anchored to your dead weight. What difference will it make bartered off to maintain peace, to keep the wolf at the door?

The clipboard man slides over a new contract. The woman gives you her pen. They never had to hide weapons in their clothing when all they needed to control you was the promise of your own dreams.

The motions have become familiar. You sign, and it's easy.

The ink turns red. And then all you see is red.

Your hand moves quickly across the page.

"May I have my pen back, please?" the woman snaps, her polite phrasing belying her cutting tone.

You still cannot say *no*, so you settle for the next best response. "Shut your mouth, madam."

There's some sort of reaction to your rudeness among the panel, like a wave of squawking spreading through a hen house. But you aren't listening to them anymore. Something inside you has been broken, set loose, and it rattles like a cog unhinged.

You finish your drawing and pull from whatever is left within you. The paper roars to life, flames bursting into existence atop the long table.

The guards thunder toward you. Before they can aim their guns, however, your vermilion fire lunges greedily, licking up their limbs, sucking in their guts, until there's nothing left of them.

The woman snatches at her pen, but you've already moved on to the next picture. Your hand glows red as the bruises leap from paper onto the woman's outstretched arms. She howls as the welts sink deep into her body, oozing ruby blood.

Your work isn't finished. One more illustration inked onto the page, and the fungal stalks shoot past your scarlet hands to the moustached man. Filaments braid themselves into his facial hair and scurry up his nostrils. He chokes, coughing, and crimson tendrils emerge out of his mouth, feeding on him.

When you face the man with the clipboard through your haze of red, he cowers into his plush chair. "Please," he begs. "Don't kill me."

"What do you have to give me for your life?" you ask.

"Anything!" he says. "Anything at all."

You watch him snivel. You know what you want from him, of course, but it's quite enjoyable witnessing his distress. Finally, you say, "Erase my debt. All of it."

He nods vigorously, pulling various contracts from his files that have tracked your loan over the years. These are the documents that tally up the numbers you owe. They're not the agreements that delineate your collateral payments, since you didn't ask him for those. One by one, he tears them up and tosses them into the embers of your fire, eager to please. "There, all done."

"Oh, but you forgot a page," you say.

"No!" he insists. "Which one do you mean?"

"That which might have spared your life, had you thought to commit our little deal to paper."

He screams. But the bellowing inferno, revived by the caress of your scarlet fingers, swallows him whole.

In the charred remains of the chamber, three contracts survive. You consider them all before ripping only one to pieces.

Your tongue stretches into the new and old space. "It's so nice to say no again."

Preservation of an Intact Specimen

Premee Mohamed

IT WAS AN ENORMOUS RAT. For one blissful moment Camilla allowed herself to believe it was something else—a fox terrier, perhaps, accidentally released by a careless patron. But the illusion could not hold. As the rat struggled in the inadequate trap that had failed to crush its spine, its forequarters bulged as if it were a circus strongman doing a press-up. It was simply so horrifying that Camilla could only stare—before realizing that it was about to push the bar clear.

She slipped on her archival gloves and darted forward, seizing the rat behind the neck just as it wrenched itself free. It was hideously powerful, like grappling with a python instead of a rodent, and for the split second that it writhed in her grasp she felt certain it would overpower her. Sheer revulsion seemed to fling her arm away, swinging the brute against a marble pillar, but not hard enough for a killing blow.

It rose bloodied, snarling, and raced towards her across the black-and-white tile. Without further thought she brought he

Panting, she examined the corpse for signs of revival, and only several seconds later became aware that she was not alone.

"Ah, Miss Sheridan," wheezed the museum director, Godfrey. He looked unusually pallid and grey, and groped in his waistcoat for a handkerchief. "If. . . if you're. . . quite finished? I, er. . . could you attend me in my office? At your earliest convenience?"

"Of course, Mr. Godfrey."

He staggered away, surprisingly quickly given his age and the slippery floor; possibly, Camilla thought, so that she would not overhear him being sick into one of the potted palms. Well, she couldn't help him, and the rat was beyond help.

She recovered the corpse by the tail, and pondered the dermestid beetles in the Hera Wing, but really, what was the *point* of a rat skeleton. If only it had been a more exotic pest! She made a mental note to order rattraps to supplement the mousetraps and set off for the incinerator.

Owing to its somewhat eccentric benefactor, who owned the island upon which it had been built, the museum was much the same shape as its landmass—an upper-case L with an exaggeratedly long downstroke and the smallest of cross-strokes. As such it was impossible to short-cut from one end to the other, of which Mr. Godfrey was well aware. Camilla therefore did not rush through the various wings, from Mammals to Lizards, Fish to Insects to Minerals to Fossils, Vegetation to Miscellaneous, through the discreet door to Maintenance and Hygiene, down the stairs to the two big incinerators.

She nodded to the caretaker, then threw the rat into the larger incinerator, followed by her gloves. Must order more of those as well.

Mr. Godfrey's office was lofty of ceiling and cramped of footprint, like the rest of the museum—but, unlike the public spaces whose appearance Camilla strictly controlled, it was a mess, all cobwebs, half-eaten sandwiches gone to mould, spilled ink, and heaps of papers and books obstructing the exquisitely-crafted stained-glass creatures on the windows. Part of a turquoise leg and one orange antenna gleamed above the largest shelf. "Ah, Miss Sheridan," he said; his colour looked a little better. "Cup of tea?"

She eyed the green-furred teapot. "Thank you, no, Mr. Godfrey. If this is about earlier, I—"

"Oh! No, no. Acquitted yourself quite well I thought. It's just. . . well, your duties keep you here dawn to dusk, one can't help but notice. First in, last out. *Hours* after closing." He gestured vaguely at the window, drawing attention at last to the fair-haired visitor lurking in a most ungentlemanly fashion behind a shelf. "I thought an. . . assistant was in order."

Camilla's stomach sank, but she managed to keep her voice level and professional. "I appreciate your concern, Mr. Godfrey. However, if you felt that the standards of my care were slipping, I'm sure you would have communicated that to me before now."

"No, never! Your care for the museum is—is exemplary, I assure you! It's only, you know. . . not that I don't appreciate your devotion! Or the Board, you know the Board is *very* pleased with your work. I only worry about your health. These long hours. Supposing you wanted to. . . marry, begin a. . ."

"I assure you, Mr. Godfrey," she said icily, "if I were to take up any activity that would affect my curatorship, you would be the very first to know."

"All the same," he sighed, "I have taken the liberty of bringing on a second for you. Miss Sheridan, this is—"

But the visitor was turning, and grinning, and she mechanically named and numbered each tooth in his head as if she meant to knock them out and exhibit them in a velvet-lined case. And it was not so much this that appalled her as the realization that she had thought *knock out* instead of *extract*. As if only the sight of his bloodied, empty mouth were cause for joy, and not the completed artifact under her oversight and care, forever.

"*Doctor* Sheridan," she corrected him. "Lucas Bainbridge, isn't it? My, what a small world. Haven't seen you since our St. Daumany's days."

"Doctor Bainbridge," he said; he made some attempt to grasp her fingers, but she quickly turned it into an ordinary handshake, releasing his hand at once and not bothering to hide wiping her palm on her skirt.

Godfrey looked between them, bewildered; perhaps he had imagined a fond reunion between two schoolfellows, not this crackling current of loathing filling the place like a downed wire. *Get rid of him at once*, she imagined herself shouting. *I don't care what the Board says. Poison his tea. Drown him in the lake. Do you know what a viper you have brought into my nest?*

"Yes, well, when I heard you were curator here, I hunted out a position at once," Bainbridge was saying breezily, sitting on the edge of Godfrey's lopsided desk and crossing his ankles to better display his expensive shoes, glossy oxblood wingtips very unlike Camilla's sensible boots. *American* shoes. "I always knew you'd make something of yourself, Camilla."

"One doesn't like to boast," she said flatly. "And it's *Dr.* Sheridan if you're to be performing your duties under me."

"These modern women," Bainbridge said, winking at Godfrey. "I do look forward to *performing* my duties *under* you, Dr. Sheridan. Though not for long."

She smiled icily. "Well. I'll leave you two to make office arrangements, shall I?"

Bainbridge! There had been a time, not so long ago, when she had used his name as a curse. Even as she stalked back to her office, she was paging through the tidy files of her memory, seeking any of a thousand ways to get rid of him. It shouldn't be difficult, she reflected, shutting and locking the door, then leaning against it.

She was on the verge of tears, and that infuriated her. *Bainbridge!* He had protested against her very admittance at St. Daumany's—from the first day he had pulled strings, finagled meetings with the deans, even their local MP, trying to keep her from enrollment, then classes, then laboratory sessions, eventually even final examinations, after it became clear she would not be bullied out by his constant rumour mongering.

What had been his first one? That she had disguised herself as a boy to get in—untrue; she had had to clip her hair short due to an incident with the newly-installed coal range at her aunt's house. Then he had gone lower. . . claiming she offered various revolting favours to professors in lieu of experiments or papers, that she would offer them to anyone else on campus.

How many times had she been woken by one of his toadies hammering on her door, shouting, "Oi there, chambermaid! My cock needs polishing! Get up!" Meanwhile, Bainbridge and his lies, Bainbridge and his horses and estates and his hired friends and underlings, Bainbridge spending mummy and daddy's money— the man missed all his classes, regularly abused every female member of the university's cleaning and laundry staff, was *known* to pay others to write his papers. . . how had he graduated? Surely, she thought, his vendetta against her left little time for actual studies.

And all the professors looking the other way, year after year, as she stumbled into class late with the contents of his inkwell splashed over her uniform, unslept from his verbal assaults, grim, determined, till both her ambition and her anger hardened into a kind of diamond shard in her heart that did nothing to protect her but flashed out ever more regularly at her tormentors, until she had managed retaliatory—what had administration called them? Pranks? against all of his underlings. But Bainbridge himself had been too slippery.

Still, still. . . she had evidence of so many of his wrongdoings. Once she chose the method of his elimination, only a few letters need be written, retrieving various documents from her safe deposit boxes. She was not one to throw out anything interesting from the past. One never knew when one might need it. It was why she had campaigned so ferociously for this position—the first woman curator of the most prestigious, most well-funded, well-respected natural history museum on this half of the globe.

She knew the Board had been displeased with a woman replacing the old curator—let alone such a young one, let alone one without title or estate, a hereditary nobody with the kind of stolen accent that only fooled the lower classes, not those who had been born hearing those cut-glass syllables. She was clinging to this curatorship by her fingernails, and it would not be Bainbridge—bloody Lucas Bainbridge!—who shook her loose. Give her a better nemesis, at least!

Camilla took a deep breath and reached for envelopes and notepaper. The herons of her own stained-glass window danced gracefully across her desk, blue and grey and green. Steady, steady. Godfrey would see sense. If she presented her case with detachment, merely as something she happened to have discovered about her new assistant. . . well, Bainbridge would find something else soon enough. So long as it was far from here, Camilla did not care.

That night she dreamt a legion of rot-furred rats skulked through the museum, toppling cases and gnawing specimens, ignoring her screams of anger, ignoring her weaponless and impotent pursuit, till one turned on her, leapt, began to devour. She woke tasting her own blood and waited for the dream-memory to fade and reality to return: a beautiful summer day, and another twelve hours of work at the place she loved best.

"Well, I suppose it seems authentic," Godfrey said slowly, holding the letter close to his desk-lamp to check the watermark. "But I certainly don't think it's anything to. . . to sack him over, really. Boys will be boys, after all, Camilla."

She didn't bother correcting him, only went still. All morning she had been rehearsing her speech—*So very sorry, one doesn't like to tell tales, assure you this was verified by the Dean's assistant himself, surely the Board*—and rehearsing her entire demeanour. Apologetic, unemotional, scientific.

"Why don't we, in fact, call him in here and ask him to—" Godfrey began, and recoiled as Camilla approached his desk.

"I don't think that's necessary, Mr. Godfrey," Camilla said softly, hoping to calm his obvious terror. In retrospect, perhaps she had moved too suddenly. "It's my mistake. . . I thought only of our reputation. That our benefactor and the Board might object to a noted plagiarist at the museum."

Godfrey chuckled uncertainly. "I do appreciate your fervour, but, well, if we were to sack everybody who'd gotten up to a little trouble in their schooldays, there would be no one left to run the museum! Eh? Would there?"

"No," she heard her mouth say; her mind had fled elsewhere, shrieking down cold corridors filled with awakened spirits of fury and frustration, seeking the old shard in the armoury. "I daresay not. None of us are perfect, after all. Are we?"

Bainbridge maintained an obnoxious proximity the next day—exhaling his foul breath upon her, all rancid milk and stale pipe smoke. "I would rearrange these alphabetically," he said late in the afternoon, poking the glass of the tarantulas exhibit and leaving a smudge. The angled light from the window showed worse inside the cabinet: tiny glittering hairs like flecks of gold, knocked loose from the delicate preserved spiders by his blow. "What on earth have you got them arranged by 'geographic area' for? No one understands that."

"The scientists visiting for research do." She huffed on her silk handkerchief and rubbed at the fingermark. No good; she'd have to arrange for one of the cleaning staff to come with a rag and some diluted ammonia. "*Bainbridge.* Smoking is not permitted. The residue destroys the surfaces of the cabinetry and stains the exposed specimens. As you well know."

"Ah, come on, Camilla," he whined, the pipe already between his lips. "No one's looking. It's hardly setting a bad example for the staff. Most of whom are of more advanced age than you," he added, reaching for his matchsafe, "*and* smoke like chimneys."

"Not inside the building," she said. "They know better than that by now."

He rolled his eyes. "Daresay you gave them a harpy's dressing-down. Must've broken some windows. Sent bats plummeting out of the air."

"Whatever I did is none of your business," she said. "And it worked. *No smoking, I said.*"

He narrowed his eyes; she refused to look away. After several seconds, he struck a match against the nearest pillar, leaving a streak of red colorant across one of the ammonites. "What are you going to do?" he said. "Go running to Godfrey again? Hmm? As if I wouldn't tell him what a little whore you were in university. Taking lessons from that history professor in his room. What now?"

"The insubordination will certainly be entered in your record," she said, her voice as pleasant as possible, staring at the ammonite. It was so *easy* sometimes, wasn't it, making up one's mind? Balancing on a fence was painful; one shouldn't make it a habit. One should pick a side and step off—no, leap.

He had been nudging her for a month. Now she had jumped.

She added, "Not that, if you don't mind my saying, it would affect your employment here, Bainbridge."

He blew out a chestful of smoke with the slightest incline of his head, letting it settle on her hair. Through the haze she debated slapping the pipe out of his mouth. An earlier image returned to her: the mouth bloody, empty, all the teeth on the floor or in her hand. His sharp, yellow teeth. Like the teeth of a pig. But no. Better to give no warning.

"Alphabetized," she finally said. "Well. I'll certainly consider it."

"You do that," Bainbridge said, sucking in another mouthful of smoke. "Or I will myself, when I'm curator of this place. As you say. Shouldn't be long."

It's just a position, a voice said urgently in her head. *You can find another position, for God's sake.*

Find another one? After being *driven* out of this one? This one, that she had earned almost at the cost of her own life for all those bloody years? This one, where she had to smile and smile and smile at those revolting old men, where she had to sail clear of every other candidate by miles, and any man would have gotten in by inches? *Another* position?

No. This one is mine. This museum is mine. I worked too hard for this, and it belongs to me and if he intends to take anything of mine, I will not show the restraint I did when we were students. No one is watching me now. Only God, so they say; and He will, I think, forgive me this. Surely it is not a sin to remove a sinner from the face of the Earth to prevent future sins. Think of everything Bainbridge has done. Think of the oceans of blood on his hands.

And the tiny, tiny bit that would be on hers.

It was madness, it was all madness; but she examined the madness from every angle and it seemed good and sound, like an old tool of forged iron. She saw no weaknesses in it. It was merely the removal of something worthless from the museum—it was *curation*. She and Godfrey could find a more suitable assistant. It would only benefit the institution.

As she waited in the darkness, her voice sounded clear and calm inside her head. The accent she had learned and stuck to for all these years. Crisp and false.

She told herself: natural selection. Survival of the fittest. Benefit to the group not the individual. The population.

Camilla stood behind one of the pillars, sensing on her face the movement of the cross-drafts. They were necessary, familiar, and welcome; a shut-up museum ensured the accumulation of humidity and therefore the dreaded mould that would destroy specimens, exhibits, books, the stone itself. It felt like the friendly breath of a large animal, interrupted by the brief eddy of the main doors opening.

Bainbridge was late not only because he was inconsiderate, she knew, but also because she had locked the staff access doors using the skeleton key, a copy of which Bainbridge would have possessed if he had listened to her that first day. But she had seen his eyes glaze over, and tonight she knew he would have tried the staff door, screamed and shouted and sworn a blue streak, and then gone to the main doors.

From there, he would have to walk almost the full length of the museum to make his appointment with Godfrey—"To discuss," her note had read in Godfrey's familiar, looping hand, "a promotion to curator, and discussion with the Board." It had even been signed. The fool's presence tonight showed her that he had been too impatient with greed to imagine Camilla had anything to do with it.

She waited to feel fear, to feel her heart hammering. But she sensed only that unbreakable spear of anger, transparent, glittering. They had all looked away, all of them. Everyone who should have said something. Everyone who should have punished him, disciplined him. Expelled him. Prosecuted him. But no one cared about his victims. No one cared.

Here he came, his heels clacking on the tiles. She knew this place and it sounds well enough that she need not leave her spot to know where he was. The echoes rang past the bones of the elephant and the mammoth, the giraffe, the rhinoceros, the tiger; then the softer sounds from the preserved lion, the wildebeest sharing its plinth, the beautiful new grizzly bear; closer, closer, the heel-clacks muffled in the spread plumage of the preserved owls, the hawk and its rabbit forever frozen in that terrified leap. There.

Camilla waited for the screaming to begin before she stepped out from behind the pillar. The bear trap had arrived 'accidentally' in a case of rat and mouse traps; she had overseen the opening of the crate herself, and *tsk-tsk'd* at the mistake. She would return it to the supplier, of course. Well-cleaned, good as new. Simply unethical to waste budget on a mistake.

Bainbridge howled and writhed as she approached. "My *God! God! God!* Camilla, is that you? Camilla? Whoever you are, *help me!* Look at—I can't see—what *happened*, what is it?"

The pool of blood surrounding his shattered legs would wash easily off the polished tiles, she knew. But such a lot of it! The black-and-white painted tarp she'd draped over the trap hadn't soaked up as much as she had expected.

She stooped. "Yes, Bainbridge. It's me. You've had an accident. Help is on the way."

His uncomprehending screams tapered off to whines, redoubling as she removed the scalpel from its case. Thrashing about for escape, he managed to drag himself by his arms perhaps a dozen feet, whimpering. Camilla followed a few paces behind, and when she judged him spent, knelt again.

A mistake. Even in his pain and shock he had been calculating, saving up what little he had to spring at her—she brought up the scalpel reflexively, felt it scrape across the bones of his fingers, but even as the tendons loosened he used his remaining fingers to snatch it and fling it aside.

The moment she was disarmed he was on her, howling with pain, horribly heavy, his tweed forearms across her throat. White lights exploded in her vision as the back of her head met the tiles, hard enough to stun but not, thank God, knock her out. Where was the scalpel? Christ almighty! She kicked and thrashed at the deadweight atop her, the familiar outlines of the exhibits around her going fuzzy as she clawed at his arms.

This is how they felt, wasn't it? the voice in her head murmured as she kicked frantically at his stomach, too close to do any damage. *Just like this. Those girls at university. In the laundry. In the kitchen. . . we all knew. It would have been me if he had ever caught me. Like this.*

His face was inches from hers, exuding a terrible odour of vomit and smoke, blood splattering her face.

Like this, like this.

Not me. I refuse.

She closed her eyes. Opened them. Lunged upwards with the last of her strength, the very last, and closed her teeth on his throat, just under his jaw. Flesh tore; her bottom lip split; he redoubled his shrieks and drew back.

She gasped an enormous breath of air, rolled free, staggered to her feet, and glanced around for the scalpel. Gone in the enormous splatter of blood. He hissed at her and reached up.

Without thinking, she stamped downwards.

"Ah, Miss Sheridan. . . you haven't seen Dr. Bainbridge this morning, have you?"

"No, Mr. Godfrey." She blinked innocently up at the clock in her office, a modern black and white model glowing bright red, at the moment, with one of the leaping fish on her window. "He *is* terribly late, isn't he. He sent me no word. Yourself?"

"Hm. Hmm. No." Godfrey accepted a biscuit and a cup of tea, settling into her visitor chair. "I do hope he's not ill at home. . . unable to drag himself in."

"I'll start without him," Camilla said. "He can catch up."

"Ever devoted." Godfrey chuckled, dunking his biscuit. "This place would fall apart without you."

"Thank you, Mr. Godfrey. I appreciate that."

"I. . . are you quite all right yourself? Your, er, your. . . face. . . "

"A little accident on my bicycle coming in. Nothing to worry about."

The tea ritual completed, she began her rounds, clipboard in hand, pausing graciously to speak to the other staff and passing researchers, lingering only once—had anyone marked it—near the taxidermied grizzly, studying it more closely than her usual wont.

No sign of her stitching was visible; no blood had leaked out of the fresh stuffing to mar the artificial grass below its paws. Sensibly, she had considered the incinerator; but at last, inclining a head to that voice in her head that would not fall silent, she decided one more act of insensibility would not be too much; and who would ever believe young Camilla Sheridan, of all people, capable of this gruesome murder?

That the act would be discovered she had no doubt; but it would not be during her curatorship, and that, she was determined, would be a lifetime appointment. After her passing, she did not care. The place was hers again, and safe.

"Miss Sheridan? Have you a moment?"

She turned, smiling. "*Doctor* Sheridan. Of course." She hoisted her clipboard and stepped back into the sunlight, her boots clicking loudly across the tiles.

Those Shining Things Are Out of Reach

Octavia Cade

Some schools are too dangerous to name. I will not be naming this one—I need this job. For now.

I was lucky to get it. My mother was a cleaner here, scrubbing the floors and toilets of a school she could never have attended herself, and part of the compensation for poor pay was a tuition waiver for her child.

All that polished wood, all those gleaming surfaces. My adolescent self trusted none of it. It was no place for a kid who wasn't also polished and gleaming, who didn't inhabit the same body of behaviour from birth. Tuition waivers don't extend to dentistry or dermatology or afterschool clubs, and we might have all worn the same uniform, but mine came from charity and everyone knew it.

No one was unkind about it. None of the other students spoke of it at all. I think they thought it was a politeness, pretending not to see. Sometimes they were even friendly. Sometimes I was even grateful. None of us knew how to bridge the gap. I think my presence here was acknowledgement that there *was* a gap. I think it was also supposed to be enough.

The gratitude chipped away when we found that it wasn't

enough after all. The kids in my class, all of them, got internships with the friends of their parents. Those internships were good preparation for college. They'd look good on transcripts. They were also completely unpaid, which was fine for everyone else—but it took money to get to the law offices and investment firms and advertising agencies that hosted the interns, and I couldn't afford the transport.

"The corporate world isn't for everyone. You might want to consider a career with the potential to give back," said the careers counsellor, as if my presence was a bargain to be repaid. "Don't you want to help people?"

The next group assignment I'd asked around. "Did she ask if you wanted to help people?" The answer was always *no*.

On my next visit to the careers office, I'd been more prepared. "I think I'd like to be a librarian," I said. "I want to help other people to learn, like they've helped me." There was a lot of smiling, and a lot of bullshit: I said that everyone in the world should have access to a library, and the right to ask a librarian for help finding out the things they didn't know. "Information is a valuable tool for self-improvement," I said. "For making the world a better place."

It was all true. It was everything a school like this wanted their students to say. And it was all *such* a lie, but even as a child I was good at lying. The lie was eaten up, and I was granted a position assisting in the school library, a couple of hours a day after school. It solved the question of transport. I didn't need to scramble for ticket money, or to wait at bus stops after dark. I could just get a ride with my mother when she was finished scrubbing and I had finished shelving.

When that schooling was over, I had good marks, but not good enough for scholarships. I stayed instead. Part-time attendance at an affordable local university and a position of school librarian opening up, and that was my repayment: never being able to leave.

"You could have left," said Elena. That's not her real name. She's not even a real person. Elena is a construct of all the kids who have come through the library doors. . . all the kids like me. The scholarship kids, the outsiders. The ones that everyone is so very kind to, because they don't belong and they won't be around forever and they're easier to tolerate than societal restructure—and kindness, under those conditions, costs nothing.

It's true. I could have. It's less *never being able* than it is *never being willing*.

I want to know what it is I destroy.

"Staying in one place too long can be limiting," I agree. "But limitation can breed opportunity. Sometimes you've got to live something to know that you can't survive it and shouldn't try."

"You look like you're surviving just fine," she says. It's a sardonic response that lasts until that same careers counsellor asks whether she has considered the military as a future option.

"This school prides itself on service," Elena repeats, and I note she doesn't bother to ask her classmates if their expectation of service is deemed equivalent to hers. I'd make a crack about survival, but under the circumstances that would be tasteless, and she doesn't need me to remind her of what she already knows. My response is different, because this school is where I learned to reflect; reflection, I have learned, is a valuable tool. As is reciprocity.

"She asked if I wanted to help people," says Elena. "I asked which people I was supposed to be helping. I don't think that was the right answer."

"It was the right answer," I tell her. "Just the wrong audience."

She and Henry are working on a group project in the history section of the library. Henry is also a construct, representative of his kind. When I bring them books to help with their presentation on technological development in World War II, it is Henry who is, of the three of us, the outsider. He doesn't seem to notice that he's not among peers. He's enthusiastic about the subject.

Elena isn't surprised. "His father's in defence," she says, low-voiced, when Henry darts away for coffee. Hot drinks aren't allowed in the library, but that father has made enough from contract work to donate a laboratory to the school, so the staff look away from the rest. "I think he finds the possibilities that war can give exciting."

"Who wouldn't?" I say.

Elena scowls, and scowls further when she sifts through the shelves and locates a lack. She brings the absence to me like it's news. Atomic testing on Pacific Islands, the forced relocation of Indigenous residents. "Not everyone was excited," she says. "Though you'd never know it from what's here."

Henry talks earnestly and well of big pictures and the price of progress. His sympathy is warm and entirely divorced from experience. He's been raised to be tactful, to be diplomatic, so he doesn't say anything as crass as omelettes and eggs, but his early instinct is towards shareholders and profit, so the things he is too polite to say will bear out in his choices anyway. Elena realises this too, I think, and when I give her a copy of *Iep Jaltok*, I know she's not going to share it. A collection of poems from a Marshallese author, and I leave her alone to read it, knowing what she's going to find. There's a poem in there I've always admired, one that speaks of the anger that came from knowing the public response to animal experimentation—goats tethered to radiation exposure on islands that had already been depopulated—when that depopulation itself sparked no such protest. There's a desire, too, to see the injustices of one era visited on another.

Sometimes people can only learn the hard way. You learn that in good schools. Other places too, of course, but academia is where it starts. That's where the complacency begins, the assimilations. I don't tell students like Elena that their education here is mostly in mimicry, and the subtleties of compromise. The ones who are capable of realizing that should be allowed to draw their own conclusions. I'm not really interested in the ones who can't.

Fortunately for conclusion-drawing, there's a war on. Those are always good for educators. Usually I have to make do with historical conflict for effective illustration. Days of remembrance every year, school projects, and that was how I got histories of chlorine gas on the shelves.

Elena takes the chemical warfare books and hides them in the agriculture section. She leaves little doodles of livestock inside the back cover. No one notices. The library's skimped on agriculture; there are few farmers being educated here. And gas is old news— but then so's the bomb, and there's a renewed interest in that. The new war, starting up, is an iteration of an old war. It's localised action and wider inaction, careful limits set up to prevent the application of nuclear weapons. I've always thought creating those bombs was a monstrous thing to do. Even more monstrous, perhaps, than using them. There was an argument for that, and I've read all the discussions about loss of life and its comparisons, the lesser repercussions than conventional warfare. There's a strong possibility that atomic weapons ended that particular war sooner, saved more lives overall. That's what Elena argues, anyway, in her debate class. I helped her find the books for research. I watched as she practiced her speech: the one that talked of omelettes and eggs, the one that was a little crass, but a little crassness is forgiven from kids like her, when they smile and smile and repeat arguments that go against their own interests.

I know that speech. I gave that speech, or one very like it, back in my own school days, when I realised that *Don't you want to help people?* very likely resulted from the belief that I would sympathise with the eggs. I thought that my debate teacher would appreciate a more considered approach. I got full marks: a sign that my education was really paying off.

Elena gets full marks too. Henry asks to borrow her notes. I hear them talking: he speaks respectfully of the military; says he heard that she was considering it as an option. Elena asks if he's interested in it for himself, or perhaps for his sister. Service is so important.

"He laughed," she says afterwards. "Like it was a joke. He wasn't mean about it. He thought I was being funny."

"I hope you charged him for those notes," I tell her, and she grimaces. That'd be against school spirit, apparently. Not that either of us really gives a damn about that, but it's sensible to pretend. Scholarships can always be offered to more grateful students, and students like Elena are all too familiar with the calculated cost of mathematics.

"It's my best subject," she says. I'm not surprised. It was mine as well. People who are invested in numbers are often drawn to outcomes, to categorisation and diagrams of unions and intersections and sets that don't overlap in any way at all.

I give her a copy of *This Changes Everything*, bookmarked at the chapter that discusses geoengineering: a retreat where scientists brainstorm large-scale solutions to climate change. The regions that will benefit, and the regions that won't. There's always someplace to be sacrificed.

"I wonder what it would be like to make that decision," says Elena, doodling goats in the margins of the book (in other books she has scribbled omelette pans and eggshells, or clouds of poison gas inching up the page and coming down again as precipitation— but always coming down on the other side of the page, so that the rising up and the coming down can never be seen at once).

"You're a mathematician," I tell her. "What sacrifices would you make?"

This is a school, and the educators here are encouraged to be interdisciplinary. If this fucking institution has taught me nothing else, it left me with an effective understanding of transgression.

It comes down to numbers. To science, and to consequence. Anyone with a decent library can see it if they look closely enough. There's an analogue to volcanism, and the effects that massive eruptions have on climate. All that particulate matter in the atmosphere, cooling the planet. That's something that might be useful: *Frankenstein* has never gone out of fashion. It's checked out regularly, and I'd bet that nearly all of the students who haven't borrowed it know the story. They may not know that *Frankenstein* was written in what was called "The Year Without a Summer," because climatic effects from the eruption of the Indonesian volcano Tambora had global consequences. Crop failure, famine, freezing temperatures. Talk about interdisciplinary. . . this is something that brings the English and the science teachers together. They do so enjoy systems, and I have come to appreciate the systemic. So has Elena. I load her up with books on famous volcanic explosions. Tambora, Vesuvius, Taupō. *Krakatoa: The Day the World Exploded.*

"It's for extra credit," says Elena, when Henry asks her. "Something to do over the holidays." Henry's politely interested. His own holidays will be spent on tropical islands. "Before they go under," he says, and it's rueful and charming and calculated, that the future rarity of the experience increases its value now. Elena's face freezes into its own calculated lines when his back turns; I can see in her eyes examination and internal assessment, the marked conclusion of enumerated sacrifice.

It's a short stretch from volcanic to nuclear winter.

I know I'm not the only one to see the possibilities. There are lots of Elenas. I was one myself. We learned to fit in, in so many useful ways.

It started as an interesting exercise. A little mental puzzle: how much particulate matter would there need to be, in the atmosphere, to mitigate the effects of all that carbon dioxide? How much winter could a planet like ours possibly survive?

Of course there would be some losses. It's the mathematics of survival, the sheer necessary logic. If I were a doctor I'd call it triage, but I'm a school librarian, and so I call it information gathering. Information dispersal. And work should be checked among peers, just to make sure that no one's reckonings are subject to bias, or to sloppy application.

"Theoretically," says Elena, "this is how I'd do it." Hypothesis, introduction, methodology. Conclusion. The objective, rational communication prioritised by schools like this one. We've learned it so very well.

"I used carbon footprints to decide," she says. It's a common starting point. My own first attempt was similar. I'd argued for the destruction of the largest cities of the countries with the largest per capita footprints.

"The most polluting populations are the most efficient to dispose of," Elena says. I remind her that Palau has a large per capita footprint, but they're hardly careening us all into a Year Without a Winter. That's the problem with limited information. Carbon footprints are useful measures of assessment, both in total and per capita, but they're not enough on their own.

"Maybe it's better for the rest of us to get rid of the largest populations altogether, then," Elena muses. That, too, is a blunt assessment. It doesn't take into account the difference between rural and urban emissions within a population, or whether the generally low emissions per capita of one metropolis makes it a less effective target than another, smaller community with higher emissions. There are so many variables. It's taken a long time to calculate them correctly; longer still to gather the necessary information to make the calculations, but that's what a librarian is for.

Service is so important, and we have a responsibility to our community.

"That depends on the community. Hypothetically, of course," says Elena. She speaks as if she's learned to appreciate omelettes, but she also speaks as someone with very definite ideas about where the eggs should be coming from, and hers is a hypothesis that would not bear full marks from this particular institution. Still, I'm curious.

"Would you miss Henry? Hypothetically."

"I'd miss him like I'd miss a goat," she says, and that's the upside of academic mentorship, I find: the ability to teach what one has already been allowed to learn. We make our networks where we can, and school has always been a good place to begin finding those who are like ourselves, and those who can't be made to get along.

I tell her she's made a good start. And because this is a school, and because I am its librarian—a job I obtained by arguing for the provision of information to those who need it—I tell her where she can go to find plans that are more. . . advanced.

Not all Elenas stay in school.

Her Finished Wings

Marisca Pichette

Kali listened to breathing on either side of her. Georgie had been out since nine thirty, a sleep mask and earplugs ensuring she fell asleep before Kali got back from the library. But Fran, her other roommate, hadn't returned until ten fifteen.

Their beds lined up along the wall, *Madeline*-style. As the last person to move in at the end of August, Kali found herself stuck in the middle, doomed to perpetually feel like she was in someone else's way.

She closed her eyes, Georgie's steady breathing on her left, Fran's softer breaths on her right. Were they both asleep? She focused on Fran, listening for almost a full minute for a change in the rhythm. Nothing. She must be asleep.

Kali resettled her comforter, easing her hand down into her sleep shorts. In the first few weeks of college, she'd perfected the art of quiet masturbation. She tilted her head back and thought about a girl in her first-year seminar.

Sarah had beautiful hands. Smooth skin that almost shone, trimmed fingernails and always a couple of rings. Kali imagined easing those rings from Sarah's fingers, sliding her hands under her sweater, twining her tongue between the piercings on Sarah's left ear.

Partway through her fantasy, Kali opened her eyes to check that her comforter was hiding the motion of her hand. She shivered, fighting the urge to sneeze. She always felt the need to sneeze while masturbating. She hoped it wouldn't happen when she eventually had sex.

Something moved down by her feet. Kali blinked, her hand slowing. She watched for a few seconds, but the comforter remained as it had been before.

Must've been the tree moving outside, casting shadows. She closed her eyes, finding her rhythm again. Her breathing sped up and she forced herself to hold it in between trembling inhales.

Her fantasy dissolved as she came, rigid and breathing out in barely contained gusts. She opened her eyes, the sounds of campus more amplified in the aftermath of orgasm.

Outside the window the tree's branches swayed in a cool breeze that smelled faintly of weed. Kali worked her breaths back into a steady in, out, in. As she watched the shadows on the wall where her desk sat in between Georgie's and Fran's, one shifted. Too big to be the tree.

Kali half sat up. For a moment it had seemed like there was a person sitting on her desk. She glanced at the beds on either side of her. Neither of her roommates stirred, their breathing unchanged. She returned her gaze to the far wall. Nothing.

Kali settled back down in bed. Minutes passed. She closed her eyes.

The touch was so light, she thought it was part of a dream. Sliding up one leg, then the other. Pleasure rippled through her. She opened her eyes.

The streetlight illuminated a bare shoulder, a hip and leg crouched over her, naked. Too pale for Sarah. Kali focused on the figure, wondering if she was really dreaming or. . .

Then she saw the wings.

The girl who wasn't Sarah had wings like a crow, black feathers rustling in the night. Eyes glowed gold in the dark. Kali thought of screaming, but her mouth refused to move. Nails dug into her arms deep enough to leave bruises. She gasped, heat rushing down her neck and up her legs.

Cold lips closed over hers, stealing the breath from her lungs.

"Thank you!"

The sophomore pushed her laptop into her backpack and left the writing center, the corner of her coat trailing behind her on the floor.

Kali watched her go, trying to convince herself that the girl had been nice; there was no reason to hate her. She retreated to the table reserved for mentors and sat in front of her computer, exhaling. Whenever someone signed up for a session, she felt anger. Her pulse quickened, heat flushing her face, her hands. There was no definite source, just deep loathing for the person responsible for wrenching her solitude away.

If no one signed up, Kali could spend her shift doing homework or reading. She felt calm, able to breathe with no one asking her questions, forcing her to *think*.

She took a sip of her London fog, glancing at the clock. eight thirty. She had half an hour left in her shift. She skimmed an anthro reading, doubting that she would hold onto any of the information.

Throughout history, the cultural belief in monsters is tied closely to notions of divergence, subversion of societal norms, and an unacceptable embrace of otherness.

Some examples in folklore include the Baba Yaga, kelpie, and the succubus—known for corrupting chastity and purity in nightmarish visitations.

Kali scrolled through the PDF, highlighting the first and last sentence of each paragraph. She was halfway through a paragraph on sexual deviance when the secretary flipped the sign on her desk, indicating that the writing center was now closed. Kali highlighted *abnormal sexual relations (or fantasies resulting in aberration)* before saving her changes and closing her laptop.

Gathering her stuff, she walked through the library. Evening studiers curled on couches and chairs, their work sprawled in front of them. As she crossed the reading room, Kali glimpsed Fran, her laptop casting a greenish pallor on her face. Kali recognized two of Fran's teammates seated with her.

Kali's pulse started racing. There wasn't any real reason to hate Fran, but as Kali approached—too close to get by on a distant wave and vague smile of recognition—she wished her roommate had never been born.

"Hey," Fran said. "You just get off work?"

Nodding, Kali ended the conversation before it had a chance to develop. "See you in the room."

She walked away, conscious of the echoes her steps made on the stone stairs leading from the reading room to the library atrium.

Outside, she drew a deep breath, cool air wiping the fire away.

Before starting at Mount Holyoke, Kali had bought into the fallacy that everyone was best friends with their roommates. Then she got stuck in a triple. Georgie barely left the room, except to go home on the weekends. Fran was never there, *except* on the weekends. Kali spent most of her time in one of the common rooms, dreaming up ways to get one or both of her roommates to move out.

Her anger subsided as she walked past the clock tower, clanging, as it always did, almost five minutes after the hour. She took steady breaths of cold air, trying to relax her shoulders. She didn't remember being like this before college.

She never hated anyone in high school. Now, her anger was a coiled thing, striking at faces, voices, bodies around her. She just wanted to be alone—more than she ever had before. She didn't feel connected to the people around her, or her academics. Everything was too loud, too bright. She wanted silence, darkness, cold.

Few students passed Kali as she cut across the green to her dorm. Free from the nearest streetlamps, she looked up at the stars. They were fainter here than at home. She yearned for the boundless sky above her house, cradled in the boughs of the trees.

She reached her dorm too soon, lights intruding on the sky. Not eager to go up to her room and change into her pajamas in the closet, Georgie in all likelihood already in bed, Kali headed for the door at the other end of Abbey-Buck, prolonging her walk by maybe thirty seconds. As she drew close to the dorm, she saw someone smoking in front of the windows, definitely not abiding by the 25-foot rule.

They shouldn't put the ashtrays at the door if they want people to smoke further away. She cast a couple of glances at the smoker, skirting the cloud that surrounded her.

The girl was thin, her black hair cut in a spiky style. Her hand was so pale it almost glowed. She pinched a cigarette between two ringed fingers. When she drew, the glow illuminated her face.

Kali faltered. The girl exhaled smoke in Kali's direction. She stopped, lowering the cigarette.

"Hi."

"Hi." Kali swallowed, surprised that the girl didn't immediately piss her off. She found herself starting a conversation. "Do you live here?"

The girl shook her head. Kali could see now that her eyes were light brown. *Not gold.* Black lipstick framed her teeth. "Just visiting."

"You in the Five Colleges?" *Why am I still talking?*

"Not really." She jerked her head to the Abbey side of the dorm. "My partner lives here."

"Oh, cool." Kali drew her card from her pocket and swiped in. She couldn't figure out how to end the conversation, so she went inside, the door swinging shut behind her. She looked back out through the window, her pulse calm, hands unclenched.

The girl continued to smoke, gazing into the night.

Fran got back to the room close to midnight. Kali lay on her side, watching the glare of Fran's phone flashlight through her eyelids. It took almost half an hour for Fran to get in bed, and after that Kali was too tired to masturbate. She rolled onto her back, thinking about the girl outside.

Where was her partner? How was she supposed to get back into the building without a card? Kali pushed the thoughts from her mind, but the girl's eyes stayed with her. Her hands, and the cigarette.

In the gap between conscious thought and dreaming, weight dropped onto Kali's chest. Her nose filled with the scent of smoke.

Lips, colder than they should have been, covered her mouth.

Kali opened her eyes. The girl wasn't wearing anything. Her skin was waxy, reflecting the light outside. Two gold spots shone in the dark.

This wasn't a dream. This was real.

She struggled under the naked girl. Over her head, something rustled. Feathers drifted down onto the comforter.

Kali threw her head to the side and screamed as loud as she could. The girl backed up, sitting between Kali's legs. Her nipples stood out, hardened by the cold.

Kali struggled up the bed into her pillows. She looked to either side of her. Fran and Georgie were there, sleeping.

"I thought you didn't want them to hear," the girl said. It was her—the girl outside—only her eyes *were* gold, and wings sprouted from her back.

Kali sucked in a smoky breath. Her pulse raced, shifting from fear to something more familiar—arousal. "How did you get in here?"

When she said nothing, Kali grabbed her phone, unplugged and plugged it into the charger. The screen refused to light up. She pressed the power button over and over again. Nothing.

She looked at the girl. Wings cast shadows on the far wall. "Who are you?"

"Sagitta." The girl tugged the covers towards her and toyed with them. Her nails were short and painted gold. They reminded Kali of Sarah's.

Cold fingers brushed Kali's toes, sending a shiver through her. "You're angry. You're angry, because you're starving. Unfinished."

"What?" Kali's throat burned. She wasn't sure she could scream again. "I don't know what the fuck you're talking about. Or what you are."

Sagitta's fingers twitched over Kali's feet. "I'm like you."

"You have. . ." Kali looked from the gleaming eyes to the shadowy wings. The burning moved down her chest to her gut. "You're a fucking monster."

Fran and Georgie slept on, shrouded in blankets and darkness. Had Sagitta somehow deepened their sleep? *It doesn't make sense. This has to be a dream.*

"They won't wake up," Sagitta whispered, her nails drawing lines up Kali's shins. "If you don't want them to."

Kali didn't move away from Sagitta's touch. Heat slipped down between her legs as Sagitta's fingers reached her knees. Kali stared at her nails, gold and hard enough to make bruises.

There hadn't been bruises on her arms this morning; she'd checked. Last night was a dream. She loosened her grip on her knees, her feet sliding down the mattress.

It was nine o'clock on a Tuesday: Kali's favorite time to shower. Aside from her, the bathroom was empty.

She leaned her head back, massaging her scalp.

Sagitta had bit, scratched, sucked on her. Every morning Kali's bed was the same; her skin held no marks from the previous night. And no matter how much noise they made, Fran and Georgie slept on.

She told herself it was a fantasy. Sagitta was predictable because Kali constructed her every move.

But her anger had retreated. She didn't tense up when Fran talked, when Georgie started getting ready for bed at eight thirty. She still floated from class to class, but her professors' voices grated less, and assignments seemed more manageable.

She rinsed her hair and turned off the water, wrapping a towel around herself and stepping out of the shower into the empty bathroom. She carried her caddy back to the shelf and glanced in the mirror.

Something glimmered over her shoulder. She leaned up close to the mirror, angling herself to see better.

A blade stuck out of her back. She turned, looking at her other shoulder. There was a blade there, too.

"What the fuck..." Kali rubbed at the spot. Her skin felt fine, but the reflection didn't go away. Her skin prickled with cold. There was a distant, indistinct ringing in her ears.

Back in her room, Kali dropped her towel on the floor, inspecting herself in the floor-length mirror on the back of the closet door. Two blades stuck out several inches from her back, scythe-curved and as reflective as the mirror. She walked over to her desk and grabbed her phone with shaking fingers, switching on the camera. She held it behind her back and took a burst. When she looked through the photos, her back was bare.

"The fuck."

She went back to the mirror, goosebumps covering her still-damp skin. The blades were there in the mirror, unmistakable.

Kali spent the next few minutes sitting on her damp towel on the floor, googling hallucinations and their causes. She didn't have any of the common side effects that came along with seeing things. And it wasn't like she felt pain or saw blood. It was just a trick of the mirror. It was just her imagination. Stress, maybe.

She got dressed for her ten o'clock class. Her backpack sat evenly on her back. As she walked across campus, the gazes and voices of her classmates floated over her, leaving no impression.

That night as Sagitta lay on top of her, Kali pulled her head back, looking into golden eyes. "Is there something on my back?"

Sagitta cocked her head to the side, her tongue running across her lips. She slid her hand over Kali's collarbone and across her shoulders. Her fingers trailed down Kali's back. "Did you see them in the mirror? Your wings."

"I'm growing wings? Like yours?" Kali felt like she should be more freaked out. She hadn't told Sagitta about the mirror.

"Not like mine." Sagitta's finger circled a point in the center of Kali's shoulder blade. "They'll be your own. Everyone grows different wings."

"Yours are like a bird's. These are—" She wasn't sure how to describe them. Knives weren't natural or soft. Knives only meant one thing.

Sagitta smiled. "They suit you. Like me."

Kali swallowed. Her spit tasted like smoke. "What happened to your last partner? The one you were waiting for, outside."

Sagitta's fingers ceased circling the spot on her back. Her gaze slid to the window. "She finished. Stopped hungering, stopped needing me."

"Where is she now?"

Sagitta looked at her. "With someone else."

She drew her hand away. As she did so, Kali felt a slight pressure—not against her back, but somewhere behind her. Like a piece of her that wasn't yet attached. Sagitta brought her hand between them.

A cut ran across her palm, blood filling the creases in her skin. In the moonlight, it shone black.

By midterms, two more blades had sprouted from Kali's back. No one but Sagitta could see, yet Kali felt different when she sat in class, her surroundings a fog of inconsequential faces, muffled voices. She could feel the blades protruding, guarding her like a cactus' spines.

Her professors stopped calling on her. If she missed an assignment, no one seemed to notice. She almost never had sign-ups in the writing center and had started spending her shift in the café instead. Every drink she ordered tasted vaguely of cigarettes.

By December, Kali's wings reached almost to her calves. They were made entirely of blades, each curved like a scythe, laid in perfect lethal layers. She stood in front of the mirror and spread them, staring at the many reflections they cast.

Each night her sheets soaked up Sagitta's blood, cuts marking her hands and arms. At first it was frightening, but Sagitta felt no pain, and Kali soon associated lust with the scent of blood.

In the morning the stains were gone. When Sagitta returned, the cuts were gone, too, her skin as smooth and cold as it had always been.

When they kissed, Kali tasted her smoke. It filled her better than any meal.

The Tuesday before finals, Kali stood in the shower, contorting herself so she could shave her legs in the tiny space. Her wings folded against the wall, blades clinking with each stroke of her arm.

A drop of black hit her knee. She stopped shaving and it fell onto the drain, slipping out of sight. She inspected her knee, then her arm. When no cut revealed itself, she switched to her other leg, shaving her shin.

Splat. Another.

Splat. Splat. Kali looked up as the shower head turned black, one stream of water darkening, then another.

The smell of soap was swallowed by the scent of octane. Oil coated her legs. It gathered at the shower's base, slick and reflective. Kali saw herself in the quivering mass, naked, wings rising over her shoulders.

And her eyes.

For the first time in months, her pulse quickened to a pounding in her ears. She tore the shower curtain aside and grabbed her towel, wiping off as much oil as she could. She left the shower running as she rushed into the main section of the bathroom.

She threw her caddy onto the shelf and stood shivering in her towel, staring at her blackened feet.

"Girl, you ok?"

Kali looked up, startled. She'd gotten used to not being noticed.

Another girl from her floor had just come out of one of the stalls. She regarded Kali with a mix of concern and confusion.

For the first time since meeting Sagitta, Kali found herself creating a conversation where there didn't need to be one. "That shower's fucked up," she said, pointing back to the oil-stained curtain.

The girl frowned. *Hope.* Kali remembered her name. She'd read it off her door as she passed on her way to and from class. Hope was one of the people who left her door ajar while she sat at her desk working, an essential oil diffuser filling the air with the scent of lavender. Unlike Kali, she lived alone.

Hope looked through the curtain. "Did it dump cold water on you? I hate it when that happens."

She reached inside, oil coating her arm. Kali felt sick, as if she hadn't eaten in hours—in months. Hope switched the water off and stepped back. Oil dripped from her fingertips to stain the floor.

She can't see it. Kali looked in the mirror. She was covered in oil, her bladed wings shaking. When she looked at Hope's reflection, there was no oil. Only water dampened her arm.

Kali turned from the mirror to Hope. She was covered—both in her reflection and outside of it—but Hope wasn't. *Which is real?* She rubbed her face, smearing oil across her cheeks. She couldn't feel it, like she couldn't feel her wings.

"Sorry."

She ran out of the bathroom, leaving spots of black on the tile that nobody but her could see.

She threw her towel into the hamper and climbed into bed. *Fuck class.* No one would notice if she wasn't there. She couldn't even remember where she was supposed to be at this time of the day. All her subjects had blurred together. She'd stopped doing assignments, stopped reading or studying. She only went to class because it was something to do while she waited for night to fall.

Kali burrowed under the covers, rubbing her back against the mattress. Her wings didn't stop her from lying flat. She didn't feel the blades at all.

But they cut Sagitta. Kali pulled the comforter over her head, head swimming. She was starving, so hungry it hurt. But she couldn't face getting dressed, leaving the room. She'd stay here until dark. Until Sagitta came. Sagitta's lips would fix the pain.

Hours passed. Kali drifted between light sleep and listlessness. Her sheets were covered in oil. It dried in the recesses of her cuticles. She scratched away what she could. The rest stayed.

Dinnertime came and went. Georgie returned to the room. She didn't even glance at Kali. It was as if she wasn't there.

Kali hadn't spoken to her roommates in over a week. She'd gotten used to invisibility, like she'd gotten used to Sagitta.

Hope saw me.

At nine, Georgie got into bed. Kali turned to face Fran's bed.

Ten o'clock. Georgie was asleep. Fran still wasn't back.

Kali lay on her back, counting the minutes. Sagitta never came until both her roommates were in bed. When she inhaled, she smelled octane.

Eleven o'clock. Fran came into the dark room, finding her way with her phone flashlight. By eleven thirty, she was asleep. Kali opened her eyes and sat up.

Her heart thrummed. She hugged her knees, wings clinking in the dark.

Midnight, and still no Sagitta. Kali couldn't stand it any longer.

She pushed the covers back and walked naked to the closet. She was about to open it and grab clothes when her reflection in the mirror stopped her. She turned, looking at her wings. The blades shimmered between light and shadow. Each reflected a tiny flash of gold.

Kali squinted, trying to find the source of the light. It seemed to be brightest where she looked. After a few seconds, she gave up chasing it. Her gaze settled back, mirror eyes meeting her own.

She found herself staring into two shimmering points of gold. She ran her tongue across her lips. They were black. Had the oil made them like that?

Across campus, the clock chimed exactly five minutes after the hour. Kali flexed her wings. The heat had gone from her, but hunger remained.

The door made no noise in the dark. Kali walked down the hallway, her bare feet leaving black prints on the carpet, goosebumps rolling over her skin.

She stopped in front of Hope's door. Lavender mixed with the scent of oil, and the clink of blades.

Those Who Teach Pay Knowledge Forward

R.J. Joseph

Georgia stared at the empty desk where her student Calvin should have been sitting. He had missed a lot of classes recently. She scanned the room to see if she could pinpoint another student she could ask about him. Her gaze met that of the youngest child in the room. The girl wore an elaborate tunic, and she fidgeted with the hem of the garment with one hand while twirling her long braid with the other. She stared wordlessly at Georgia. Georgia smiled. The girl did not smile back.

Calvin did not have any friends or neighbors who lived close to him, only social acquaintances she saw him interact with superficially during recess and class activities. He probably would not have been friends with the little girl, who was far too young to engage with him. Her concern for Calvin deepened at the realization that he was as solitary as the young child who walked out of the room into the bright Texas sun.

Most of the children in her small, one-room schoolhouse had quite a few obstacles to overcome in getting their education. Some came from families who did not see the value in an education beyond being able to count money and plant crops. Others had to complete chores on their homesteads before they could attend the classes. Some of the older children had jobs throughout town, and only through her incessant pleas since she had arrived there three years prior had the business owners been persuaded to allow the young people to attend class for at least a couple of hours each weekday.

For those students who did not have job duties preventing them from attendance, other financial circumstances often came into play. The vast majority of the families in the town and its surrounding areas were of meager means. Through her conversations with parents, she quickly realized many of the children would be allowed to attend classes only so they could take two of their daily meals at the schoolhouse. The same importunities she had directed towards the wealthier citizens to maintain student attendance had also yielded food and firewood donations.

Resources would always be an issue, especially when depending on the generosity of fellow humans. For now, Georgia was able to provide warmth, meals, and all the knowledge she had to share with her pupils. The country was on the precipice of being a grand nation, and she wanted her students to be educated as she had been, to go on to college, and then do the best they could to gain visibility in the nation that had not always afforded such to most people of color.

Calvin was a bright kid who submitted all his assignments. Georgia worried he would fall behind in their coursework when he neglected to physically attend school as frequently as he had taken to doing. She could only send the work to his grandparents' home so many times before the gaps in his education would start to show due to his missing the organic discussions and impromptu alternative journeys they often took in the classroom. She consulted her attendance log and marked Calvin's fortieth absence in it. Georgia shook her head. That was a full third of their entire school year, and they were nowhere near the end.

She understood he had lived with his grandparents on the

outskirts of town since he was an infant, his mother having passed away during one of Texas's rare harsh winters, years ago. She had only had the chance to chat with the two elders on a few occasions, and it was clear they cared for Calvin and wanted him to get an education. However, they no longer farmed their land, having leased out the farming rights to another family in return for a slim, but steady, income and food provisions in their later years.

Georgia grew concerned about how Calvin was really spending his time. He had no interest in farming, anyway. He had expressed this sentiment to his classmates and Georgia on numerous occasions. He wanted no parts of bartending, blacksmithing, horse tending, or construction—most of the occupations available to young Black men in their part of the country. The fact he was likely not employed anywhere in town fueled Georgia's concern for him. Calvin wanted to be a doctor. To do that, he had to graduate from school and apply to, then attend, college.

Georgia often shared what information she gleaned about medical school training in the US and abroad with the boy. Although a Black physician had recently graduated from Dartmouth College, Calvin could not rely on any fleeting benevolence from the admissions board to guarantee him admittance. He would likely need to attend medical school in Europe.

She felt in her spirit that working as a healer was Calvin's calling. He was smart enough to meet the educational requirements and compassionate enough to care for his patients. She would do whatever she needed to make sure he got into college. What was required of her at that moment was checking on Calvin and his grandparents.

She saw her students as more than just bodies to be talked at and reasons for her to keep a job. Georgia very much cared about actually helping them to learn all they could about the world they lived in, especially their still developing country. She had spent her childhood in Ohio, wishing to get away from the stench and overcrowding of her rapidly growing town. When she graduated from Oberlin College, her only desire was to head out west and find a rural community that needed a teacher.

Georgia Watkins had ended up in Texas, where she would live out her remaining days. And her deepest desire was that the students she taught would do the same as she had, answering a heartfelt call to go back and help other community members to build lives of joy and accomplishment. Others would escape to different parts of the world to thrive in productive lives. Georgia smiled when she thought of her part in the whole educational cycle.

Her expression turned contemplative when she returned her thoughts to Calvin. Yes, there was something very special about the boy, besides his personhood and how quickly he picked up on anything he wanted to learn. She did not know exactly what it was, though she had her suspicions. She only knew she had to talk to him and persuade him to return to school.

Georgia stepped gingerly through the fallen corn stalks that covered the gradually disappearing trail. She had worn her most serviceable boots to protect her feet. The Johnsons' homestead lay beyond the well-worn path leading out of town in that direction. She would have to travel through high grass in some places and while she was unafraid to do so, she did not want the basket she carried to tumble from her arms. The school's left-over yeast rolls, sliced ham, and fresh carrots she carried as an offering to the Johnsons would likely go a long way towards helping out, even if the family saved the food for the next day.

She waved at the two older gentlemen walking through the distant remnants of the cotton harvest on the other side of the field. Neither waved back, although they both stood from their bent positions to watch her as she passed them. The fields were not pretty in the aftermath of the harvest season, but Georgia loved the smell that emanated from worked land, once it had given up its life sustaining produce, leaving only the remains—subsequently returning the remnants to the ground from which they had grown, making the soil richer for the next harvest.

Where outsiders to their rural community saw desolation and poverty, she saw less gluttonous hoarding of wealth and a community that provided for its members in ways those outsiders rarely understood. This farming community of theirs wanted everyone to have a fighting chance to make it through the hard times plaguing them all.

A woman dressed in a serviceable calico dress and bonnet held the hand of a small boy as they fell into step a good distance away from Georgia. Their feet fell without sound on the grass. Georgia nodded her head in greeting. The two looked in her direction and continued along their journey without disturbing her pace. She smiled at the dogs chasing each other ahead of her.

She stopped for a second in overwhelmed exhilaration, surrounded by life and death and everything in between. People outside their little town seemed to forget they lived whole life cycles in the rural communities, just as those who lived in the larger towns did. Folks were born, made the best life they could, and died, just the same as their human brethren across the world. The interactions between the living and the dead existed in beauteous wonderment that never ceased to amaze Georgia. She wanted Calvin to go on to college and continue his own life cycle while helping others through theirs.

The schoolwork and meeting the learning objectives were not Calvin's obstacles. She had created an advanced, individualized curriculum just for him when he had devoured the lessons she gave to the other students. He was thin and sometimes dozed off in class, but many teenage boys were similar. She suspected the family could likely use extra food every now and then so they could eat well and Calvin could get more adequate sleep. She made a note to reach out to a few merchants in town to see if they could help out with extra provisions for the Johnsons if it came to that.

Georgia had just felt the beginnings of sweat rivulets running down the middle of her back when she finally arrived at the modest Johnson home. As she knocked on the heavy wooden door, she scanned the fields surrounding the home, taking note of the beautiful mature trees dotting the land. She also noticed the few other people walking in the general vicinity, none of whom were the Johnsons. There were no other homes close by.

After a respectable amount of time passed from her first unanswered knock, Georgia knocked again. She shifted her weight from one foot to the other and peered unobtrusively through a small gap in the faded muslin drapes on the dusty front window. An elderly woman sat upright, motionless, on the edge of a beautifully worked, detailed wooden bench. Her wrinkled hands rested on her thighs. She never looked in the direction of the front door or window. Georgia raised her hand to knock again when the door creaked open, and Calvin's face appeared in the crack.

"Ms. Watkins?" His surprised question held a hint of something else. Fear.

"Hi, Calvin. I came to check on you."

He lowered his eyes and mumbled. "I'm fine. You ain't. . . you didn't have to come all this way."

"Oh, but I did. When the Sun told me you might have been kidnapped by Hades, I had to come in search of one of my top students."

The boy smiled. "I haven't been kidnapped. If I had, I wouldn't eat any old seeds."

"That's a relief. Then I and your classmates will not have to split time with you here and in the underworld." She moved the basket to her other arm. "We've missed you in class."

He lowered his gaze again. "I have to take care of things here." He made no move to open the door further.

"I understand. But how will you ever go to college if you miss so much school? There are communities around the world that will desperately need the medical training you must get." Georgia could see Calvin weighing her words.

"Remember how we talked in class about paying knowledge forward? About helping our people. Teaching—leading?" Georgia prompted the boy's memory.

She then lowered her voice so only he could hear. "I was hoping I could talk to you and your grandparents about your absences." She then raised her voice back to a regular level. "You aren't in trouble. You're a brilliant student, and I just want to make sure you all have everything you need."

The fear she'd originally seen in trace amounts moments ago came through heavily on the teenager's face.

"MeeMaw and Pops ain't really up for company right now," he mumbled.

Georgia placed her hand on top of his where he gripped the door underneath the wooden plank lock.

"It's okay. I won't stay long. I really need to talk to you all."

Calvin continued to stare at a point below him. Finally, he mumbled again.

"Just give me a couple of minutes. You can sit in here while I go get them from the back room." He opened the door slowly and ushered her inside a dark front room.

Georgia nodded in greeting towards where the old woman sat, while allowing her eyes to adjust to the darkness.

The small, overcrowded room looked pretty much like most of the others in their community, excepting the homes of the wealthier townsfolk. Large, expertly crafted wooden furniture scattered throughout the space, almost—but not quite—too large for the small area. Bric-a-brac filled every available surface and corner, odds and ends from lives of material scarcity and emotional wealth. An ornate wooden cross hung above the open fireplace, where a low flame burned to take the chill from old bones.

One group portrait hung on another wall. She could not make out the individual faces in the picture, but she could feel the pride emanating from the figures, vague outlines commemorating family history. Sacrifices made to purchase the luxury of a new innovation.

The lingering odor of pork neck bones wafted through the air and Georgia's stomach grumbled. Her eyes began to water, and she swallowed down the growing lump in her throat. She missed her mother. She missed the loving comfort of her childhood home, which often smelled of various cheap cuts of meat, seasoned and cooked so well they tasted better than more expensive food she got elsewhere. Food was love all across the diaspora. The positive energy in the home helped assuage her worry about Calvin: his grandparents' house was full of love.

Georgia finally heard shuffling from a hallway and Calvin slowly walked back into the room, flanked by his grandparents. Both elderly people walked slowly, Calvin guiding them towards the bench. His grandfather stared straight ahead, following Calvin's murmured direction. Stiffly, he sat down first. Calvin's grandmother took a few extra, guided steps to a point further on the bench, then sat where Georgia first saw her sitting through the window and when she had entered the room. Calvin sat between them in the tiny space left between the two.

Georgia cleared her throat. "I'm sorry to bother you, Mr. and Mrs. Johnson. Thank you for giving me a little bit of your time this evening." The Johnson family remained silent, the elderly members not looking directly at her but somehow *through* her. Neither of them accepted her greeting or asked if Calvin was in trouble.

"Calvin is a wonderful student, and I enjoy having him in class."

"Thank. You." The two words uttered by Mr. Johnson

sounded like two different sentences, slow and raspy. His voice held the remnants of a robust tone now gone flat.

"I'm concerned about his absences. He mostly keeps up with the assignments, but he misses a lot of the material we cover in class. I'm sure Calvin has discussed his plans for college with you and if he is to attend in the next year, we have to get him back in class."

"Our Calvin is a good boy." Mrs. Johnson's voice hissed into the room.

"He is a good boy." Georgia's gaze lingered on Calvin, sitting quietly between his grandparents. In the dim light, she could see a light sheen of sweat starting to cover his forehead.

"I just wanted to check in with you to see if there was anything you needed to help get Calvin back to school regularly."

"Thank. You." Mr. Johnson repeated.

Calvin wrinkled his eyebrows into a frown. His breath came in shallow bursts. The older man opened his mouth and closed it again and again several times, like a fish gasping to breathe air outside the water. Georgia continued to watch, her focus shifting to Calvin.

Mrs. Johnson moved her lips again. "Our Calvin is a good boy."

Georgia held Calvin's gaze for long moments before she replied.

"Yes, ma'am." She stood up. "I can see that Calvin is well cared for and you have a beautiful home. I know you both will do whatever we must to keep him on track to graduate next year. You all have a good night."

When she got to the door, she asked, "Calvin, after you get your grandparents settled again, could you please come for a short walk with me?"

The boy wiped his still glistening face with the back of his forearm. "Yes, ma'am."

Georgia stepped off the porch and waited for him, watching a mid-sized black bird sitting motionless on a low branch in the large tree in Calvin's yard. When the boy joined her, she waved him over to the tree.

"See that bird there?" She pointed to the branch.

He squinted. "What bird?"

"Focus your eyes on that other tree across the field. Then pay attention to what shows in your peripheral gaze." Georgia guided Calvin so he fully faced the focal tree, with the closer tree to the side of him.

He did as she instructed. After several moments, his eyes opened wider. Then, he turned his head back to the tree, to the house, to the tree again. "There *is* a bird there! Why can't I see it straight on?"

"I'll have to help you train yourself to see that way." Georgia ran her foot softly through the grass underneath the tree. She picked up a feathered carcass that lay there.

She took her free hand and alternated between making a circle around the body and a sweeping motion towards the branch until the feathered wings began to flutter weakly. The bird opened its eyes but made no effort to leave her hand.

"Ms. Watkins. . . how?" Calvin reached out and touched the bird. He suddenly dropped his hand and glanced at the branch. Tears filled his eyes.

"You know what I was doing with MeeMaw and Pops." He spoke quietly.

"I do."

"Please don't tell. I'm not doing anything bad. Am I? I don't have anywhere else to go and I gotta stay in school and graduate."

"I won't tell," Georgia promised.

Calvin visibly relaxed, only to suddenly tense up again.

"You can do it, too."

"Yes. I can do a lot more." Georgia waved her hand over the bird's body and the feathers stopped moving. The creature's soul returned to the branch. She gently lowered the corpse back onto the ground.

"The souls of the dead stick around for a bit after their bodies die. They don't really know what else to do, sometimes." She began to walk out towards the field surrounding Calvin's house. He fell into step next to her.

"If the body remains close, people like us can place the souls back inside and keep the body reasonably functional."

Calvin nodded. "Yes. I figured that out with my grandparents. They got sick and then passed away two days later. I didn't know what to do. They didn't want me to go get doc to come out, and I had no one else to help. I didn't want to leave them. They died. I couldn't help them." He ended on a swallowed sob and took deep, shuddering breaths.

"I begged them not to leave me and they opened their eyes again. But I couldn't see them around the house, like you did, when I would lay them down." He swiped at the tears on his face.

"I saw your grandmother sitting in the front room before you let me in. I suspect your grandfather is also around. Their spirits haven't left the house. Now they wait for you to need them and help them back inside their bodies. As long as you have their bodies, they'll stay."

"How—how long can they exist this way?"

"It depends. If you feed their bodies a little bit and let their spirits back inside them every now and again, they'll last a good while. At least for the year you need to finish school and get ready to go to college." She placed her hand on his shoulder to force him to look at her.

"But you don't want to keep them like that for any longer than you must. They aren't at rest like this. At some point, you have to release them so they can find peace."

Tears welled up in his eyes again. "I don't know how to live without them."

"You may not have to live without their spirits. See those men in the field there?" She pointed to the men she had passed earlier. "And that lady with the little boy?"

Calvin took a few moments to focus, then nodded.

"You learn so quickly! They stay because their bodies are long buried, but they found some type of peace here. After their bodies are buried, your grandparents may decide to remain here, around the loving home you all have."

The boy nodded. "Will they worry about me? Will they be sad?"

She raised her arm to run her hand over the kinky curls on top of his head. "They'll always worry about you, as parents do. But they won't be sad. They have each other. And they'll always be proud of you, going out into the world to find your destiny."

They stood in the field for a few minutes longer. Calvin nodded again.

"They'll be fine when you're not here. We'll start telling the townspeople that they've mostly taken to their bed so folks won't try to disturb them. I expect to see you in class tomorrow."

"Yes, ma'am."

"Make sure you eat the food I brought so it doesn't go to waste."

"Yes, ma'am."

"Good evening, Calvin. Everything will be fine."

The next morning, Georgia stood outside the door of the schoolhouse to greet her students with biscuits and milk for breakfast. The little girl in the tunic stood next to her. Georgia caught sight of Calvin in the distance, hands in his pockets, a mid-sized dog lumbering slowly next to him. As they drew closer, she could see that the dog had one eye and moved in an odd way that only she would notice. She smiled widely at the boy.

"Good morning, Calvin. I see you have a new friend. He's welcome to stay out here to wait for you."

He grinned back. "Yes. This is Chester." He waved to the little girl. She waved in return and followed him inside the classroom.

"Well, okay then." Georgia shook her head and chuckled, following them. "Make that *two* new friends."

WILTED PAGES

About the Authors

75 Sheets · 150 Pages
5 x 7 in / 12.7 x 17.78 cm

About the Authors

Hussani Abdulrahim is a Toyin Falola Prize winner, Gerald Kraak finalist, and a winner of the 2019 Poetically Written Prose Contest. He was a semifinalist for the Boston Review 2019 Aura Estrada Short Story Contest and shortlisted for the 2019 ACT Award. His works are forthcoming or have appeared at 20:35 Africa, praxismagonline, KSR, and Memento (an anthology of contemporary Nigerian poets). He lives in Northern Nigeria. Find Hussani at twitter.com/hussaniabdul4

Octavia Cade is a New Zealand speculative fiction writer. She's sold close to 70 short stories to markets including *Clarkesworld*, *Asimov's*, and *F&SF*, and she particularly enjoys writing stories about the horrific application of science. Her next book, *You Are My Sunshine and Other Stories*, is due out in September from Stelliform Press. In 2023 she is writer in residence at Canterbury University, where she's putting together a book of creative nonfiction essays about NZ ecology. Find Octavia at ojcade.com

Amber Chen is a Singaporean-Chinese author of SFF and contemporary fiction. She spends much of her free time living within Chinese fantasy novels and dramas, and also drinks one too many cups of bubble tea. Her debut silkpunk fantasy novel, *Of Jade and Dragons*, is forthcoming from Penguin Teen in Summer 2024. Find Amber at ambercwrites.com

Brian Evenson is the author of a dozen books of fiction, most recently *Song for the Unraveling of the World* (Coffee House Press 2019), the story collection *The Glassy, Burning Floor of Hell: Stories* (Coffee House Press 2021) and the novella *The Warren* (Tor.com 2016). He has also recently published *Windeye* (Coffee House Press 2012) and *Immobility* (Tor 2012), both of which were finalists for a Shirley Jackson Award. His novel *Last Days* won the American Library Association's award for Best Horror Novel of 2009. His novel *The Open Curtain* (Coffee House Press) was a finalist for an Edgar Award and an International Horror Guild Award. He lives in Los Angeles and teaches in the Critical Studies Program at CalArts. Find Brian at brianevenson.com

Cyrus Amelia Fisher writes queer tales of shipwrecks, mycelium, and horrors of the flesh. After years of driving around the United States in a beat-up minivan, they finally returned to the mossy fens of their birth in the Pacific Northwest. Now they while away the hours communing with their fungal hivemind and writing about cannibalism. Naturally, they also love to cook. Find Cyrus at twitter.com/hubristicfool

Jennifer Fliss (she/her) is the writer of the story collections *As If She Had a Say* (2023) and *The Predatory Animal Ball* (2021.) Her writing has appeared in *F(r)iction*, *The Rumpus*, *The Washington Post*, and elsewhere. She can be found on Twitter at @writesforlife or via her website, jenniferflisscreative.com

Ana Hurtado is a Clarion West 2022 alum. Her work has been published by Strange Horizons, Uncanny Magazine, The Magazine of Fantasy & Science Fiction, among others. LeVar Burton chose one of her stories for his podcast LeVar Burton Reads in 2020. Find Ana at anahurtadowrites.com

Gabino Igelsias's work has been nominated for the Bram Stoker Award and the Locus Award, and won the Wonderland Book Award. He is the author of *The Devil Takes You Home*, *Zero Saints*, and *Coyote Songs*. Find Gabino at twitter.com/gabino_iglesias

R.J. Joseph is the author of the Bram Stoker and Shirley Jackson Award-nominated *Hell Hath No Sorrow like a Woman Haunted*. Find R.J. on various social media platforms @rjacksonjoseph

Jo Kaplan is the award-winning author of *It Will Just Be Us* and *When the Night Bells Ring* (bronze medal winner of the IPPY award for horror). Her short stories have appeared in *Fireside Quarterly*, *Black Static*, *Nightmare Magazine*, *Vastarien*, *+HORROR LIBRARY+*, *Nightscript*, and Bram Stoker award winning anthologies. She has also published work as Joanna Parypinski. In addition to writing, she teaches English and creative writing at Glendale Community College and plays the cello in the Symphony of the Verdugos. Currently, she is the co-chair of the Horror Writers Association's Los Angeles chapter. Find Jo at jo-kaplan.com

John Langan is the author of two novels and five collections of stories. For his work, he has received the Bram Stoker and This Is Horror awards. He lives in New York's Hudson Valley with his family and an office full of surly books. Find John at johnpaullan-gan.wordpress.com

R.B. Lemberg is a queer, bigender immigrant from Eastern Europe and Israel. Their work has appeared in *Lightspeed*, *Strange Horizons*, *Beneath Ceaseless Skies*, *Unlikely Story*, *Uncanny*, and other venues, and has been a finalist for the Nebula, Ignyte, Locus, Crawford, and other awards. Find R.B. at rblemberg.net

Premee Mohamed is a Nebula, World Fantasy, and Aurora award-winning Indo-Caribbean scientist and speculative fiction author based in Edmonton, Alberta. She is an Assistant Editor at the short fiction audio venue Escape Pod and the author of the 'Beneath the Rising' series of novels as well as several novellas. Her short fiction has appeared in many venues and she can be found on Twitter at @premeesaurus. She is represented by Michael Curry of DMLA.

Suzan Palumbo is a Nebula finalist, active member of the HWA, Co Administrator of the Ignyte Awards and a member of the Hugo nominated FIYAHCON team. She is also a former Associate Editor of "Shimmer" magazine. Her debut dark fantasy/horror short story collection "Skin Thief: Stories" will be published by Neon Hemlock in Fall 2023. Her novella "Countess" will be published by ECW Press in spring 2024. Her writing has been published or is forth coming in Lightspeed Magazine, Fantasy, The Deadlands, The Dark Magazine, PseudoPod, Fireside Fiction Quarterly, PodCastle, Anathema: Spec Fic from the Margins and other venues. Find Suzan at suzanpalumbo.wordpress.com

Marisca Pichette collects nameless monsters. More of her work appears in *Strange Horizons, Vastarien, The Magazine of Fantasy & Science Fiction, Fantasy Magazine, Flash Fiction Online, Pseudo-Pod,* and others. She is the winner of the 2022 *F(r)iction* Spring Literary Contest and has been nominated for the Pushcart, Utopia, and Dwarf Stars Awards. Her speculative poetry collection, *Rivers in Your Skin, Sirens in Your Hair,* is out now from Android Press. They spend their time in the woods and fields of Western Massachusetts, sacred land that has been inhabited by the Pocumtuck and Abenaki peoples for millennia. Find them on Twitter as @MariscaPichette and Instagram as @marisca_write.

Michael A. Reed is a dyslexic English teacher from Las Vegas. He thinks spelling is for robots and loves all things speculative. His writing can be found at Factor Four Magazine.

Ayida Shonibar (she/they) is an Indian-Bengali immigrant who grew up in Europe and currently works in North America. Their short works appear or are forthcoming in *Asian Ghost Short Stories* (Flame Tree Publishing), *Nature Futures, Luminescent Machinations* (Neon Hemlock), *Transmogrify!* (Harper Teen), and *Night of the Living Queers* (Wednesday Books), among others. Find Ayida at ayidashonibar.com

Simo Srinivas lives in Colorado with their spouse and two senior tabby cats. Their short fiction has appeared in Strange Horizons, Fantasy Magazine, khōréō, Dark Matter Presents: Monstrous Futures, and Archive of the Odd, among others. Find Simo at srinivassimo.com

Steve Rasnic Tem has published over 450 short stories over the course of his 40 year writing career. Additionally, he has published poetry, plays, and novels in the genres of fantasy, science fiction, horror, and crime. His collaborative novella with his late wife Melanie Tem, The Man On The Ceiling, won the World Fantasy, Bram Stoker, and International Horror Guild awards in 2001. He has also won the Bram Stoker, International Horror Guild, and British Fantasy Awards for his solo work. A transplanted Southerner from Lee County Virginia, Steve is a long-time resident of Colorado. He has a BA in English Education from VPI and a MA in Creative Writing from Colorado State, where he studied fiction under Warren Fine and poetry under Bill Tremblay. Find Steve at stevetem.com

About the Editors

75 Sheets · 150 Pages
5 x 7 in / 12.7 x 17.78 cm

About the Editors

Ai Jiang is a Chinese-Canadian writer, a Nebula Award nominee, and an immigrant from Fujian. She is a member of HWA, SFWA, and Codex. Her work can be found in F&SF, The Dark, Uncanny, among others. She is the recipient of Odyssey Workshop's 2022 Fresh Voices Scholarship and the author of *Linghun* and *I AM AI*. Find Ai at aijiang.ca

Christi Nogle is the author of the Shirley Jackson Award nominated and Bram Stoker Award® winning First Novel *Beulah* from Cemetery Gates Media as well as the collections *The Best of Our Past, the Worst of Our Future* and *Promise* from Flame Tree Press. She is co-editor with Willow Dawn Becker of the Bram Stoker Award® nominated anthology *Mother: Tales of Love and Terror* and co-editor with Ai Jiang of Shortwave Publishing's *Wilted Pages: An Anthology of Dark Academia*. Find Christi at christinogle.com

Special Thanks

Abby Moeller • Abelardo Valdez • Alan Calvert • Alan Mark Tong • Allison L. Matthews • Amanda Cook • Amber Carreau Davidson • Amenze Oronsaye • Andrew Hatchell • Angie S. (strangersights.com) • Ann Kucharski • Ashleigh H. • Ashley Brennan • Ava Strough • Axel Lazuli • Bethany Jezerey • @BewitchedSunflower • Bridget D. Brave • Brooks Moses • Carley Doty-Dutcher • Carolyn @akaTheReader • Carrie Finch • Carrie Lee South • Cathy Green • Cemetery Gates • Chad Bowden • Charles E. Wood • Chelle Parker • Chris McLaren • Chris 'Vulpine' Kalley • Chris Wolff • Christie Marie Lauder • Christopher Wheeling • Clare Janke • Cody Mower • Colleen Feeney • Corey Farrenkopf • Daniel Beer • Daniel Mowery • Darren Lipman • dave ring • Dave Urban • David A. Quist • David Worn • Debbie Phillips • Derek Anderson • Don C • Dorothy Taylor • Elizabeth Ling • Em Liu • Emily Gray • Emily Walter • Emmy Teague • Eric de Roulet • Fester L.D. MacKrell • Gabriel Casillas • Gemma Church • Goldie Peacock • Hatteras Mange • Isaac E. Payne • Jason H Miller • Jason Sizemore • JD McKeehan • Jean Strickland • Jessica Richards • Jim Brownrigg • Joe Butler • John Dale Beety • John G Rowe • John Winkelman • John WM Thompson • Jon Paul Hart • Jonathan Gensler • Joseph Jerome Connell III • Joshua McGinnis • Jude Deluca • Kaela Valle • Kai de Roulet • Kaitlin Geddis • Kaitlyn Wells • Kelsea Yu • Kevin Kastelic • Kiera McNutt • Kristina Meschi • Leah Ning • Leo Korogodski • Mady Hays • Marie Croke • Marisca Pichette • Marissa van Uden •

mathew wend • matt • Matthew Stepan • Megan • Melanie B. • Michael Axe • Michael Mock • mochi • Monica Louzon • N Queen • Nicholas G. Marconi • Nicole Dieker • Olivia Montoya • Patrick Barb • Richard Novak • rob alley • Rob Jarosinski • Ronald H. Miller • Rowen Hutchins • Ryan Marie Ketterer • Ryan Power • S. "Jet" Pak • Sam Logan • Sarah Duck-Mayr • Sasha Chilton • Scott Schiffmacher • Seane • Shannan Ross • Sheena Perez • Sirrah Medeiros • Solomon Forse • Steve Gold • Steve Rasnic Tem • Susan Jessen • Tanya Pell • Tanya Sutton • Taylor Grothe • Thérèse • Tim Jordan • Tina Alberino • Traci Belanger, PhD in training • Trainor Houghton-Whyte • Ute Orgassa • Weird Little Worlds Press • William Jones • Willow Redd

A Note from
Shortwave Publishing

Thank you for reading *Wilted Pages*! If you enjoyed this anthology, please consider writing a review. Reviews help readers find more titles they may enjoy, and that helps us continue to publish titles like this.

For more Shortwave titles, visit us online...

OUR WEBSITE
shortwavepublishing.com

SOCIAL MEDIA
@ShortwaveBooks

EMAIL US
contact@shortwavepublishing.com

ALSO AVAILABLE
FROM
SHORTWAVE PUBLISHING

MELON HEAD MAYHEM

KILLER VHS SERIES #1

ALEX EBENSTEIN

Cousins Carson and Sophia find an unfamiliar VHS tape tucked away in grandma's house. When played, the video summons the movie monsters—local urban legends called melon heads—into their very real lives!

The destruction caused by the blood thirsty melon heads has Carson and Sophia fighting to survive and sets them on a deadly path to the shores of Lake Michigan, home of the beasts. They vow to destroy every last one of the melon heads and make sure these monsters never get a sequel.

OBSO LESC ENCE

ALAN LASTUFKA & KRISTINA HORNER

27 New Tales of Technological Terror!

The unique camera lens that exposes hidden monsters. The blue-collar robot that would do anything to not become obsolete. The app that knows your needs better than you know them yourself.

In OBSOLESCENCE, technology gets repurposed, subverted, and re-defined. OBSOLESCENCE features new stories by Eric LaRocca, Clay McLeod Chapman, Ai Jiang, Caitlin Marceau, Rob Hart, Gabino Iglesias, Hailey Piper, Christi Nogle, Laurel Hightower, David Niall Wilson, and more...

DEATHREALM SPIRITS

STEPHEN MARK RAINEY

Deathrealm: Spirits is a new horror anthology, edited by Stephen Mark Rainey, featuring stories from genre legends Joe R. Lansdale, Brian Keene, Elizabeth Massie, Eric LaRocca, and many others.

This is the first anthology of new Deathrealm stories since the original magazine ceased publication in 1997. Once called one of the most important horror lit magazines being published at the time by acclaimed editor, Ellen Datlow, Deathrealm printed a wide variety of dark fiction.

This collection specializes in ghostly stories that explore supernatural themes with a prevailing sense of personal dread.

ALSO AVAILABLE
FROM
SHORTWAVE PUBLISHING

 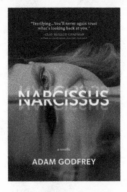 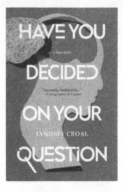

ALSO AVAILABLE FROM SHORTWAVE PUBLISHING

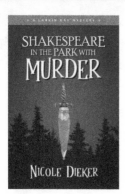

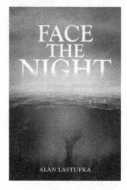

ALSO AVAILABLE FROM SHORTWAVE PUBLISHING

Content Warnings

- The Girls of St. X — Sexism, family dysfunction, child death
- Hugging The Buddha's Feet — Implied child death
- In Vast and Fecund Reaches We Will Meet Again — Violence, themes of oppression, classism, animal death, suicide
- Higher Powers — references to the occult, suggestions of sexual harassment, emotional abuse, violence, child endangerment, mention of suicide
- Twisted Tongues — bigotry, graphic imagery, violence, gore
- The Allard Residency — mental health
- The Library Virus — Brief graphic imagery, minor body horror
- Parásito — sexism, sexual harassment, body horror
- An Inordinate Amount of Interest — exploitation, violence
- Preservation of an Intact Specimen — animal death; off-page sexual assault; graphic violence including broken bones and blood; murder; desecration of a corpse
- Her Finished Wings Finalized — sexual themes (dubious consent), body horror, including cuts and blood. There is also a short imagined passage of literature that contains discriminatory ideas through a historical lens.